Volume 1

Satisfy your desire for more.

On **Bonnie Hamre's** story: "Bonnie Hamre is every bit as good as Amanda Quick and certainly a hell of a lot sexier."

—**Bertrice Small**

On **Alice Gaines's** story: "...a delicious, and very sensual fantasy."

—**Bertrice Small**

On **Ivy Landon's** story: "...an absolutely delightful and yummy erotic tale."

—**Bertrice Small**

On **Jeanie LeGendre's** story: "These stories take you beyond romance into the realm of erotica. I found Secrets absolutely delicious!"

—**Virginia Henley**

Reviews from Secrets Volume 1

"Four very romantic, very sexy novellas in very different styles and settings. ... The settings are quite diverse taking the reader from Regency England to a remote and mysterious fantasy land, to an Arabian nights type setting, and finally to a contemporary urban setting. All stories are explicit, and Hamre and Landon stories sizzle. ... If you like erotic romance you will love *Secrets*."

— **Romantic Readers** review

"Overall, for a fan of erotica, these are unlike anything you've encountered before. For those romance fans who turn down the pages of the "good parts" for later repeat consumption (and you know who you are) these books are a wonderful way to explore the better side of the erotica market. ... *Secrets* is a worthy exploration for the adventurous reader with the promise for better things yet to come."

— **Liz Montgomery**

Reviews from Secrets Volume 2
Winner of the Fallot Literary Award for Fiction

"*Secrets, Volume 2*, a new anthology published by Red Sage Publishing, is hot! I mean *red hot!* ... The sensuality in each story will make you blush—from head to toe and everywhere else in-between. ... The true success behind *Secrets, Volume 2* is the combination of different tastes—both in subgenres of romance and levels of sensuality. *I highly recommend this book.*"

— **Dawn A. Long, America Online** review

"I think it is a fine anthology and Red Sage should be applauded for providing an outlet for women who want to write sensual romance."

— **Adrienne Benedicks, Erotic Readers Association** review

Reviews from Secrets Volume 3
Winner of the 1997 Under the Cover Readers Favorite Award

"An unabashed celebration of sex. Highly arousing! Highly recommended!"

—**Virginia Henley,** *New York Times* Best Selling Author

"*Secrets, Volume 3* leaves the reader breathless. Each of these tributes to exotic and erotic fiction offers a world of sensual pleasure and moral rewards. A delicious confection of sensuous treats awaits the reader on each turn of the page. Sexy, funny, thrilling, and luscious, Secrets entertains, enlightens, and fuels the fires of fantasy."

— **Kathee Card**, *Romancing the Web*

"*Secrets, Volume 3* is worth the wait... and is the best of the three. This is erotic romance reading at its best."

— **Lani Roberts**, *Affaire de Coeur*

"From the FBI to Police Detectives to Vampires to a Medieval Warlord home from the Crusade — *Secerts Vol. 3* is SIMPLY THE BEST!"

—**Susan Paul**, Award Winning Author

Reviews from Secrets Volume 4

"*Secrets, Volume 4*, has something to satisfy every erotic fantasy... simply sexsational!"

—**Virginia Henley**, *New York Times* Best Selling Author

"Provacative...seductive...a must read! ★★★★"

— *Romantic Times*

"These are the kind of stories that romance readers that 'want a little more' have been looking for all their lives without crossing over into the adult genre. Keep these stories coming, Red Sage, the world needs them!"

— **Lani Roberts**, *Affaire de Coeur*

"If you're interested in exploring erotica, or reading farther than the sexual passages of your favorite steamy reads, the *Secret* series is well worth checking out."

— **Writers Club Romance Group on AOL Reviewer Board**

Reviews from Secrets Volume 5

"*Secrets, Volume 5*, is a collage of lucious sensuality. Any woman who reads *Secrets* is in for an awakening!"

—**Virginia Henley**, *New York Times* Best Selling Author

"Hot, hot, hot! Not for the faint-hearted!"   — *Romantic Times*

"As you make your way through the stories, you will find yourself becoming hotter and hotter. *Secrets* just keeps getting better and better."

— *Affaire de Coeur*

Reviews from Secrets Volume 6

Satisfy Your Desire for More... with *Secrets!*

Did you miss any of the other volumes of the sexy **Secrets** *series?*
At the back of this book is an order form for all the available volumes. Order your **Secrets** *today!*

Bonnie Hamre

Alice Gaines

Ivy Landon

Jeanie LeGendre

Volume 1

Secrets

Satisfy your desire for more.

SECRETS Volume 1
This is an original publication of Red Sage Publishing and each individual story herein has never before appeared in print. These stories are a collection of fiction and any similarity to actual persons or events is purely coincidental.

Red Sage Publishing, Inc.
P.O. Box 4844
Seminole, FL 33775
727-391-3847
www.redsagepub.com

SECRETS Volume 1
A Red Sage Publising book
All Rights Reserved/December 1995
Second Printing, 2000; Third Printing, 2002; Fourth Printing, 2003; Fifth Printing, 2004; Sixth Printing, 2006
Copyright © 1995–2006 by Red Sage Publishing, Inc.

ISBN 0-9648942-0-3 / 978-09648942-0-4

Published by arrangement with the authors and copyright holders of the individual works as follows:
A LADY'S QUEST
Copyright © 1995 by Bonnie Hamre
THE SPINNER'S DREAM
Copyright © 1995 by Alice Brilmayer
THE PROPOSAL
Copyright © 1995 by Ivy Landon
THE GIFT
Copyright © 1995 by Jeanie LeGendre

Photograph: Copyright © 2000 by Greg P. Willis; email: GgnYbr@aol.com

Cover design, layout and book typesetting by:

Quill & Mouse Studios, Inc.
2165 Sunnydale Boulevard, Suite E
Clearwater, FL 33765
www.quillandmouse.com

Contents

A Lady's Quest

by Bonnie Hamre

To My Reader:
Have you ever wondered what it would be like to experience exquisite lovemaking with the perfect lover? Antonia Blair-Sutworth did and look what happened! Enjoy along with Antonia…

Chapter One

Antonia heard the breathless murmurs and glanced beyond her dance partner's shoulder. Across the crowded Wolfington ballroom, guests gathered at the foot of the sweeping staircase to watch a man descend.

Head erect, broad shoulders straight, he made his leisurely way down the steps, seemingly at ease with being the center of attention. Even the dancers slowed to observe the tall man with the regal bearing. Like the dominant lion whose coloring he shared, he moved with the sinuous, controlled grace that spoke of might held under strict restraint.

He reached the bottom of the steps. The crowd parted before him. Ladies dipped in welcoming curtsies, men lowered their heads as he made his way between them, ignoring the sussuration that encircled and flowed in his wake.

As he joined her, Countess Wolfington all but swooned. She rose from her curtsy, puce skirts puddling from her broad hips, clasping the hand he extended.

He lifted her fingers to his mouth. "Countess. Beautiful as always."

More than twice his age, she simpered like a young girl in her first Season. "Your grace, such an honor to have you attend our simple entertainment."

Dougal MacDonald, seventh Duke of Sutherland, lifted an eyebrow. The Wolfingtons were known for their extravagant and ostentatious parties and this one promised to be no exception. He glanced around at the gaudy ballroom, at the scores of flickering silver candelabras, and the elaborately dressed hordes milling about hoping to catch his attention.

"We heard you were back from the north, your grace," the countess ventured.

"Aye. I rode hard to be here tonight."

She raised a fan to cover a coy titter. "Oh, you flatter me."

Let the woman think what she wanted. Covertly, Sutherland searched the faces of the guests. Even on his isolated estates, he'd heard the news that Lady Blair-Sutworth had dismissed Effingdale and he had wasted no time returning to London. Now that she was free, he meant to make her his.

Immediately.

His gaze traveled past an ensemble dancing a quadrille, then snapped back. There. No mistaking that glorious chestnut hair piled atop that slender neck. Her gown, a deep blue, clung to her figure, subtly revealing the curve of her hip, the tantalizing hint of her thigh. She wore no adornment other than the glowing gems at her throat and ears, yet her simplicity drew him far more than the ornately decorated gowns of the other women.

For an instant their eyes met, then she looked coolly away from the interest he let show on his face. He frowned. The lady was no blushing virgin, but a sophisticated woman well aware of her own sensuality. Why then did she look away in a deliberate snub?

He accepted a glass of champagne from a passing footman and moving out of the way of the dancers, he took a position where he could watch her without interference.

She moved gracefully through the steps of the quadrille, her fingers just resting on those of her partner. Though she smiled as she danced, and nodded and acknowledged acquaintances who shared the floor, she showed no particular preference for any man that Sutherland could discern. That pleased him. However, she steadfastly refused to look his way, which did not.

When the music ceased, she smiled at her partner, rested her fingertips on his arm and allowed him to escort her from the floor. Sutherland straightened his shoulders and made his way to her side.

He intercepted her as she turned to join another group. "Lady Blair-Sutworth."

Antonia glanced up and stiffened. "Your grace." She made him the smallest curtsy imaginable.

He hid a smile. "Have I offended you in some way?"

Casting her emerald gaze somewhere beyond his shoulder, she murmured, "I cannot imagine why you should think so."

"Almost the cut direct should do it, wouldn't you agree?"

She slanted her head in inquiry.

"A few moments ago, while you were dancing?"

She paused, as if in reflection. "I don't believe I noticed you."

"I am wounded."

Her gaze flicked up and away. "Is there not a sufficient number of women here to fawn over you? Perhaps our hosts would be good enough to import some additional female guests."

He laughed. "One will do. Shall I tell you who?"

"That is not necessary, your grace. If you will excuse me?"

"Not yet."

Her mouth tightened. Sutherland studied the set look to her face, Why was she so eager to rid herself of his presence? Though he found it more irritating than complimentary, he couldn't pretend he knew nothing about the usual reaction of women to his attention. He didn't flatter himself that it was for himself alone, for Dougal MacDonald, that some women flirted and chatted gaily to attract his attention to their charms. It was common knowledge that he would have to marry soon to protect the title and fill his nurseries. More than one woman hoped to become his very wealthy Duchess.

But not yet. Marriage and children would have to wait. First, he would lay claim to Lady Antonia Blair-Sutworth. Anticipating the outcome of his intentions, he studied the tender flare of her lips and wondered how they would feel under his. His loins tightened at the thought.

The music began again. A waltz, perfect. He turned to her, but she took a step back.

"I've promised this dance to Talbot." She looked past his shoulder. "Here he is, now."

Sutherland turned his head and waited until the other man, a young fop by the looks of his intricately tied neckcloth, approached. Calmly, he said, "Lady Blair-Sutworth has pledged me this dance."

She caught her breath. "Oh, but I didn't—"

The younger man cast her a startled glance and bowed. "My error, your grace."

"Wise of him," Sutherland commented as the younger man retreated. He turned to lead Antonia to the floor.

"Do you always get what you want?"

"Always. Make note of that, my lady."

"I do not wish to dance a waltz with you, sir."

"Why not?"

Antonia knew he knew exactly why she did not want to dance with him. The waltz, only recently accepted by the patrons at Almacks, would allow him to put his hand on her waist, to hold her facing him, to command her steps. How could she maintain a distance between them when he held her? "I prefer to choose my own partners," she said firmly.

"As do I." He looked into her eyes. "I have chosen you. Will you waltz with me or cause a scene? Already people are staring at us."

"They look at you, your grace. They always do."

She tensed as he took her into his arms and held her much too closely. She withdrew immediately to the acceptable distance between partners. His grip loosened, but she heard the slight rumble of laughter deep in his chest.

"Jealous?" He took the first slow, graceful steps, immediately establishing his mastery of the dance. "You are beautiful, witty, always in demand. Surely you are used to people watching you? Particularly men?"

"As the women watch you, your grace? Your reputation far exceeds mine."

He laughed, a low sound meant for her ears alone. "Perhaps we shall add to our reputations."

The implications of his statement whirled in her head as he moved her around the dance floor in flawless rhythm. She had no trouble following him. He performed the scandalous dance as though it were invented to show off his lean physique, his manly command of his partner's body. Even with the proper space between them, she knew intuitively that their bodies would fit perfectly.

The music swirled through her. Closing her eyes, she let the melody and the man sweep her in wide, circling turns. Her body throbbed to life as the thought of the sensual possibilities this man offered.

Indeed, for a moment, she allowed herself the pleasure of imagining a far more intimate dance. Once or twice, as their thighs brushed together, she felt the hard muscles and envisioned his phallus, rigid and ready. Desire, heated and heavy, rushed through her. She felt her limbs go limp, knew only that his arm supported her, and savored the feeling.

But only for an instant. Abruptly, she forced the pleasure away. She knew only too well the risk of allowing her desire to govern her head. She could not allow this dance to be any more than it was, a brief moment out of time, an exquisite interlude.

Much as she would prefer to let the passion sweep her along, she could not allow an instant of weakness to threaten her liberty. If she allowed her heart to interfere with her head, if she let herself relax the vigilance that had served her well, she'd lose all that she had gained. In the three years of her widowhood, she'd become used to managing her own affairs and being in control of her inherited income.

Though there was nothing to say that Sutherland would be anything other than a passionate liaison, she knew herself too well. If she once allowed herself to indulge in the pleasure of making love with him, she wouldn't be content with a mere affair. She would want everything, the man, marriage and a life together. In return, she would be expected to surrender everything to him. The thought of submitting that authority over herself to a husband was enough to discourage any idea of matrimony.

She longed for the music to end, to release her from this sensual torment of being near him, yet she dreaded the moment when she would have to move out of his arms. She shivered at the touch of his hand on her waist. Through the material of her gown, and the delicate undergarments, she felt the warmth of his palm. The heat insinuated itself through her skin, to flicker like fire through her body. It penetrated her defenses. She longed to move closer, to lay her head on his broad chest and feel whether his heart thundered as hers did.

"I believe I knew your husband, madam. Died at Waterloo, didn't he?" His voice, deep with the rolling resonance of the Highlands, brought her to her senses. She collected her wavering defenses and gathered them closely about her. Her only hope lay in discouraging him, of being so cold that he would seek feminine company elsewhere. "Yes."

"A hero. No doubt you miss him greatly?'

"As any woman grieves for her husband, your grace."

This time he didn't hold back the laughter. It boomed out, drawing attention to them. She grit her teeth in frustration, resenting the intrusion into her brief moment with him. Why hadn't he the good sense to keep silent until the dance ended?

She started to withdraw from the circle of his arms, but he tightened his grip on her gloved hand. "My apologies," he stated as he twirled her around. "In my observation of the ton, grief is the last thing young wives feel when their elderly husbands cock up their toes."

"Perhaps you have been observing the wrong people," she said, a crisp edge to her voice.

"Perhaps. I would rather observe you. Those sapphires about your neck become you. They enhance the smoothness of your throat. Like fresh, sweet cream. I wonder, will it be as delicious to my tongue?"

"Your grace!" Her gaze darted up to meet his intent brown eyes. Once again she was reminded of the lion stalking his prey, all sinuous stealth and deadly determination. She felt impaled on that gaze, unable to move, to run, to protect herself.

"Yes? Surely men have complimented you before?"

She made herself speak lightly. "Not quite that way. At least, not in public."

"Quite so. When we are alone together, I shall compliment you in great detail—"

"There will be no opportunity for you to do so."

He smiled slightly. "Make no mistake, madam. You and I shall become intimately acquainted."

"I have no wish to continue this discussion, your grace. Pray release me."

"When the music is over."

She glanced up at his steely tone. She saw the predatory expression on his rugged face and despite her wish to escape the enticement of his arms, her heartbeat faltered. Temptation made her feel faint. She had to escape from his sensual lure before desire made her lose her good sense.

With relief, she heard the closing strains of the waltz. Sutherland could not expect another dance without causing speculation and that would protect her, at least for this evening. She would take care that they did not dance again.

They came to a halt not far from the grand staircase. He released her with a slight nod.

"Until we meet again."

A moment later, to her surprise, he was halfway up the stairs, leaving her feeling strangely abandoned. The buzz of gossip surrounded her as her fellow guests discussed the Duke's extraordinary departure and directed their curious glances at her. Holding her head high and her shoulders back, she, too, ascended the stairs, and called for her wrap and her carriage.

"Clarry! You must help me!"

The older woman paused as she carefully placed Antonia's jewelry into their velvet lined case. "What's the matter, milady?" She scrutinized Antonia. "You look all flushed and shivery like. Did you forget your shawl?"

"I must find a lover. There is no time to waste!"

Clarry bustled to her side and touched Antonia's forehead as if checking for fever.

"What's amiss?"

"Sutherland intends to make me his mistress."

Clarry's eyes lit up. "Sutherland? Now there's a man to keep you warm at night. I've heard that the women he beds wear smiles for a week—"

"This is no jesting matter," Antonia protested.

"What's wrong with his grace, I ask? I've heard he's a tiger—"

"Not a tiger," Antonia corrected. "A lion. He intends to make me his next meal."

"And about time, too."

"Clarry!" Antonia couldn't help smiling at her servant's plain spoken ways. The old woman had been her maid for many years and knew every one of her secrets and sins, yet sometimes Clarry still managed to surprise her. "Never him."

"And why not, milady? Now there's a real man for you—"

Antonia shut her eyes to avoid seeing the look on her servant's face. If Sutherland could make even elderly serving women look that rapturous, what more damage could he do to her heart? To her hard-won control over her own life?

"I will not have that man. Any but him"

Clarry's lips set firmly. "You are a fool, milady."

Antonia took no offense. "No doubt. You must help me find a new lover."

"Me?" Clarry all but squeaked.

"You've never failed me yet, Clarry. I count on you to help me." To take my mind off Sutherland, to assuage my need, to submerge myself in all the pleasure I can stand so that I no longer wonder what it would be like to make love with that Scot.

"You're sure about this, milady?"

"I am," Antonia stated. Her blood quickened at the memory of the duke's body so close to hers. "There is no time to lose."

Clarry sighed. "On your head be it."

"Oh, no," Antonia murmured to herself once Clarry had left her alone. "It's my heart that will pay the price."

Chapter Two

Antonia removed her hat and veil and gazed around the salon in the suite of rooms Clarry had secured. "You've done well, Clarry. You and the footmen will wait here while I am otherwise engaged." Clarry nodded. "It's not too late to change your mind, milady. The first of the lot isn't due for another half hour."

"No. I must do this. For my own sanity, if nothing else," Antonia murmured, her mind filled with the erotic dreams she'd had of Sutherland ever since the Wolfington ball. He wouldn't let her sleep. Now, more than ever, she needed a lusty lover to replace the thoughts of him.

She moved forward and opened the door leading to the bedroom. She studied the dimly lit room, the wide bed draped in gold brocade hangings, the thick Oriental carpets under her feet and the plump pillows piled invitingly on a well-upholstered chaise. "Oh, Clarry. This is beyond description!"

A low fire warmed the room, while aromatic candles provided just enough light to set a sensual mood. The room promised seduction. At the end of the bed, an emerald silk robe, richly embroidered in gold thread, lay next to a matching emerald silken scrap. Antonia picked it up and saw that it was a full head mask, with openings for the nose and mouth delicately outlined in matching gold floss. She smiled and lifted it to her face. "I can't see through it. Good."

"Nor be recognized," Clarry commented, her voice betraying her misgivings.

"Everything's just as you said, milady. There's your bell, there, if you need us. Ring, and we'll come running."

"I hope that won't be necessary."

"You never know, I say. Though I picked them carefully, some of these men aren't what you're used to. Some of them aren't gentlemen," she sniffed. "Why you can't stick to your own kind—"

"Because they are too full of themselves," Antonia said. "We've been over this before."

Clarry sniffed. "These men are common!"

"Just so they satisfy my requirements," Antonia reminded her. "I want no one who will remind me of Sutherland."

"No chance of that. Only thing these 'applicants'," she said in a voice laced with scorn, "Have in common with his grace is a yard."

Antonia frowned at the vernacular for a man's penis. "No need to be crude." She dropped her reticule on a small table and studied her servant's face. "You are sure you know what to tell them?"

"I know. Nothing more foolish I've never heard, but I'll tell them right enough."

"Good." Antonia removed her pelisse and started to undo the buttons of her high-waisted walking dress. "I had best get ready then."

She paused when Clarry drew it from her. A sudden chill swept across her, leaving her shivering. It's just nerves, she reassured herself. She'd come this far, she could go through with it.

Before she could change her mind, Antonia hastily undressed and donned the emerald robe. It fell over her breasts in a silken shimmer to sweep to her feet. She placed the mask over her face, adjusted the mouth and nose openings and tied the strings at the back of her head. She experimented with the mask until she was comfortable. "There. That should do it."

Clarry drew back the perfumed sheets. "You'd best get into bed, milady. That is if you insist on doing this."

Antonia said nothing as she arranged herself artfully on the soft mattress. "I'm ready."

She heard Clarry's rustles as the maid bustled about, tweaking a blanket here, plumping a pillow there, placing Antonia's clothes in the armoire. Antonia composed herself against the oversized pillows, until at last, they heard a knock on the outer door.

She sat up, her backbone straight.

"Shall I send him away, milady?" Clarry sounded hopeful.

"No." Antonia made herself relax back against the pillows. "When you are ready, allow him in."

Clarry left the door partially open. From her position on the bed, Antonia could hear the murmurs as Clarry spoke with the applicant. The voice was rough edged with none of the cultured tones of the peerage, but it was young and enthusiastic.

"First off," Clarry stated, "You are not to ask milady's name. You are to know nothing about her unless she tells you. If you are rough with her, or if you hurt her, heaven help you, for these two won't."

Antonia envisioned her two footmen bristling at the young man. She and Clarry had chosen them for their absolute loyalty to her, for their strength and ability to protect her.

"If milady says enough, or if she rings her little bell, you are to stop at once and leave her. If you do not, then it's that sorry I am for you." Clarry's voice carried the threat of what would happen to him if the applicant ignored his instructions.

"Aye. When do I meet the lady?"

"You understand what you are to do?"

"I'm to pleasure the lady—"

"That's all. You are not to do any more, do you understand?"

"I can't—"

Clarry interrupted him, her voice firm. "No."

"But, that's not natural, like. It's the man who's to say when and how—"

Antonia tensed. "Those are milady's rules," she heard her servant state. "No questions.

If you go in that room, you do as she says."

"And if I pleasure her, and she likes it, then I get to—?"

"Not this time. If she likes you enough, she'll tell you to come again."

"But if I do all that, when am I to—?"

Clarry snorted. "If you can't control yourself, man, then when she's done with you, you can go into the room beside hers and do what you must."

"Crazy fool notion," he grumbled, then his voice brightened."I can do what I please with her?"

Antonia held her breath until she heard Clarry reply, "You may touch her to give her pleasure. You can do whatever she lets you do. But you're not to harm her, you understand?"

"All right. Where do I take my clothes off?"

"You don't. Your jacket and those great hob boots is all."

Antonia heard the heavy boots drop to the floor, one after the other. Her breath quickening, she lay back against the pillows and waited.

The young man came through the doorway and closed the door behind him. "Milady?" he whispered.

Now that the moment was upon her, Antonia felt nerves overtake her, then remembered that this was her plan. She was in control. If necessary, she had only to call out and her servants would rush to help her. With that reassurance, she remembered why she had to take a lover. How else would she subdue her desire for Sutherland? Perhaps this applicant would be lusty enough to drive the thought of the Duke from her mind. She beckoned. "Come closer."

His footfalls muffled by the thick carpet, he approached the bed and stopped at the edge of the draperies. Antonia could hear the slight rustle of the draperies and his breathing change as he waited for instructions.

"Do you know what to do?" she murmured.

"Pleasure you," he said after a moment. "But how?"

"How do you usually do it?"

"Kiss her 'til she says she wants me."

"Kiss her where?"

"On the mouth, o'course."

"But you may not kiss my mouth. Where else would you kiss me?"

She felt the bed jiggle as he edged closer.

"Can I touch you?"

"Yes." She felt the tip of a callused finger against her nipple. "That would be nice, but a little later. Where else could you start?"

His fingers trailed down her body to the chestnut curls. He hesitated, then dipped between her legs, looking for her little bud.

She closed her thighs. "Too fast," she corrected him. "Think again."

This time, his fingers trailed down her legs to her knees. She felt him drop beside the bed and then felt first his warm breath, then his lips hover over her knee. "That would be a good place to start," she agreed.

His mouth was warm, his tongue agile as he pressed kisses to her calf, her knee and then licked his way up her thigh. "That's the right idea."

His kisses grew hotter the closer he got to the juncture of her thighs. She relaxed, but not enough to give him access. Taking his cue from her, he bypassed that area and moved his mouth across her hipbones, down into the hollow of her stomach, then nudged his way past her ribs. He nuzzled between her breasts, and when her nipples began to peak, he lapped at one, then took it firmly between his lips and suckled.

As the tugging at her breast grew stronger, she sighed and relaxed. With this encouragement, he climbed on the bed with her and lay at her side. He continued to feast on her nipple.

She lifted a hand to stroke his shoulder. "That's very nice," she murmured. "Don't forget the other one needs attention, too." He let the one go and turned obediently to the other as her hand drifted over his corded muscles. "How old are you?"

He lifted his mouth just enough to say, "Three and twenty."

His endurance wouldn't be a problem, then. "You're very strong."

He nodded. The motion pulled at the breast, making her feel the sensation deep down inside. It felt good to concentrate only on her own feelings, without having to worry about pleasing her companion.

Gradually, she let the strangeness of the situation be forgotten as she delved deeper into the pleasure. While his technique lacked polish, his willingness to take direction satisfied her. Now that he had an idea of what she wished, he seemed determined to fulfill her requirements.

With his mouth still busy at her breasts, his hands roamed her body, learning the curves and indentation of her hips and buttocks.

He trailed a warm finger between the half moons of her derriere until it eased into the moist heat between her legs. She moaned and flexed her thighs, opening herself to his inquisitive touch.

With a gentleness that surprised her, he caressed her inner flesh, his breath quickening as he felt the dew of her desire. Seemingly spurred on by the evidence of her acceptance, he eased a finger into her, stroking softly, then harder as her hips lifted to him.

"Yes," she whispered. "That's it. More."

He obliged, fitting himself more securely on the bed that his hand might pleasure her more deeply. He maintained the stroke, alternating that with a flicking motion of his thumb on her nub. His breath came harsher, hotter, as she responded to him.

Against her thigh, Antonia felt his erection grow and strain against the coarse material of his trousers. The length of it pleased her as she thought of the depths he could reach and caress with his hard manhood. All at once, the memory of Sutherland's body, so close to her in that unforgettable waltz, spurred her into her a mild fulfillment.

When the inner contractions stopped, she lay on her bed, unsatisfied. The young man had done as she bade him. It wasn't his fault that the thought of Sutherland intruded at such an awkward moment, yet it was apparent to her that this applicant would be incapable of banishing Sutherland.

She sighed with disappointment. "Go now."

"But, I pleased you." He eased into a sitting position. "You know I did. What about me?"

"You may take care of yourself elsewhere."

"Aye, but next time?"

"You will be informed if there is to be a next time."

She felt him hesitate, as if debating with himself whether he should press the issue. Then with a muttered curse, he heaved himself away from her. She listened to his heavy footfalls as he left the room, then heard him draw on his clothing.

She heard the clink of coins, and imagined the look on his face as Clarry paid him.

"That's it, then?"

"If my mistress wants to see you again, I'll let you know."

Moments after the outer door closed, Clarry wasted no time in going to Antonia.

"You're all right then? He didn't hurt you?"

Antonia pulled the mask off and shook her head to free her hair. The chestnut tresses tumbled to her shoulders. "No, but he won't do."

Clarry put her hands on her ample hips. "He didn't satisfy you, then?"

Regret tingeing her voice, Antonia said, "No, not enough."

"You want to go on with this, then?"

"I must," Antonia said simply.

Clarry muttered under her breath all the while she helped Antonia refresh herself and dress. She took a moment to tidy the room, then ushered Antonia, in her veil once more, down the stairs to the waiting carriage.

Antonia hid a yawn behind her black lace mitt as she sat in the ornate salon of the Howard's town house. Feeling the strain of interviewing potential lovers by afternoon, and maintaining her social calendar by night, she longed to put an end to the intimate testing.

Though each of the applicants had pleasured her, some more so than others, none measured up to her requirements.

Tensing her jaw against another yawn, she noticed movement to her side then glanced first at a pair of trousers barely skimming the hard muscled thighs beneath them, then up at the man wearing them. Not again!

"Hate these musicales, myself," Sutherland murmured as he took the gilded white seat next to her. "Hear Lady Howard has them weekly. Poor Howard."

She said nothing.

He leaned closer and lowered his voice. "You are yawning, my lady. Perhaps you are fatigued by your busy days?"

She froze. Could he know? Feverishly, she thought over the arrangements. Clarry had vowed secrecy. Sutherland could not possibly know anything. Reassured, she kept her eyes on the trio of musicians. "My days are always busy."

"More so lately."

She shot an alarmed glance at him. He regarded her with casual ease, but she didn't miss the narrowed brown eyes, the craggy cheek bones made more pronounced by the muscle ticking at his jaw. He was angry? With her?

Antonia looked around None of the other guests seemed interested in them. She kept her voice low and forced a polite smile. "My activities are no concern of yours, your grace."

"And if I wish to make them mine?"

"There is no reason to do so."

His mouth tightened. "Let us discuss this more privately."

"There is nothing to discuss. Pray do not disturb me any longer."

He hooked his hand under her elbow, and forced her to rise with him. Stepping carefully past the people seated next to them, he drew her to the aisle, then out into an adjoining foyer. With one grim look, he dismissed the footmen.

Once they were alone, she tugged her elbow free. "What do you think you are doing?"

"Merely ensuring you listen to me." His voice softened and he looked at her with something like amusement. "Did you know I came haring to London when I heard you had ousted Effingdale?"

Antonia shrugged. "Gossip travels exceedingly fast, your grace. What does that prove?"

"Do you know why I came so quickly?"

She shivered at the intent look on his face. His amusement had faded, replaced by a look more akin to possessiveness. He stood so close that she could feel the warmth of his breath upon her cheek, feel the heat of his body next to hers. Once again she felt like his quarry and stared back, mesmerized, into his predatory eyes. Her blood began to simmer. She moved away, hoping her casual manner betrayed none of her inner turmoil. She gestured with her fan. "I'm sure your reasons have no interest for me."

He moved closer. "On the contrary, they concern you."

"How odd. I can think of no reason why you should involve yourself with me."

"No?" He took another pace closer. "Shall I tell you why?"

She edged behind a small round table. "I am not interested, your grace." She cocked her head as the music floated to her. "Lady Howard will wonder what has become of us."

He came forward, rounding the table after her until she found herself with her back against the wall. Though several inches remained between them, Antonia felt surrounded. His body blocked out the sight of anything behind him. She was conscious only of him, of the heat of his body, of the determined way he stared at her, eyes narrowed and intent. Her heart beat faster beneath the low décolletage of her evening gown.

Desperately, she tried not to let him see how his nearness affected her, but her body sensed the lure of his and responded. She told herself she was susceptible only because she had thought of him at a critical time only that afternoon, but what she felt now made her earlier feelings tepid and dull.

The warmth spreading through her softened her, making her moist and ready. Her breathing became jerky under his intent and powerful gaze. Her breasts expanded as her nipples bloomed against the delicate lace of her chemise. The tiny chafing made her wonder how Sutherland's mouth and tongue would ease the small hurt.

"I can tell you what will become of us, Antonia. We shall be lovers."

"How absurd." She tried a laugh, but it sounded more of gasp. "I choose my own liaisons."

"And so you shall. You shall choose me." Bending slightly forward, so that his voice reached only her ear, he asked, "Can you imagine what it will be like between us? Pure flame. You are a passionate woman, not in the least afraid of your womanly desires. Do you know how rare that is? I am a man who appreciates and rewards sensuality in a woman. We shall do wonderful things together."

He smelled of rare and marvelous spices and ointments, of aroused masculinity held rigidly in check. Antonia wanted nothing more than to put out the tip of her tongue and trace the underside of his jaw and his throat, to sample him, to see for herself if he tasted as she imagined.

She eyed the tanned flesh of his neck above the snowy white cravat and wondered if his skin would be as tawny everywhere else. Would the pelt on his chest be as silk to her hand, or the rougher fur of the lion he resembled? Would he be as dominant, as forceful in bed as he appeared to be out of it?

She swallowed past the dry lump in her throat. "Nonsense," she demurred though the heat rose in her blood and melted her resistance. She swayed on her feet, leaning toward him in an irresistible longing to feel even more of his warmth, to feel his body next to hers, to savor the pleasure his few words had conjured up. More than anything, she desired to put his claim to the test. Would they indeed go up in flames together?

"You are in need of a lover, Antonia. Even now your body is ready for mine. Why not accept me?"

His words cooled her faster than an icy bath. In another instant, she would have succumbed to desire and ruined everything. "I...no."

"Be warned, Antonia, I am not a patient man."

Chapter Three

"How many more applicants are there?" Antonia peered over her morning cup of chocolate as Clarry brushed crumbs away from the bedcovers.

Clarry jumped and tipped the silver pot. She fluttered with a napkin, mopping up the few drops that had stained the pristine white cloth.

"Is something the matter?"

"No, not so's you'd notice, milady."

Antonia studied the older woman's face. She appeared uneasy and strangely reluctant to speak. "Then, what is it?"

"Don't go on with this any more. You'll regret it."

"What ever is the matter with you this morning, Clarry? You look like you're going to collapse. Sit down, here, next to me." Antonia moved her legs to make room for Clarry's ample rump. "Now, talk."

Clarry fidgeted with a fold of her skirt. "I don't want you to go back to that place. Not again. No telling what'll happen if you do."

"I have to," Antonia murmured. "Are there any more applicants, then?"

Clarry looked away. "Just one."

"That is all? I thought you'd said that you had to turn them away."

"I did." Clarry faced Antonia, her old face indignant. "I turned dozens of them away, all of them with their tongues hanging out."

Antonia winced. "I don't understand. What has changed?"

Clarry devoted her attention to her skirt again. "Maybe the word's out that the masked lady is too particular like. That no one can please you."

Her words reminded Antonia of Sutherland. Despite herself, warmth coiled low in her abdomen. She lifted the cooling chocolate to her lips and sipped.

Clarry continued, "Why don't you choose one you've already tried out and let it go at that?"

"I can't." Antonia replaced the cup on the tray and sank back against her fluffed pillows. "None of them will do." She thought of the fumbling applicant she'd last interviewed and without volition, her mind instantly compared him to Sutherland. Until she found someone who could erase Sutherland from her mind, she had to continue. "Perhaps this last one will do the trick."

"He'd better," Clarry muttered.

"Is everything arranged?"

"Your bath is ready."

"That is not what I'm asking, Clarry, and you know it."

Clarry turned away from her ladyship's gentle voice. At the knock at the door, she opened it and took a folded note from the footman. She saw the ducal seal and took it to Antonia with trembling fingers.

Antonia broke the seal and read the few words. Admiration for his perseverance and dismay that he persisted warred within her. She glanced up at Clarry. "It's from Sutherland. He wants me to ride with him this afternoon."

"Good idea, that. You could use some fresh air."

"I will be busy at that time, Clarry. Remember?"

Clarry pursed her lips. "Wouldn't hurt to cancel."

Antonia rose and went to her small desk where she penned him a polite refusal. "Send this back, will you?"

"Why are you refusing the duke? He's perfect for what you want."

Antonia's shoulders slumped against the desk chair. "That's the trouble. He's too perfect. Oh, Clarry, he could ruin me."

"How?" Clarry asked bluntly. "He's got enough of everything. More than enough, if you can believe the gossip. Pots of money. An income to make the Prince his best friend. And he's not half bad to look at, either."

"How do you know all that?"

"It's no secret that the Prince of Wales is always short in the pocket. Borrows from all his friends, he does, but not much chance of his ever paying them back."

"No, I mean about the Duke."

Clarry hesitated. "I hear things. That's why you wanted my help with all this foolishness, isn't it?"

"That's true." Antonia looked thoughtful. "What else have you heard?"

"About his grace?"

Antonia nodded.

Clarry sat and settled her weight comfortably, as if preparing for a cozy chat. "Well, he's got estates in Scotland. Way north, where the sun never shines."

"He is brown from the sun," Antonia demurred.

That didn't stop her maid. In full swing, Clarry continued. "Pots of money, like I said. He's good to his household staff. Only one mistress at a time. He's faithful, like."

Antonia laughed. Somehow the description Clarry offered didn't resembled the tawny lion she knew. She made him sound like a trusty hound, content to lounge at her feet in front of a warm winter fire, while the man she knew was all lion, roaming his domain, intent on maintaining his rule. Her laughter faded as she considered her situation. She couldn't afford to see him again. She didn't dare, never knowing when she'd swoon at his feet and hope that he'd pick up and care for her heart as well as her person.

"Well, let's get on with it, then." Antonia shrugged out of the lace and satin gown and

let it drop to her feet.

After her bath and a simple coiffure that wouldn't be mussed later, Antonia donned an elegant afternoon gown and pelisse. She picked up her heavily veiled hat.

Clarry opened the door. "You don't have to go," she offered on a hopeful note.

Antonia shot her a thoughtful look. Clarry was up to something, but she didn't have time to find out. Later, after the afternoon interview was over, then she'd get to the bottom of this. An hour or so later, once more wearing only her emerald silk robe and the matching mask, Antonia reclined on the bed in the boudoir of her rented rooms and waited for the last applicant to arrive. She heard the knock at the outer door, then muted voices as Clarry instructed him. After a few moments, Clarry knocked and entered.

"He's here."

"Show him in, then."

Antonia heard Clarry close the door and waited. Knowing that this man was her last applicant made her all the more aware that everything must go well. The strident calls of street vendors hawking their wares, the heavy wagons and carriages passing by were muted by the thick drapes at the windows and seemed very far away.

A log shifted in the grate. Antonia heard the hiss of new flame, then the steady flames and imagined them licking eagerly at fresh fuel. The man, if he had indeed entered the bed-chamber, was so still that Antonia began to wonder. Senses straining for some indication that she wasn't alone, she shifted position on the bed and wondered why he waited. "Is someone there?"

There was no answer, but she became aware of a presence, no more than the barest hint of another person breathing. A curious anticipation filled her as she detected the slightest disturbance in the air and then the soft footsteps. He approached the bed and stood silent beside it.

As though it was already her lover's touch, she felt his gaze on her body, nude except where the emerald silk artfully revealed her. She couldn't repress the warmth suffusing her skin.

"You may begin," she whispered.

He dropped on his knees beside her. Now she could hear him breathe, a slightly ragged sound that reassured her. He paused, as if contemplating what his first move would be. Antonia waited, excitement building. He exhaled, as if calming himself. His warm breath wafted over her. She shivered.

With a forefinger, he touched the tender skin of her bent elbow, then traced the delicate curve to her wrist. He bent and touched his mouth to the pulse there. Her throat went dry at the feel of his warm, firm lips on her skin. With just that simple beginning, she knew that this was no ordinary applicant.

He lifted his head. Linking his fingers with hers, he brought her hand to his mouth and pressed tiny kisses over the back of it, then turned her hand and repeated the kisses, nibbling now and then again, on the soft palm and each of her fingers.

They quivered in his. He took one into his mouth, sucking gently, twirling his tongue around the tip of it, then nipping. He laved the tiny hurt with his tongue, and suckled harder. Antonia sighed blissfully, anticipating how that would feel on her breasts.

He left her hand to trail kisses up to her elbow, until the sleeve of her robe stopped him. He switched his attention to her other arm, repeating the same kisses and nips until Antonia squirmed and changed her position on the plump pillows.

He undid the sash at her waist. With one hand, he parted the sides until the gap revealed her breasts and the curve of her waist and abdomen. His breathing told Antonia that he liked what he saw. She expected him to push the robe farther out of the way, but instead he left it where it was and with a touch so light that she imagined she barely felt it, he smoothed his fingertips over the soft down of her body. The tiny hairs, invisible to the eye, quivered at their passing. Antonia felt the slight stroking caress all the way to her bones. She trembled, waiting for more.

Only when he had caressed all the skin visible to him did he nudge the robe out of the way, an inch at a time. He continued his massage, fingering now the curves and planes he had left untouched before, making her aware as never before of the sensitive arch where arm met chest, of the tenderness of the sides of her breasts. He traced each of her ribs from side to front, learning her, until her eyes closed and her breath came shallow. He feathered her breasts and nipples, making her arch against his hands, mutely asking for more. Instead, he moved the robe out of the way and lightly touched her armpits. Ordinarily ticklish, Antonia felt no desire to laugh. She gasped when he turned her, removing the robe in one swift motion.

On her stomach, she felt vulnerable and exposed to him, but the instant his fingertips returned to her body, she forgot her qualms. She wanted more. With the tip of his finger, he followed the curve of her back to her buttocks, stopping to explore the indentation of her spine. By the time he reached her buttocks, she was moaning.

The delay was excruciating. Antonia wanted more, and she wanted it all at once. That he made her wait while he pleasured every inch of her skin was unbearable, both thrilling and frustrating. She heard his breathing change as he varied his method and replaced his fingertip with his tongue.

She stiffened at the first moist touch on the swell of her hip. Her shoulders came up off the bed as her head lifted. He pressed her back down into the mattress with both hands, a gentle inexorable pressure, until she subsided and lay supine for him.

With long, slow strokes of his tongue, he covered every inch that he had previously massaged with his fingertips. Antonia felt ready to scream. He followed his moist lapping with a gentle exhalation. The cool air on her skin after the warmth of his mouth almost drove her out of her mind. She gripped the pillows at her head and hung on.

He moved away only long enough to shift her to her back again. Antonia lay with her eyes closed, waiting expectantly for what he would do next. He didn't keep her waiting long as he bent his head to her and continued laving her, until he had attended to every inch of her except her most intimate feminine recesses. She waited for him to caress her there as well, but he skirted her mound, to move on to her belly, which quivered under his ministrations.

She felt stretched on the rack of sensuality, unwilling to stop and equally unwilling to have it end. Heat pooled deep within her, building to an inexorable ache. She was afraid that if he continued, she'd burn alive under his touch, yet she feared with an equal dread that if he stopped, she'd hang quivering, nerves stretched to breaking point. He was the most imaginative, tender and stimulating man ever to provoke such a response from her, and all he had used was his hands and his mouth!

She moaned softly as she stretched under his touch. Her legs parted, inviting him, but he nuzzled at her neck through the silken mask and made her earlobes the focus of his attention. After a few moments, Antonia realized that she'd never put on another pair of earrings without thinking of this man. Vaguely she wondered where he had perfected his lovemaking technique, but her curiosity ended abruptly when he withdrew and sat by the side of the bed. She waited, barely breathing, for what he would do next.

His hand stroked her from throat to mound. Antonia knew he waited for permission to continue. She hesitated. He had shown her things about herself that she'd never known. How much more could he teach her?

"Please continue." Her voice sounded low and sultry even to her own ears.

Immediately, he bent his head and touched the tip of his tongue to a nipple. Already hard and ripe, the nipple ached and grew even more swollen. He eased his lips around it, sucking gently, etching circles around it, then suckling. A red hot burst of desire shot through her. She clutched his shoulders.

Even with her attention occupied by the marvelous sensations at her breast, she felt the hard muscles beneath his skin and gripped harder, her nails biting into him. When he raised his head to attend to the other breast, she eased up on him enough to smooth her palm over her back.

"Take your shirt off," she whispered.

He complied. She put her hand on his chest, smiling beneath her mask at the feel of him, all hard muscles rippling and the thatch covering him from flat male nipple to belly. She circled his nipple and murmured her pleasure in how quickly it hardened under her touch.

Her hand traced the silky curls until they disappeared under his waistband. He drew in his breath but said nothing. She let her hand follow the flat planes of his belly until it came to the unmistakable hot length of his turgid shaft. She cupped him through the material of his trousers, entranced by the unseen promise of his erection. It pulsed, hot and heavy, in her hand, as if eager to be free of the confines of his clothing. Through the delicious haze, she wondered how it would feel to have him enter her, to stroke her, first slowly and provocatively, then fast and furiously.

She smiled, a slow satisfied smile at the knowledge that she wasn't the only one affected by his lovemaking. "You like that?" she murmured.

He said nothing but the way his member grew, harder and longer, in the palm of her hand told her everything she needed to know. "What would you like to do next?"

In response, he moved his palm, cupping her mound in return. He toyed with the curls, drawing them through his fingers as the skin of her belly contracted. He stroked her muff, his finger at first gentle and slow, then moving faster as her body responded. He slipped a long finger into the moist warmth, gently separating the plump outer lips until he found her bud. He stroked it once or twice, then circled it, and traced the opening to her inner passage. She clawed at the sheets as pleasure shuddered through her. Sensation centered in that one throbbing bloom.

She moaned when he took away his hand, but as his mouth replaced his fingers, Antonia breathed out, a long shuddering exhalation. She sighed in relief, then felt the inner contractions that surrounded his finger even as he did. He had to know it.

Instead of continuing, he withdrew. She moaned in distress. He palmed her once again, drawing her moisture into his hand, then spread it in sensuous circles around her navel. He followed his hand with his mouth, licking every drop away from her quivering skin. She arched under him, offering him more, begging for more.

As if he had heard her plea, he returned to her privities, licking and nipping in tiny bites. She thrashed on the bed, head tossing from side to side, strung out on a rack of desire and aching for release. She lifted her knees and parted her thighs to make room for him between her legs, but he ignored the blatant invitation and stuck to his instructions. Her breath came in short pants and the flames threatened to consume her.

"Now," she cried. "Oh, please, now!"

He pushed one long finger within her, then two, stroking hard, mimicking the thrusts his body would make. He put his mouth to her breast and suckled one while his hand attended to the other. Wracked with pleasure, every susceptible nerve in her body hummed with passion. She closed her inner muscles around his fingers, pulsing around them, milking them, until her last shivering cry died away.

His breath coming as harshly as hers, he pulled free. She barely noticed how he arranged her lax body and rested briefly beside her. They lay quietly together until their breathing calmed.

When she turned her head to thank him, he pressed his lips to hers. Sated, exhausted and pleasured beyond belief, Antonia had no strength left to protest. She felt the desire, fiercely controlled, within him, and pushing the mask aside, she opened her mouth to him.

He refused the invitation, and left her.

Chapter Four

That evening, Antonia hid a yawn behind her hand as she waited for her partner to draw another card. Though she had slept for two hours after the applicant left her this afternoon, her body was still lax and exhausted. She would have sent her regrets to Lady Fox's whist party, but that would have disarranged the numbers, and Maude Fox was unforgiving when it came to disrupting her card evenings.

She gritted her teeth against the need to yawn again. The man, whoever he had been, had satisfied her like no other lover. His touch had made her body come to life and go up in flames before he had finally allowed her release. Just thinking about the way he had pleasured her made her legs go limp. Thank goodness she was sitting down.

If he could make her feel as she did without his body entering hers, what could he do when their bodies were joined? She felt a flush creeping up her breasts to her throat and placed a hand over her bosom to cover it.

"Are you feverish, Lady Blair-Sutworth?"

Her hand dropped as her gaze flew upward to the man standing by her table. Dougal MacDonald, that insufferable seventh duke of Sutherland, looked down at her with a quizzical smile on his leonine features. With his tawny hair perfectly in place, his evening attire clothing his body like a lover's caress, he appeared to be very much in control.

She stiffened. "I am quite well, your grace. How kind of you to inquire," she added cooly when she saw the curious looks cast their way.

"Not kind at all," he denied. "Your skin is quite flushed." He bent closer and studied her. "Your eyes have a strange look to them. Quite dreamy. Are you sure you are not ill?"

She leaned away from him. "I am not ill. It is a shade too warm in here."

He straightened but didn't take his gaze from her. "Perhaps a breath of fresh air?"

Though she hadn't noticed the temperature of the room before now, it was suddenly unbearably close. A few moments out on the terrace would be just the thing to clear her brain. Excusing herself, she rose from the card table and took Sutherland's arm. He guided her through the mass of tables to a set of doors open to the night air.

She tried to ignore the feel of his muscled arm beneath her hand, but the heat rose through his clothing and added to her feverish sensation. Though he was the soul of discretion as he moved her through the crowded room, acknowledging acquaintances and friends, she knew he was intent on getting her alone. It didn't bother her this time, since she was now immune to his sexual lure. After all, with a lover like the man she'd tested this afternoon, she had no reason to succumb to Sutherland's masculine allure.

She confidently stepped outside and she the cool evening air into her lungs.

"Better now?"

She glanced at the man at her side. "Very much so."

Grateful for the dark that hid his intense interest, he turned slightly away from her and gestured to a couple strolling off a path into the darkened arbor. "Those two have the right idea. They'll come to an agreement in the shrubbery. He'll emerge with a satisfied look on his face, I wager, while she will come forth with her hair and clothing awry and an equally satisfied expression."

She had to laugh. "You are far too observant."

"Perhaps we should find our own bit of greenery," he offered in an off-hand voice.

"I have no desire to be mussed, thank you."

An image of her body sprawled in sensual pleasure whipped

through him. Her lush body, slender and yet voluptuous, would tease and arouse him until his control threatened to snap under the weight of just a murmur, or one movement of silken limbs. Her legs, long and shapely, enticed him. He imagined them clasped around his waist as she begged him for release. Her breasts, full and just the right size for his hand, made him sweat.

He would muss her, he vowed. And she would love it.

"Pity," he drawled. "I would make sure you emerged from the bushes with more than a satisfied look on your beautiful face."

"You have a vivid imagination, your grace."

He hid a grin. She'd had only a taste of his inventive mind. He could hardly wait until their next meeting. "Do I?" he asked in a languid voice though his body was taut and hardened with desire. "Shall we compare our fantasies, then? I'll tell you one of mine, then you shall tell me yours."

She flicked him a small, seductive smile. "I think not, sir. I have heard of your legendary prowess with the ladies. I am afraid that I could not compete."

"I don't want your competition, madam," he said in a voice suddenly harsh. ""I want you.""

Chapter Five

Sutherland entered the dim bedchamber and paused while his eyes adjusted to the dark. The sumptuous room lured him in with promises of sensual delight. The mingled aromas of fresh flowers, subtle perfume and the lingering scent of sexual release made his nostrils flare.

He made his way to the reclining figure on the bed. Wearing the emerald green mask and gown she hid behind, Lady Antonia Blair-Sutworth presented a most delicious sight. She rested on an elbow, the gown slipping off her shoulder to reveal pale skin that gleamed like vanilla satin in the candlelight. One knee was drawn up, the other leg extended with the gown draped just so, enough to tantalize him with glimpses of her shapely legs and the merest hint of the chestnut curls between her thighs.

His mouth went dry with anticipation of the things he would do to her this afternoon. He'd come prepared. As he neared the bed, he saw that the green mask fluttered as she breathed. The cloth rose and fell with her bosom. So, she, too, was eager. That made his task all the more pleasant and rewarding.

He'd vowed he'd keep his mind cool and uncluttered, that he would delve the depths of sensuality with her without he himself becoming affected. In short, he vowed he'd teach her a lesson, a dangerous lesson, about the depths of depravity and decadence. After today, she would know better than to allow anyone but himself into her bed.

Without waiting for her permission, he stripped off his fine linen shirt and tossed it carelessly on a nearby chair. In his buckskin trousers, he placed one knee on the bed and allowed himself one tender touch, just for his pleasure, before he steeled his nerve to carry out his plan.

Her skin was warm, smooth to his fingertips. She quivered at his touch, telling him wordlessly that she was already aroused. Good. By the time he was done with her, she'd know all there was to know about arousing unfulfilled desires. He almost smiled at the thought of himself, Dougal MacDonald, randy seventh duke of Sutherland, so besotted with her that he'd stoop to playing stud for her.

"Good afternoon," she murmured in the low and throaty voice that enchanted him. "Are you going to speak today?"

When he said nothing, she continued, "No? Then I shall speak for us both. I was content with yesterday's interview. Have you something new to show me today?"

He grinned. Taking her hand, he held it to his cheek as he nodded yes.

"M'mm, that's good. Would you like to begin?"

Again, he indicated he would. He kissed her hand, then replaced it on her hip. She settled more comfortably into the plump pillows at her back as she waited for him to start making love to her.

He considered, then reached for the small leather case he'd placed on the table next to the flickering candle. He opened it, eyed the contents, and withdrew a plume with soft, eider down feathers. He tested it on his neck then drew it slowly along hers.

"What is that?" she gasped.

In response, he drew the feather down the edge of her robe, now tracing the gold embroidery, now skirting the edge of the material to brush her bare skin. She shivered.

He feathered every inch of exposed skin, making her skin tremble under his touch, until he reached her toes. She laughed as he tickled the soles of her feet, but her laughter changed to a pleased murmur when he found the sensitive spot behind her knee.

"You are a devil, aren't you?" she all but moaned when the feather reached the back of her thigh and teased the chestnut curls.

Sutherland grinned. She had experienced only the beginning. With the tip of the feather, he drew the robe back slowly, caressing her as he exposed her. She parted her legs for him, inviting more, but he ignored the offer and drew the robe back up over her thigh. He paused to exchange the soft downy feather for a stiffer one, a fine egret. With that, he traced the enticing curve of her hip, pushing the robe back as he went, until her entire hip and the swell of her buttock was his.

She murmured, low in her throat.

He pulled the robe from her in slow motion, using the silken fabric as an additional caress on her skin, until she lay open and naked for him. He moved her to her stomach, positioning her the way he wanted her, with one leg slightly bent and the other extended. Satisfied with the way she was open to him, he ran the egret feather from ankle to thigh. Her skin, soft and finely textured, quivered as he passed, increasingly so as he reached the curve of her blind cheeks. He ran the feather between the twin mounds, first up toward the base of her spine, then back again, slower this time, lingering, tantalizing, making her moan, until he reached the softest flesh of her outer lips.

He withdrew the feather and brushed it over the back of his hand. The feathers were damp with her dew. Gratified, he placed the feather back in the case and while one hand rested on her hip to keep her in place, he selected a small jar of lotion.

He uncapped it, sniffed it and replaced it. Choosing another, he tested it again and pleased with this one, he left the cap on the table while he poured a small amount of the lotion into the hollow above her buttocks.

She tensed at the feel of the cool lotion, then relaxed as he began to smooth it in slow circles, kneading away any remaining tension. The scent of almonds filled the air about them as the lotion warmed under the combined heat of his hand and her back. He felt her muscles go limp under his ministrations and nodded with satisfaction.

He loved the way she responded to him. Granted, he was using all the seductive tricks he knew to batter her senses, but as she responded so willingly and wholeheartedly, he found his determination not to feel anything weakening. His rigid cock chafed against the confines of his clothing. He gritted his teeth against the ache and set his mind again to ignore his own lust.

He continued the sensual massage until every inch of her back, shoulders and legs had been covered with the scented lotion. He eased her over on her back and paused to view his handiwork. In the candlelight, he saw her full breasts and the dark aureoles surrounding her already hard and extended nipples. Pouring more lotion into her navel, he began his massage again.

When he had covered every inch but her breasts, he sat back on his haunches a moment to contemplate his next move. By the way she moved against the sheets, he knew she was eager for more. Her skin was flushed, warm from his ministrations, aromatic with the scent of almonds, her own perfume, and the scent of aroused woman, what the French called *cassolette*, perfume box.

"Don't stop now," she pleaded.

Smiling, Sutherland bent his head, placed his open mouth on one breast and did nothing for a moment but inhale her fragrance. His head reeled with the seductive, sensual scent of a woman who was not afraid of her own sexual nature, who even now was urging him on to greater heights of sensuality.

Obliging both her pleas and his need to make love to his woman, he traced the aureole, gently at first, then varying his touch, loving the firm texture and the way her skin puckered and her nipple grew even harder and longer in his mouth. He nipped gently, small love bites that increased her sensitivity and her pleasure. He sucked, gently at first, then harder as he suckled, taking what he vaguely understood and then accepted as both lustful and a more enduring nourishment from her.

He turned to the other breast, giving it the same dedicated, thorough attention while his hand caressed the breast he had just left, keeping it satisfied and the nipple hard under his palm.

Her breathing grew heavier.

He left her breast for a moment to nuzzle the sweet, tender flesh of her armpit. He inhaled deeply, aroused by her femininity, then showered her with kisses and drew her skin into his mouth, leaving faint marks behind on her skin. She arched her back, giving more of herself to him, and he couldn't help the low growl of possession with which he accepted the gift of herself.

She lifted a knee, drawing his attention to her parted thighs. Smiling to himself at her responsiveness and eagerness for more, he now followed her hint and traced with his tongue a lingering, teasing path to the curls between her thighs. He nipped at her skin as he went, easing the tiny hurt with kisses, as he inched his way around her navel to the satiny skin below it. He followed with his hand, pulling gently at the curls, until she moaned as he cupped her mound.

He caressed the fleshy outer lips for a moment, while he positioned himself, he slipped an elbow under her raised knee, and then kissed his way up to her muff. He placed gentle, open mouthed kisses on the closed lips as though she were an inexperienced virgin he was initiating, enjoying the way she chafed under his restraint, until she reached for his head and holding him by the temples, grated, "More!"

He chuckled and obeyed.

He gave her deeper tongue strokes, parting the lips with his tongue until he came to the treasure within. She moaned with pleasure and came immediately. Her orgasm pleased him immensely. Lifting his head, he took the heady moisture and smoothed it on her belly, then lapped it up, enchanted by both her response and the fragrance of her moist perfume. She lay still under his mouth, yet her skin rippled and quivered, telling him without words that she was still aroused and ready for more.

He gave her more. Bending his head to her once more, he put his mouth on her still quivering bud and licked. When that wasn't enough, he inserted his tongue into her intimate recesses and then withdrew. She tightened her legs about him. He penetrated her again and again with his tongue, deliberately controlling his almost frantic need to replace his tongue with his yard, until she came, again and again, in great flooding orgasms.

She lay limp under him.

When he took his mouth away, she moaned and attempted to curl up on her side. He prevented her by placing a hand on her hip, keeping her in place, while the other hand cupped her mound. With a finger, he traced the path his tongue had taken earlier.

"No more," she whimpered. "I can't stand any more"

He ignored her just as he ignored his own desperate need. Wanting, needing, aching to thrust into her and relieve his own painful arousal, he penetrated her, finding the silken inner walls still contracting around his finger. He added another finger and placed his thumb on her bud, arousing her with strokes and gentle pressure until she cried out and convulsed around his fingers.

He left them there until the last shudder died away and she slept.

He stood and studied her as she lay, arms and legs tangled in the mussed sheets. Instead of feeling satisfied that he'd beaten her at her own game, he had to admit that it was he who had surrendered. He'd succumbed to her womanly sensuality and wanted her more than ever. She was everything he could ever hope for. Passionate, comfortable with her own sexual need, she'd match him in bed and demand more and more. He'd die happy trying to satisfy her.

Though he'd come haring to London to make her his mistress, knowing full well that they'd tire of each other eventually, that was no longer enough. Now that he'd tasted her, experienced how she responded to him, he'd be damned if he'd release her to move on to another liaison. From now on, no man but he would share her bed.

Like it or not, Lady Antonia Blair-Sutworth was his, forever.

Chapter Six

Late that evening, Sutherland saw Antonia going into midnight supper on the arm of the Honorable Edward St. John. A moment of fury passed through him before he regained the rigid control he cultivated. How could she look so radiant, so damned beautiful on the arm of another man after he had wracked himself to bring her pleasure this afternoon?

Jealousy, hot and violent, followed his footsteps as he strode, barely slowing to acknowledge the other guests of the Baroness of Rockingham's ball. Though she tried to detain him with thanks for gracing her home, and thus making her a name to be reckoned within the *haute ton*, he barely spoke two words to her on his way to Antonia.

He reached her side just as St. John seated her. Sutherland grasped the back of the chair the other man had intended for himself and seated himself before St. John could protest.

He nodded to the startled man. "Thanks, St. John, for allowing me to take your place."

With nothing to do but bow gracefully before the peer, St. John did just that and murmured an apology before he disappeared into the crush.

"That was very rude of you, your grace. Perhaps you should have inquired if I desired your company before you acted so rashly."

"And good evening to you, my lady. You are more beautiful than ever." He meant every word. She was truly exquisite this evening, her green eyes sparkling and her skin the color of pale porcelain, barely tinged with a subtle warmth. Her chestnut hair, burnished from the light of a hundred candelabra, was piled high in an intricate style that accentuated her slender neck and beautiful shoulders. If he looked closely, he could just detect the faint markings of the love bite he had given her that afternoon.

Gratified, he sat back in his chair and watched her. Her gown, a deep red that brought out the creaminess of her skin, had a low décolletage that emphasized her bosom. He remembered the feel of her skin, the texture of the aureoles and the way her nipples had hardened to little kernels in his mouth. He was instantly aroused.

She looked like a woman who had been loved well and long. She had that languid, sated air that kept the men surrounding her frantic to know who had bedded her and why that man had not been himself. Sutherland smiled. They might not know it, but the luscious lady was going to torment them in just that manner quite often. He would see to that.

He smiled at the thought.

She saw his smile, satisfied and proud, and frowned in return. How dare he, no matter that he was Dougal MacDonald, the utterly masculine beautiful seventh duke of Sutherland who had stolen her heart, how dare he interrupt her supper with St. John and burden her with his presence. Why wouldn't he leave her in peace!

"Has something displeased you, my lady? Perhaps the lobster patties are not to your liking?"

She scanned the plate of food she had not yet touched. Though it displayed a tempting assortment of the delicacies the Baron's chef was famous for, she had no appetite.

She glanced at the man beside her. Clad as all the other gentlemen in faultless evening attire, on him the severe black and snowy white cravat were outstanding. The fit of his coat across his broad shoulders was perfection, leaving no one in doubt that he needed no padding to enhance their breadth. The white of his impeccably tied neckcloth against his tanned skin was almost blinding. His brown eyes in his chiseled face were fixed only on her.

He didn't even look at the women, all gowned in the latest fashions, who flitted by, décolletages so low that the bodice barely covered their breasts. His gaze was fixed on her, as if he could see through her clothing to her nakedness beneath. Her throat went dry. She lifted the crystal glass to her lips and took a sip of champagne. The sparkling wine soothed her throat and calmed her nerves.

She smoothed her white silk evening glove over her wrist. "Is it your exalted rank that makes you feel you can do as you please without regard to other's wishes?"

Her cool tone, disdainful and not quite hiding her pique, interrupted Sutherland's study of her. No man spoke to him thus. He waited a moment until his pride settled down. He cocked an eyebrow at her. "If being a Duke doesn't allow me to have what I want, what good is it?"

She gasped. Sutherland smiled at her reaction to his trifling dismissal of the responsibilities and duties that accompanied the privilege of his position.

"Do not jest with me, your grace."

"Then do not speak foolishly, my dear."

"I am not your dear."

He smiled at her denial. "I would speak less quickly, if I were you."

She frowned, a tiny narrowing of her eyes. "What do you mean?"

"I shall tell you at the proper time."

Antonia's frown deepened. This smacked of the authoritarian control her husband had exerted. She had no intention of submitting to anything like it ever again.

"There will be no time, proper or otherwise, for you, your grace."

"I am afraid you are going to be most surprised. I can only hope it will not be an unpleasant shock."

She cast a quick glance at his face. His eyes glowed and his face was lit by an odd smile. What could he find so amusing? Unnerved that he should know something she did not, she wracked her brain for an explanation. She came up with nothing. He could not possibly know of her afternoon interviews.

If he but knew! She thought of the lovemaking she had experienced this afternoon, and only wished she had stayed awake long enough to inform the man of her decision. Whoever he was, she would have him for her lover.

As she thought of the final interview, the one in which she finally allowed him to take her, anticipation filled her with moistness between her thighs. This man, whoever he was, was just the one to dismiss Sutherland from her thoughts.

"Something amuses you?" Sutherland queried.

She spared him a questioning glance.

"Your smile," he explained. "It reminds me of the cat at the cream."

She laughed. How astute he was. Suddenly she was enjoying herself in his company. Now that she no longer had to worry about her heart, she could allow herself to enjoy his quick wit. "The word is about, your grace, that you are in need of a wife."

His rapidly cocked eyebrow was his only reaction to the change in subject.

"Yes. Have you thought of your requirements yet? Perhaps a wife who will keep you pleasantly occupied at home—"

"Pleasantly occupied?" he interrupted. "By that do you mean cozy evenings before the fire?"

"However you wish to enjoy yourself," she murmured, a small teasing smile on her lips. "However, I would imagine that it is time you saw to establishing your nurseries for your heirs."

"Indeed? And have you chosen my future duchess?"

"H'mm." She smiled at his serious tone. "I shall have to give that some thought. Perhaps Caroline, Lady Arbuthnott's niece. You recall, you met her at the opera one evening."

"The young lady just making her come out? She seemed interested enough," he admitted with a modest smile.

"It would appear so. She is very beautiful, don't you think?"

"Is she? I didn't notice. I shall have to make that observation myself."

Antonia stomach clutched at the thought of Sutherland looking at and enjoying other women. Evidently she had been premature in thinking she could speak like this with him and not suffer the penalty. She made herself keep her tone light. "She is of good family. Not as distinguished as your own, of course, but well established.

She would be a good match."

He nodded. "She is certainly young enough to fill the nurseries with no problem, but would she have the proper conversation to keep me entertained?"

"Ah." She paused as if giving thought to his questions. In truth, she struggled with the temptation to offer herself for his consideration. "That complicates matters. Entertaining conversation is a requirement, then?"

"Most definitely. I should hate to be bored by a wife with only one talent."

"That talent would be—" she questioned delicately.

"Providing my heir."

She exhaled. "What else would you require? Perhaps I could be of some assistance in finding the right wife for you."

He laughed. "You might at that."

"Well, come then, tell me what you want in a wife, and I shall endeavor to help you."

"Very well. Let me see. I want a woman with passable good looks—"

"Just passable?" she interrupted.

"More would be preferable, but so long as she is not a gargoyle—"

"Your grace! Very well," she managed through her laughter. "No gargoyles."

"To continue, then. A woman who I enjoy looking at, a woman with intelligent conversation, someone who will not bore me before the month is out."

"You are serious?"

"Absolutely."

She didn't know what to say. Clearly Sutherland was made of different cloth from other men.

"I should also like a woman to be well attired, but that is up to me. I shall dress her well."

Antonia took exception to that. "And if the woman you choose to dress prefers her own taste in clothing?"

"If it is satisfactory to me, I should allow her to continue. No billowing flounces or lace up to her ears."

Antonia glanced at the sleek lines of her gown and hid a smile at the image his words presented. Without trouble, she could visualize a woman smothered in lace and furbelows, with only her nose and eyes visible. At that, it wouldn't matter if she were less than passable.

"Share the jest with me," he suggested.

She did. Their laughter mingled and drew curious glances. Antonia ignored them.

"What else would you like in a wife?"

"Let's see. We have looks, heirs, intelligence, the outer wrappings. What else is there?"

"Ah," she sagely. "What about the inner woman?"

"The what?"

She gathered her thoughts. "Have you never envisioned what kind of woman? So far, we have discussed all the exterior things, but what about the qualities that must wear well to last a lifetime together?"

His gaze sharpened. "And what would those be?"

"Patience. Good humor, tolerance for one another. A loving disposition. Fidelity. Anything you would want specifically?"

"Ah. I see what you mean. Indeed, those are admirable qualities. Yes, I should want all those, and more."

"And what are they?"

"Loyalty. A spirit of adventure," he said with a private smile Antonia found intriguing. "Faith in me. An acceptance of me as the man I am, of my heritage."

She listened to his Scots burr. "You would want your wife to live on your estates in Scotland? I hear it is very cold."

"It can be. It is also wild, rugged, beautiful country. My wife would not spend all her time in the Highlands, but I would expect my children to be born on land I inherited from my ancestors."

She nodded. "That is reasonable. Is there anything else your wife would have to do in Scotland?"

"Perhaps she could learn to fish?"

Her eyes widened. "I understand fishing is a solitary, silent activity. Would you want her chatter to scare away the fish?"

"Ah, but remember, my wife would have intelligent conversation." He grinned, his teeth gleaming in his tanned face. The candlelight accentuated the interesting hollows in his cheeks and flattered his manly looks. "It follows that she would also know when to refrain from speaking."

"I see. So while you are fishing together, she is to keep silent and save her conversation for the drawing room."

"And elsewhere."

"Where?"

"Bed," he said bluntly.

She felt her eyes widen. "Bed?"

"Aye. I like a woman to tell me what she likes, what pleasures her. I should expect my wife to do no less."

Antonia swallowed. "Yours will be a most unusual marriage, your grace. Quite the exception to stylish marriages."

"My marriage will be not be a Society alliance for the usual reasons, but a lifelong union. There will be no others for either of us."

"How can you be so sure, your grace?"

"You have forgotten the most important ingredient to a successful marriage, Antonia. It is my chief requirement."

She hesitated to ask, but could not bear not to know the answer. "And that is?"

"Love. My wife shall love me beyond everything."

"Oh," she said faintly. "Is that not one-sided? Will you not love your wife in return?"

"I already do, Antonia."

"It sounds as though you have already chosen your wife, your grace."

"I have."

Chapter Seven

Antonia lay sleepless. By all rights she should be sleeping soundly after her late night and the most satisfying way she had been pleasured by her anonymous lover, but her conversation with Sutherland kept her awake.

She hadn't known before how enjoyable conversing with him would prove to be. She'd reveled in their verbal sparring for the lift it gave her spirits. It had made her feel as if she danced on the edge of a cliff.

To fence with him with words always made her feel that she'd come away from a perilous encounter with all her parts in place. She'd enjoyed the danger, the element of risk in dueling with a man reputed to be as good with a blade as he was a lover. Their conversation over the delicious midnight supper had been entertaining, suggestive, and had allowed her a glimpse of what she had renounced.

She envied the woman he had chosen to be his wife. Whoever she was, she was an extremely fortunate woman. To have won his love, to have him forswear his mistresses to be faithful to her alone was singularly rare. And for him to have done this without the gossips of the *ton* at his heels was another extraordinary feat. He had them all buzzing with his pursuit of her while he was actually courting another.

Whoever the unknown woman was, she had much to be thankful for. Sutherland would kept her identity secret until he was ready to announce their engagement, protecting her privacy and her good name until he was ready to give her his.

Clever, clever man. She admired his strategy so much that she could forgive him using her as a blind for his true activities. She should resent the attention he'd paid her, the unbelievable tale he'd told of hastening back to London when he'd heard she was free of Effingdale. She should be furious for making her a laughingstock with his public pursuit of her.

Many gentlemen of the *ton* had placed wagers on the outcome of the chase. The betting books in Whites and the other clubs had page after page of entries that the Duke of S would make Lady B-S his mistress before the Season was over. She'd heard the tremendous sums being wagered on the outcome of Sutherland's public hunting her through the ballrooms and drawing rooms of their acquaintances.

She should be angry and plotting his set-down, but instead she was envious of the woman he had chosen. Envious, and more than regretful that she would have to relinquish Sutherland's company. It would be too painful to meet him when he had his duchess on his arm.

She tossed restlessly. Much good it did her now to wonder what it would be like to have Sutherland love her. For all she'd renounced marrying again, she couldn't help but wonder what it would be like to be his duchess, to share his life. Sighing, she turned on her side and drew her legs up. At least she had her wonderfully imaginative lover to console her. She'd content herself in his arms.

When she woke late the next day, Clarry was already bustling around her bedchamber. Steam from a tub of water curled up through sunshine streaming in the opened windows. The scent of roses from her garden perfumed the air as freely as the bath salts Clarry poured into the bath.

Antonia stretched. "Good morning, Clarry. How late have I slept?"

Clarry turned and placed her hands on her hips. "It's not morning any longer, milady, and if you intend to keep your appointment this afternoon, you'd better get up out that bed and into the tub."

Antonia blinked at Clarry's tone, but didn't have the heart to scold her. "What's the matter with you?"

"It's that tired I am of this constant traipsing over to that rooming house and you carrying on while I wait with the footmen. Aren't you done yet? How much longer do we have to twiddle our thumbs?"

"Today is the last time, I promise. Today I'll tell him that I've chosen him to be my lover." Antonia stretched, feeling energy rush through her body as she thought of the way she would inform him. Now he was just "him," but later, she would know his identity and have a name to put to that magnificent male body. He would be pleased, and proud, that she had chosen him out of all the others, but determined to make her happy with her choice. "I can hardly wait to see his face."

Clarry turned her back, all at once quite busy laying out Antonia's clothes. "What if you don't like him once you see who he is?"

"Why should I not like him? Is there something wrong with him?"

"Not that I know, milady, but you never can tell. He might be not what you want, after all."

"You're acting very strange, Clarry. If I weren't late, you can believe we'd have all this mysterious behavior out."

"You can ask me anything you want later, milady. I'll tell you everything."

Antonia wondered at Clarry's words while she rushed though her bath and her dressing ritual. She had nothing planned for this evening, and she would not go to bed until she had cleared up the reason for Clarry's puzzling manner.

She dressed quickly, in a simply cut afternoon gown of a deep blue that flattered her pale skin and hair. As she placed a small drop of perfume behind her ears and between her breasts, she eagerly waited her lover's reaction to her preparations for him.

She donned the veiled hat, knowing it was the last time she'd do so, and was soon on her way to her last interview. Eagerly, she rode through the streets of London until they reached the now familiar street and rooming house. Only the barely concealed smirks on her footmen's faces kept her from lifting her skirts and running up the stairs in her impatience to meet her lover. He hadn't arrived yet, which disappointed her, yet she used the time to prepare herself for one last anonymous encounter.

Moments later, reclining on the sofa instead of the bed, she heard his footsteps coming up the stairs, then the murmurs in the outer room. She stopped breathing until she heard the door open and close behind him.

She breathed again as she heard him approach the bed. Today she'd had Clarry leave the heavy drapes slightly open and the windows open to the warm afternoon. The street scents and sounds mingled with his. Together, they made a heady, earthy combination.

"Will you speak today?"

He said nothing.

"That will be acceptable for now, but later," her voice dropped as she promised, "later, you will speak with me."

She waited excitedly for him to begin. She had left off the robe, keeping on only the mask. She heard his breathing, then felt his body as he stood over her. She felt his heat and trembled with anticipated passion.

Watching her, Sutherland stripped off his shirt and trousers, leaving himself nude. He was already erect, his cock hard and aching. Willing himself to ignore his own desire, he took a deep breath and began as he had begun before, with soft, delicate touches on her skin that soon had her craving more.

Her skin heated under his touch as the fine hairs quivered under his fingertips. He'd brought none of his seductive toys in his box of sexual tricks, wanting to rely only on himself and her ardent response to his lovemaking.

Her skin was smooth and silky, delicately perfumed by both a floral fragrance and her own personal musk. The heady mixture swamped his senses, increasing his hunger for her and his determination to make their lovemaking so perfect that she'd have no cause for complaint when he drew the mask from her and she discovered his identity.

She would have no reason to refuse him.

He placed little kisses on every inch of her skin, beginning with her toes and working up to her mouth. By the time he reached it, she was panting. The silken mask presented only the flimsiest barriers, but he managed, by the merest thread, to control the urge to tear away the mask and plunder her soft recesses.

He kissed her as he had been longing to, with nips at her lips, tracing the outline of her lips with his. He savored the taste of her mouth as he had relished the taste and texture of her everywhere else. The silk mask tore at one corner of the mouth opening. He pulled it further apart to reach more of her.

She didn't protest. Instead, she opened her mouth to him and he swept in, conquering and being conquered at the same time. She was delectable and heady, like the strongest whiskey and the sweetest meadow flower. Like honey, he lapped at her until she moaned and dueled with his tongue, circling it with her own and darting into his mouth to taste him.

At last they broke apart, breathing heavily, stunned by the emotions they'd aroused in each other. Though he knew she was as lusty and passionate as he, to feel her become aggressive with his mouth stimulated him and made him crave more. He wanted everything with her.

He reached for the mask.

Antonia forestalled him. "No, not yet."

He stopped. So his lady was still unsure of him. Very well. That would be rectified. He removed some of the plump damask pillows behind her and repositioned her so that she lay sprawling against the cushions, her satiny thighs open to him and her feet resting on the thick carpet.

He dropped to his knees between her thighs and caressed her legs from ankle to thigh. When she moaned and shivered, he lowered his mouth to drink from her. She cried out as his tongue entered her, she convulsed immediately. Her orgasm delighted and spurred him onward. He kissed her repeatedly, using his tongue on her intimate folds, tasting, savoring. teasing, learning her tastes and textures and always demanding greater passion from her.

"More," she moaned, unknowingly echoing his hunger. He increased his pace, his tongue now flickering on the swollen tissues, now entering her slick passage, varying his technique until her hands clutched his bare shoulders, her nails buried deeply, as she urged him upward to enter her.

"Please, now, I need you now."

He sat back on his heels, breathing heavily, his mouth full of the taste of her as he contemplated how he would take her. He could rise on his knees, pierce her and thrust until they shattered together. If he did that, he could suckle at her breasts at the same time. The thought tempted even as he considered other positions. Draw her to the carpet with him, turn her over and enter her from behind? Stretch her out on the sofa and cover her?

While he debated which would afford them the most pleasure, she reached down and took his stiff yard in her hand. He bucked and almost spent his seed until he gritted his teeth and commanded himself to resist the fierce ecstasy.

With soft fingers, she measured and pleasured him. She played with him, alternating featherlight strokes with harder ones, then cupping his sac and rolling his testicles gently in her hand. He closed his eyes, willing himself to remain motionless, gripped by passion, until he though he'd lose control. He grasped her hand, stilling the motion, until she released him and lay back.

He stood and scooped her up into his arms. With a few long strides, he reached the bed and kissing her, leaned over to place her the way he wanted her. She let him do as he would with her. Triumphantly, possessively, he lowered himself beside her, stretching his longer length next to hers and he bent his head to take her nipple in his mouth.

Antonia trembled. Fire surged through her. She arched under his mouth, begging, pleading for him to take her. He had stretched her on a rack of sensual pleasure so keen she thought she'd fly apart. Every inch of her body was attuned to his. Each of her muscles strained to hold him closer, to urge him to rise above her, part her thighs and make her his.

His long legs, muscled and strong, enclosed hers. She felt the hair on them as a furry pelt and moaned. She traced the line of the hair on his chest as it tapered in a wide vee from his nipples to his navel, then extended down to luxuriantly cup his sex. She gasped when he lowered his chest to hers and caressed her with his body hair.

He took first one nipple, then the other in his mouth, taking as much of her rounded breast as he could until she felt as if she were being devoured by him. Passion poured through her with each pull of his lips. She moaned, "No, it's too good. No more."

Yet he did not desist. Instead he maintained his control by pushing her beyond pleasure, into the realm of rapture. He lowered his body to hers, and with one supreme thrust, entered her. She responded with instinctive tightening of her muscles around him. Her orgasms came, one after another, with such force that she cried and gripped him harder.

Once, twice, a dozen times he thrust, each lunge more powerful and deeper than the one before, until at last, with a mighty roar, he claimed her as his.

When he collapsed, breathing heavily, his body resting on hers, searing her with his heat, she lay with her eyes closed, holding him near. With one hand she stroked his back in slow, easy caresses, sated and grateful. She had been right to search for a new lover. This man more than fulfilled her every requirement.

At last, his breathing evened out and he rolled to his side, pulling Antonia with him. She went willingly, wanting this closeness as much as she had earlier hungered for the passion.

Sutherland kept one hand on her hip, and with the other, caressed her throat. He pressed a kiss on each eyelid, closing them. When she didn't protest, he slipped a finger under the material at her throat. The green silk, moistened by her perspiration, clung to her skin. The moment he drew it away on one side, it clung to the other. She made a sound in her throat, part laugh and part moan, as if she enjoyed his struggle to unmask her.

He persisted, cursing his suddenly fumbling fingers, until he managed to loosen the strings that kept the mask in place. One by one, he undid the knots at the back of her head and lifted the fabric away from her face. Feature by feature, her beautiful face was revealed to him.

He dropped the mask to one side, relieved that the masquerade would soon be over. He bent and pressed kisses on her closed eyes, on her temples, down her cheek until he came to her mouth. He gave her a kiss of promise, of welcome.

He drew his mouth away. "Open your eyes, Antonia."

Chapter Eight

Drugged with pleasure, it took Antonia a moment to focus her eyes, and then they popped open in disbelief. Dougal MacDonald, that unmitigated cad of a seventh duke of Sutherland, gazed down at her.

She sat bolt upright and grabbed a sheet to cover her breasts. "What on earth are you doing here?"

He laughed. "Surely that should be obvious, Antonia."

"Why are you here? What have you done with—" she fell silent when she noticed his nudity. "Oh, no. Not you."

"Without a doubt."

"You mean to tell me that you, that you—"

"It isn't often I have seen you a loss for words, my dear. What happened to your gift for conversation?"

She drew the sheet closer to her throat. Her pulse pounding, she closed her eyes. She had to be dreaming. When she opened them a few moments later, he was still there. "I had hoped I was having a nightmare."

He lifted a finger to stroke her cheek. She leaned away from his touch. "Come now. You can not deny that you and I have just experienced one of the most wonderful moments together."

"I do not understand. Why have you done this?"

"Ah, Antonia, where is your sharp wit? I can only hope that I have worn it to a frazzle by my lovemaking. And as to why I am here, I repeat, that should be obvious. I am to be your next, and I might add as a small warning, your only lover."

"No."

He sat upright. "You wish to renege on the arrangement, Antonia? I'm afraid I will not allow that."

She cast him an annoyed glance and then pointedly looked away from his broad shoulders and muscled chest. "You are here under false pretenses. The arrangement does not apply to you. I specifically do not want another peer in my bed."

"Could you not forget my title for a moment and consider me as any other man?"

She refused to be drawn. "I will not consider you at all."

"You have no choice," he said briskly. "You yourself set up the rules. You would allow only the man you intend to take as your lover to enter your body. I have done that. Ergo, I am your lover."

"You are quite wrong. I refuse you."

"You would change the rules that easily?"

His voice, soft with unspoken threat, made her throat go dry. She swallowed and gathered her wits. "This is not a game. Nor a duel. I alone set the rules."

"A man would be held accountable for such dishonor."

She hitched the sheet up to her throat. "Please clothe yourself and leave. Immediately."

"Not quite so fast, my lady. We have yet to set the conditions for our new arrangement."

She exhaled. "There is no arrangement between us. How often must I tell you that?"

"I have heard you." His voice turned hard, as if he would brook no further disagreement. "Now you are to listen to me."

"If I cry out, my servants will eject you immediately."

He blinked, then smiled. "If you do that, my servants will thrash your servants and I shall return in triumph."

His sense of humor worried her more than his authoritarian tone. It made her weak, vulnerable to the man as well as the lover. In some desperation, she cried, "This is not a jesting matter! Please leave me."

His voice lost its teasing tone. "You are quite right, on that score at least. This is not a humorous situation. Allow me to tell you what this is."

"And if I refuse?"

He hooked a finger under her chin and lifted her face to his. "You will not refuse."

She shuddered but she kept her gaze steadily on his.

"This, my dear Lady Antonia Blair-Sutworth, is an offer of marriage. You would do me great honor by becoming my wife."

Her mouth dropped open. With his finger, he gently closed it.

"You are mad," she breathed.

"About you, yes. I am besotted, insane with love for you. I would grovel at your feet, but I am afraid in your present mood you would take the opportunity to do me damage."

"Why? Why are you doing this?"

"Antonia, I should have thought my motives perfectly clear. I want you to be my duchess."

"Last night you said you had already chosen one."

"I was quite honest with you. I just didn't mention that I had chosen you."

She shook her head. "No. I will not marry you."

"Why not? As you yourself mentioned, the *ton* has decided that it is time I take a wife." He paused, as if reflecting on the *ton* managing his affairs, then continued. "For the first, and no doubt the only time, I am in agreement with Society. You need not worry about your future. I have wealth to support you and our children many times over. I have lands and houses at your disposal. I will shower you with jewels and whatever fripperies you wish—"

"There is no need to catalogue your material advantages, your grace."

"Many mothers have set their daughters at me, but I have held out," he continued as though she had not interrupted him. "Refusing many a tempting morsel for a chance at—"

"At the entire pie?" she asked, smiling despite herself. "Your words are not very complimentary, your grace."

He laughed. "I do admire your quick wit, my dear. Even when I am the butt of your joke."

"It is flattering to be asked to be your duchess, but I must refuse."

"Are your affections engaged elsewhere?"

Startled by the abrupt change in his manner, she paused before answering him. "No."

"Are you suffering from some dreadful disease?"

"Of course not."

"Are you already married?"

"I am a widow, as you very well know."

"Then I find no impediment, unless you find me distasteful."

She touched his cheek. "You know that I do not."

He smiled at her. "You find me attractive?"

"Very much so."

"We already know that we suit quite well together in bed. What keeps you from accepting?"

"I have my reasons."

"You do not love me?"

She sighed. "I fear that I love you to distraction, your grace."

"Call me Dougal."

She smiled at the intimacy he offered with his given name. "Dougal."

"Good." His smile was fierce, proud and possessive. "Now repeat that last sentence."

"I love you to distraction, Dougal."

He bent his head and kissed her. His lips told her he loved her. He'd cherish her to their last days.

When he lifted his head, Sutherland saw the tears in her lustrous green eyes. "Why do you cry, Antonia?"

"I cannot marry you, or any other. I have sworn so."

"A religious vow?" he asked, confusion in his voice.

"No, not that." She wiped her cheeks dry. "A vow to myself."

"I don't understand. Why do you not want to marry again?"

"It's not something a man would understand."

"Try me," he urged, his voice low and encouraging.

She studied him, her gaze lingering on each of his beloved features. "Since my husband died three years ago, I have discovered several things about myself. Things that many would consider unsuitable in a woman."

"Such as?"

"I prefer being a widow to being a wife."

"You do?" He leaned forward to rest an elbow on his knee. "Why is that?"

"I do not have to answer to a husband, for one."

He sat up. "I can see where that might discomfit a husband or two." She smiled at his wry tone. "Shall I continue?"

"Please do. This is fascinating."

"I am my own mistress, as I said. I control my own means."

"That is point two," he observed. "Is there more?"

"Quite a bit more, but it can be summarized easily. In short, I am independent."

He was silent for a moment, as if considering the meaning of her words. "If you had all of those things, and you could be married at the same time, would you consider it then?"

"It is not possible, your grace—"

"Dougal."

"Impossible, Dougal. It is a contradiction in terms. How can a woman be married and independent at the same time?"

"Let me think on it. I shall come upon a way."

"You are too confident of yourself."

"Should I not be? Do you not like it when I am sure of what I am about?"

She knew they no longer spoke of her wish for independence. She pressed a kiss on his shoulder. "How could I deny it?"

"You cannot," he agreed with satisfaction.

She continued with her kisses, making her way slowly along the musculature of his chest until she came to a nipple. She flicked her tongue on it, once twice, then sucked on it in imitation of what he had done to her.

He grasped her head in both hands and gently raised her face to his. "If you do that, I shall not be able to think straight."

"Do not think," she murmured. "Let me make love to you." One last time, she added silently. Once more to last me the rest of my days and nights.

"If you think to distract me—" he warned.

"I think you are a most wonderful, imaginative, powerful lover. Your stamina is truly impressive."

He rose to the occasion immediately. His arousal grew against her hip and she smiled with satisfaction. He lay back, putting his body at her disposition. She toyed with the hair on his chest, running her fingers through the silky hairs, pulling and tugging gently as her mouth continued its foray down his belly. She felt his heart pick up speed, his breathing grow shallow even as she felt his stomach muscles contract under her questing touch.

She pressed kisses all over his face and throat, then settled down and kissed him seriously. His mouth opened under hers when she traced his lips with the tip of her tongue and probed deeper. He tasted of sweet passion, now heady and frantic, now soft and languid. She lingered, testing every bit of his mouth, dueling with her tongue, aping the thrusts he would make soon.

By his passivity, he gave her the freedom to explore his body as he had explored hers. With every touch, she expanded on what she had learned from him. He groaned but made no move to stop her.

His chest rubbed against hers, the hair caressing her breasts. They were already sensitive from their earlier lovemaking and peaked instantly against him. She arched to feel more.

"Dougal," she whispered. "I want—"

"Yes? What do you want?"

"You, just you. Love me."

He could refuse her nothing. Complying with her whispered request, he moved closer, shifting his weight to rub against her. His cock, already hard and eager, throbbed against her thigh. She moved her hands to his shoulders, then to the back to play with his hair and stroke his neck. He responded by nuzzling her neck, leaving kisses in his wake. She murmured and lifted her chin to give him greater access.

He shifted to reach her breasts, and followed the line of her shoulder to her arm, kissing and nibbling as he went. He pushed her arm out of the way and licked his way to her elbow, then up again, blowing gently at the moist path he'd made until she moved restlessly beneath him. His hands clasped her breasts and she moaned with the joy of it as he left her arm and concentrated on her nipples.

Everything he had done to her before in the name of seduction, he did again with love. Where before his technique had evoked raw lust from her, now his tenderness and emotional approach wrought intense passion all the more lustful and ardent for being caring and tender.

She lay under his hands, coming alive in every pore, as euphoric and avid as though they had not already indulged themselves to exhaustion. Wherever she could reach him, she stroked and petted him, nipping at his skin, breathing in the scent of aroused male. She licked him, tasting the salt of his earlier exertions, and left bites of her own on his broad chest.

When he pushed himself down the bed to rest between her legs and placed his mouth on her intimate flesh, made extra sensitive by his earlier ministrations, she cried, "Oh, no more! I can't bear it."

He gentled his embrace but did not move away. His tongue barely touching her, he laved her soreness away until it was replaced by need. Her orgasm was his reward.

He moved up on her again, and rising to his knees, he lifted her legs and placed them around his waist. When he did not move, she lifted her eyes in confusion. "When I come into you now, I come as your husband."

She bit her lip, wracked with unbearable passion, yet wanting him more than she had ever wanted anything before, or would ever want anything again.

He probed at her entry with the tip of his member. "Decide now, Antonia."

She felt the velvety smoothness of the skin stretched over hard muscle and wavered. She knew it was emotional blackmail to force her to choose when she was unable to think straight, but oh, Lord, how good he felt against her!

"You mean this?" she gasped.

"I do not lie. You should know that by now." He penetrated her, barely entering her, and withdrew.

She moaned at the loss.

"Decide, Antonia, before I go mad," he ordered in an aching whisper.

She arched against him, her hips moving restlessly. The silken feel of her was more than he could bear, yet he forced himself not to move. Muscles straining, sweat beading his forehead and chest, he held himself immobile above her.

She stared up at him with wild eyes. She tossed her head back, her mouth gasping for breath. At last, she surrendered. "Yes, yes, damn you, yes!"

With a groan he penetrated her in one long thrust. They moaned together as he rested, deeply imbedded, for just a moment before he began a long, slow rhythmic stroke.

It was madness. It was sheer bliss. It was heaven.

It seemed hours that he maintained a steady rhythm, propelling them forward. She begged for release. He increased his pace and with his thumb, found her bud and stroked it. Madness overtook her. With each movement of his body he propelled her further into passion until her orgasms overtook them both and provoked his. He cried out her name as his back arched into one spasm after another. He poured himself into her.

She wept.

She raised her head to look at him. "It will be difficult for me to forget you."

"Forget me?" He forced an eye open. "How are you going to forget me when I intend to make love to you every day and most of the night?"

"You will not have the opportunity."

"I thought we had settled this. You agreed to marry me."

"You forced me to say so under duress."

"Duress?" he repeated, his tone severe.

"How could you expect me to think, much less make such an important decision, under those circumstances?"

"Listen to me, Antonia." He sat up against the pillows and made himself comfortable, then drew her into his arms. "I have no intention of letting you get away from me. I have thought of a way to satisfy us both."

"Impossible."

"You shall keep your independence, I swear."

She laughed. "And how shall I do that if I am married?"

"Do we agree that we are both imaginative, intelligent people?"

She nodded cautiously.

"Then, if we both agree to live in a certain way, who is to say us nay?"

"I don't understand."

"It's simple, my lady duchess-to-be. We shall agree, in a marriage contract if you wish it, that what you now possess shall be yours alone, to do with as you please."

Her green eyes opened wide. "You would do that?"

"I would," he stated. "And more."

"More? How could you do more?"

He cleared his throat. "Well, I admit it will take a considerable amount of adjusting on my part, but then, it's in a good cause."

"What are you saying?"

"If you had a husband who did not demand obedience, but instead requested agreement, would you still be adverse to marriage?"

"That is unheard of."

"But not impossible," he countered.

"Rather than have to answer to a husband's every whim, I am to be consulted and my wishes considered?"

He reflected. "Perhaps the proper theory is compromise. A husband and wife ought to be able to agree on the important decisions, wouldn't you agree?"

"I would," she said, cautious again.

"And if they agreed, in advance, that there were certain decisions only one would make, and the other agree to without argument, do you think that would work?"

"I think your imagination is running away with you, your grace."

"Dougal," he corrected. "Now, if this same couple had the agreement I mentioned, they should get along famously."

"Of course," she agreed with an airy gesture. "So long as she made the decisions such as what to serve for tea and which polish to use on the staircase, and he made all the other decisions—"

"You malign me, Antonia. I am speaking of a partnership."

"A business partnership?"

He winced. "I wouldn't like to think it was a cold business partnership, with hereafters, wheretofores and penalties."

She stroked the frown from his forehead. "What would you call it then?"

"A loving partnership between two people who want only the best for each other."

"Could there be such a thing?"

"We shall make it so."

"I fear you are too optimistic. What about the first time I overspend on gowns?"

"If you don't wish to pay for them yourself, I shall do so gladly."

"May I have that in writing?" she inquired politely.

He roared with laughter and pulled her closer to him. They settled back, resting comfortably. Antonia fell into a light sleep. A knock at the door interrupted his thoughts about Antonia. "What is it?"

Clarry poked her head through the half-open door, "Begging your pardon, your grace, but it's gone seven and—"

He pulled a sheet up over their nakedness. "And what, Clarry?"

"Well, it's the footmen, you see. They're wanting their supper."

He laughed. Nothing could daunt his good humor, not disrespectful servants nor recalcitrant ladies. "You may congratulate yourself, Clarry. You have done well."

"It's over, then?"

At his nod, Clarry entered the bedchamber, closed the door behind her and approached the bedside table with a fresh candle.

"Do not wake her ladyship," he warned as the light fell over Antonia.

"Humph, she sleeps like she's exhausted. You did right by her?"

Sutherland blinked. "You might say so."

"I could hear the two of you in here. Had to send the footmen below."

"Very discreet of you, Clarry."

"I see to her, you know."

"And very well indeed. There'll be a little something extra for you. Is everything ready?"

"It is, but it's so late—"

Antonia opened her eyes and stretched. "What are you two talking about?"

"It's time to get up, my love. Your servants are hungry."

Antonia glanced at the window, at the dusky light coming in through the gap in the draperies. "Oh, we shouldn't have slept so long!"

"Just out of curiosity, you understand, but are we going to let the servants' stomachs govern our lives?"

"Your lives?" Clarry asked, her eyes growing big.

"Her ladyship has consented to be my wife, Clarry. You may be the first to wish us well."

Clarry bustled closer and swept Antonia up into her arms. "Oh milady, this is wonderful news." She sent Sutherland a severe warning glance. "I hope you will be very happy."

"As happy as I can make her," he assured Clarry.

Antonia returned Clarry's hug. "Not so fast, you two. There are a number of questions to which I want answers, and I want them now."

"You could wait until we get home, milady, all cozy like," Clarry suggested.

Antonia watched the glances fly between Clarry and Sutherland. "Now. And don't leave anything out."

Clarry kneaded her skirt.

"Do not blame Clarry, my love. If you wish to cast fault at anyone, sling it at me."

"You shall have your share, I promise you that."

He laughed at the threat. Plumping the pillows behind them, he lay back with her in his arms. He didn't seem to mind that Clarry gawked at his naked chest. "I am properly abashed."

She glared at him. "Get on with it, then."

"Well, you will recall that I told you I wanted you?"

At her wary nod, he continued, "I enlisted Clarry's help. The long and short of it is that she agreed to let me pose as another applicant."

"Did she now?" Antonia slanted a long look at her maid.

"Only for your own good, milady," Clarry hastened to explain.

"Indeed." Antonia turned to gaze Sutherland.

He gave her a bland look in return. "So, you see, all is explained."

"Not quite."

"What is left to resolve?"

"A simple matter. How could you be here in the afternoons with me and then bedevil me at night?"

"With the greatest difficulty, Antonia." He leaned closer. "You have had your revenge, and all without knowing it."

"I have?"

"Aye," he whispered. "I all but expired from the ache of wanting you."

"A fitting punishment," she announced, though she couldn't help the smile tugging at her lips. "Are there to be any more of these surprises?"

"Perhaps one," Sutherland admitted. "A small one," he added.

Clarry coughed and hurried over to the armoire. Keeping her back turned to the couple on the bed, she removed Antonia's clothing.

Narrowing her eyes to see through the rapidly failing light, Antonia said, "Those are not the clothes I came in."

"I know milady. I thought you'd be wanting fresh."

"But, Clarry, that's my cream satin. Why now?"

"Just thought you'd like something pretty, milady."

Antonia started to protest again.

Sutherland silenced her with a kiss. When he moved back, Clarry had finished laying out Antonia's clothes and left the room. "She'll be back to help you dress, my love, but I imagine she thought the rest had better come from me."

"Rest of what?" Antonia asked suspiciously.

He glanced at the gown, then back at her. "If you agree to marry me immediately, those will your wedding clothes. I shall dress in the next room. No doubt my valet is also wanting his supper," he added, attempting to lighten the frown that wrinkled her lovely forehead.

"Wedding, valet? Your grace, what is going on here?"

"Dougal." He rose from the bed. "We could be married as soon as you dress."

"Impossible!"

"Not at all. The minister is waiting in the other room. I have a special license with me."

"But why the rush? I mean, what if I want a proper wedding?"

He hesitated. "Do you?"

"Well, no," she said after a moment. "I had all that with Blair-Sutworth, and look what it got me."

"Good. There is another reason for the haste, you know."

She raised her eyebrows. "Surely you don't think I would change my mind after being so uniquely coerced into saying yes?"

He drew on his trousers and his shirt before he bent down and kissed her again.

"What?" she gasped when he let her up to breathe.

"You may already be pregnant, my love. I want no one counting on their fingers when my heir is born."

She could say nothing. She'd never thought of it, but of course he was right. Once more, she was reminded of his thoroughness.

"I shall leave you now to dress. If you come through that door wearing that gown, you shall leave these rooms as my wife."

She watched the door close behind him. For a moment she couldn't move, stunned by all that had happened in the last few hours. She, Duchess of Sutherland—it wasn't to be believed!

She lay still, allowing herself time to become accustomed to the idea, then all at once energized, she rose and called for Clarry. With her help, she bathed in the warm water Clarry provided and then dressed in her elegant cream satin.

"I brought your pearls, milady, and I thought your hair down—"

"I am not a blushing virgin, Clarry."

"Maybe not, but I think the duke brought a blush or two to your face." she sighed. "Ah, he's a fine figure of a man. He'll keep you happy."

"I hope so." Antonia's legs felt weak. She sat unsteadily. Clarry picked up the silver backed hair brush and began brushing Antonia's hair.

"Oh, Clarry, am I doing the right thing? All along I've said I would never marry again and here I am preparing to go out there and —"

"Now don't you be getting all nervy on me, milady. The Duke is a fine man, and he'll make you a fine husband."

"But, Clarry, all I wanted was a lover!"

"And didn't you get one?" Clarry's face settled into a wide, self-satisfied smile. "Couldn't ask for a better end to this foolish plan of yours."

"It seems to me that I had some help with it," Antonia reminded her.

Clarry went on brushing. "It was all his idea, I swear. He came to see me and invited me to sit down, all proper like, and we had such a nice chat."

"About me?"

"Well, of course about you. Why else would the duke be sitting in your parlor chatting with me?"

"It makes me feel faint to think of it," Antonia murmured.

"Do you need your vinaigrette?" Clarry asked, a worried expression on her face. "I didn't think to bring it."

"No, no, I'm quite all right. Are you finished with my hair?"

Clarry fidgeted with one last tendril before pronouncing herself satisfied. "Now I am."

"Go and tell them I'm ready. I'll be out in a moment."

Clarry eyed her. "You make a beautiful bride. First time, you were all innocent and nervous, now you know what to expect, and you're like a blooming rose."

They hugged and Clarry left the room.

Antonia stood and paced slowly through the sumptuously appointed bedchamber. The room had served her well, but now the furnishings seemed overblown and somewhat tawdry. She glanced at the bed, still undone, with sheets and pillows strewn to the floor and the aroma of heated passion still lingering in their folds.

The room had been perfectly prepared for sex and seductions, but it suited her no longer. Now that she had found love, she wanted all the furnishings to be fresh for the two of them. She wondered what Sutherland's bedchamber was like, and what he would say when she informed him that they would not be sleeping apart. Would she need to change the furnishings?

Maybe all the furniture in his bedroom was old and meaningful to his family history. She reflected on that. Would she be able to sleep in a bed in which the first six dukes and slept? Wouldn't it be awfully lumpy by now?

She smiled at herself. She was procrastinating, she knew, postponing the moment when she would go through that door and face a new life. For just a few more minutes she wanted to relish the successful completion of her quest, with a reward far greater than she had ever expected.

For all that Dougal had promised her that she would remain independent and his partner, she knew that the promise could never be fully kept. While a small part of her regretted that, the greater part of her, her heart and mind and soul, loved him. She loved him for listening to her, for caring enough to make that pledge to her.

She threw open the door and advanced to meet her bridegroom, Dougal MacDonald, the masterful, exciting, utterly virile seventh duke of Sutherland.

About the author:

Born in Ecuador and raised in Chile, Bonnie Hamre was educated there and in the United States. She has also lived in Italy, England and Scotland, where she gained an appreciation for her Scots heritage. She now makes her home among the coastal redwoods south of San Francisco. Published also in book-length women's fiction, Bonnie finds there is nothing as satisfying as an emotionally gripping tale of two people making a commitment to each other. She writes with sensitivity, with passion and with the tough of humor that makes sensuality fun.

The Spinner's Dream

by Alice Gaines

To my reader:
The most romantic worlds are the ones that live in your imagination. I've created one here, and now I can share it with you.

Chapter One

Solitude and contemplation. Cool fog and the shade of giant trees. The goddess-mother's balm for a fire in the heart. It should have been enough.

Kareth sa-Damil selected an arm's length branch of wood from the dwindling pile and tossed it onto her small hearth-fire. The wood in the forest was plentiful. With no other human soul living in this part of the forest, Kareth had no competition for the abundance of downed timber that lay everywhere. Even if that weren't true, she was young and healthy enough to take the ax from its hook on the wall, find a log, and split it. But the perpetual chill suited her one-room cottage far better than a raging fire.

Some might choose sun and heat to burn their sins away. Kareth had run instead to the silent company of ancient trees and swirling mists. The goddess guided her here to purify herself. Why did she still ache inside?

She sat, cross-legged at her hearth and envisioned the fog seeping under her door, around the window pane, through cracks in the walls to envelope her. Cool, detached, dispassionate. She closed her eyes and sighed. *Dendra take me, school me. I am yours.*

A crashing sounded nearby—as someone raced through the underbrush just outside. Then wood slammed against wood, as her door flew open and banged against the wall. Kareth opened her eyes and found the cause. A man stood on the threshold, not much more than a silhouette in the shadows—a large figure, filling the doorway with shoulders, arms, legs—but indistinct nevertheless. She scrambled to her feet to confront him.

"So, there is someone here," he said. "With the meager smoke from that fire I couldn't be sure."

"Who are you?" she gasped.

He stepped into the room, a long woolen cape swirling around him, and shut the door. "I should think that would be obvious."

And suddenly it was, from the glint of metal around his throat. Nothing gleamed quite like a churl's collar—slick and smooth and inexorably attached to the poor soul who wore it. This man's owner had chosen brass and sapphire blue to mark his property.

"What do you want?" Kareth demanded.

The man looked at her then, really looked at her, his eyes flashing emerald fire from under brows the color of sun-bleached sand. "There are eight or ten catchers close behind me. What I want is to kill a handful of them and escape the rest."

"You'll not kill anyone here."

"Without a weapon, I won't." He glanced around him, and his gaze fell on the ax. "Ah, this will do."

He headed toward the wall where the ax hung, but Kareth blocked his path. "No," she said, staring upward into his face. "You'll not kill anyone here."

"And who's to stop me?"

"I will," she answered. "Dendra will."

"Dendra," he repeated. He slipped a finger under the chain around her neck and pulled the amulet from inside her bodice. His fingers toyed briefly with the crescent-cut crystal. "A priestess."

"A novice," she corrected.

"All the same. Only a true believer would be stupid enough to live in a wilderness like this."

From outside came shouts and the sounds of people blundering through the forest—branches breaking, ferns being trampled under-foot, a flock of curo-curas rising up on noisy wings and cackling out their alarm.

"Blast." The man grabbed her arm and pushed her toward the window. "What do you see?"

She glanced outside. As he had said, nearly ten men were making their way toward her home, hacking a path through the trees and ferns with long, ugly knives. They came to within several yards of the cottage and stopped. A large, barrel-chested man at their head motioned the others to fan out, and the rest of the party disappeared back into the woods to encircle the cottage.

"You're right," she said quietly. "Catchers, a whole patrol of them."

"Get me that ax."

"No."

"Curse you, woman. Do it."

She glared up into the murderous green of his eyes. "No," she repeated.

He dropped her arm and ducked low to crawl under the window. He made his way to the far wall and grabbed the ax from its hook. He took a wide stance, the ax handle clutched in his fists, the blade gleaming in the flickering firelight. "Let them in," he snarled. "One at a time."

"I'll not let you kill anyone."

He stared at her, his eyes wide, as much from terror as exertion. "Do you know what they'll do to me?"

She did. Dendra guide her, she well knew those knives weren't used only to cut the forest apart. They also served to slice through flesh and even to cleave bone. No wonder he wanted to carve the catchers to pieces before they could do the same to him. And from the look of desperation in his eyes, he'd do it, too. She had to find some way to save him without allowing bloodshed in her sanctuary.

She held up her hands to him in a gesture of reassurance. "I'll send them away."

"Easily said, my little brown-eyed believer. But if they smell blood, they won't stop for you or Dendra or anything else." He brandished the ax. "This is all they know."

"Hide," she ordered. "I'll protect you."

He barked out a mirthless laugh. "You? You'd blow away on the first good gust of wind."

"I'm your only hope," she answered. "Hide now, or I'll run out and leave you to their mercy."

His eyes widened ever further. "You'd do that?"

Of course, she wouldn't. But he couldn't know that. So she simply stared back at him, giving him a choice between trusting her and facing ten or so blood-thirsty churl-catchers with only an ax for protection. At that very moment, a heavy knock sounded on the door. "Open up, in the name of Lord Rabal."

Breath of the Beast. She had to do something, now. Her intruder churl still held the ax in strong hands, the muscles of his arms and shoulders bunching, clearly visible even beneath his flowing cape. If one of his pursuers got inside alone, the catcher would likely end up in pieces.

The knocking turned to pounding. "Open up."

"Lord Rabal rules not here," Kareth called back.

"Of course my lord doesn't rule here, woman," the voice grumbled outside. "We've had to travel these four days to get here from his province."

"Then you can travel four days back. I obey no one but Dendra."

"We're chasing an escaped churl. A dangerous man," the catcher shouted through the door. "You'll want us to stop him, or who knows what he'll do to you? Now, be an obedient female and open this door."

Obedient female, indeed. No man referred to a priestess of Dendra as an obedient female, even if she was still a novice. She'd show these males—all of them—who obeyed whom in her own private haven. She glared over at the churl and waved her arm toward the wardrobe. He opened it silently and slipped inside, taking the ax with him.

She walked to the door and lifted the latch. The door flew open, pushing her back toward the center of the room. One of the catchers, the leader, strode in, his long-knife raised. "Where is he?"

"He's not been here."

The man's gaze traveled slowly around the room, taking in every corner. "We saw him come this way, and he hasn't left, or one of my men would've found him."

She folded her arms over her chest. "I've seen no one."

He leered down at her. "Then you're blind as well as deaf, little mother."

That churl was making enough noise to raise my grandam from the dead."
She stood tall and lifted her chin. "I must ask you to leave."

"I must decline." He sketched a sarcastic imitation of a bow. Then
he straightened and headed toward the only place in the room where
a man could conceal himself—the wardrobe. She backed up to inter-
cept him then stood her ground.

The man continued until he stood nearly on top of her, until she
could easily make out his stubble of beard and the grease stains on
his shirt, from Dendra knew how many dinners. In a moment he'd
push past her to the wardrobe. And when he opened the door, he'd be
greeted by a swinging ax.

She rested her hand on his chest and let herself sway into him.
Then she let out a loud cough. He caught her shoulder in his free
hand and shoved her away from him, staring down into her face.
"Here, what's wrong with you?"

She covered her mouth with her hand and coughed some more. More
emphatically this time, long and hard, giving him her best imitation of
someone fighting for breath. "Nothing," she wheezed. "Only..."

She wavered again and made as if to lean into his chest, but he
backed away. "I've not been well," she muttered. "Nothing. A fever.
I'll cure myself soon."

His eyes went round. "The pestilence."

"No. Only a fever," she said. "But there are some soiled things in
there," she added, nodding toward the wardrobe. "Not pestilent, not
at all." She took a gasp of breath. "Still, I wouldn't have another
person see them."

He backed up another step, staring at the wardrobe as though it
imperiled his very life. And indeed it would, if she were pest-ridden,
if her wardrobe did contain unclean bedclothes and dressings.

"I'll leave you then, mother." He lifted his knife as if for protection and backed toward the door. "To cure yourself."

She coughed again and nodded, following along to be sure that he
took not an extra moment to leave. She needn't have worried. He made it
to the door and jumped across the threshold, nearly knocking down one
of his cohorts.

"Easy, Brath." The other catcher reached out and steadied his leader. "Did you find him?"

"No," Brath answered. "You?"

The second catcher shrugged. "Nothing back there but a privy-house. Empty." He made as if to enter the cottage, but Brath caught his arm.

"Don't go in there."

"But we haven't found him out here," the second man protested. "He must be inside."

"He got past us somehow," Brath said.

"Impossible," the other one replied, again moving to step over the threshold. Brath held on, now almost throwing the man back down the path they had carved through the forest.

"What's got into you, man?"

Brath gave him another shove. "We've disturbed the mother enough." Brath nodded toward Kareth.

She coughed one more time and nodded back.

"Round up the others," Brath ordered. "We'll continue the search."

The second man let out a loud whistle, and the two catchers headed away. Kareth closed the door, turned, and leaned against it.

The wardrobe door opened slowly, and a blond head peeked out, followed by broad shoulders and then the head of the ax. "Are they gone?"

"Yes," Kareth answered. "And now you can go, too."

The churl sidled to the window and peeked outside. "A clever bit of deception, the pestilence tale." He glanced over his shoulder at her. "That was a deception, wasn't it?"

"I'd not have let you into that wardrobe if it wasn't." She glared at him. "Pest-soiled linens would kill you faster than those men would."

"Thank you."

"I'm not in the habit of lying, and I don't thank you for forcing me to it."

He turned to peer out the window again. After a moment he set down the ax, leaning the handle against the wall. Then he ran his hand over his eyes. "They are gone."

"Now your turn has come."

He slumped against the wall. "In a moment."

"No." He couldn't stay, not with his shining golden hair and flashing green eyes. Not with that jaw and those hands and the muscled thighs that filled his breeches. He'd bring it all back if she let him—the urges, the weakness that had led her astray. He wasn't Jahn, but still...he was so..so male. He couldn't stay.

"Four days." He sighed. "Little sleep, less food." He yanked on the tie that held his cape, and it dropped to the floor. "And this..."

Dendra guide her. A rust-red stain colored most of one shoulder of his shirt. Blood. "How..." she gasped.

"Lord Rabal himself." He laughed through gritted teeth. "Got a dirk into me on my way out of his wife's bedroom window."

"His wife?"

"A long story." He closed his eyes and swayed. "For later."

"We have no later. You have to leave, now."

He didn't answer but brushed past her and walked to the room's sole chair. Sighing deeply, he dropped onto the seat, tipped back his head, and closed his eyes.

She crossed to him and stared down into his face. She took one look at the pallor of his skin and the tiny lines of pain around his mouth, and her fingers itched to touch him. To brush the platinum hairs from his face and stroke his brow. Soft feelings, these urges, but they would lead to others. "You can't stay here," she whispered.

"You can't make me leave," he answered, his eyes still shut. "As a priestess you can't turn me away. Or does your goddess' kindness only go to the powerful of this world?"

"No," she protested. "Dendra cares most for the helpless, the hungry."

He opened his eyes and smiled at her, stealing her breath with his beauty. "I'm helpless, little mother. I'm hungry. Care for me."

She stood and stared at him, lost in the heat of his gaze.

He reached out slowly and took her hand in his. He brought it to his face, studying her fingers, caressing them with his own. "Heal me."

His words, his breath fanned over her skin—warm and sweet.

No, not sweet. She couldn't taste him, wouldn't let her imagination run in those directions.

She jerked her hand back. "Very well. I'll heal your wound. Then you'll have to go."

He sagged against the back of the chair. "Fine."

She reached to his shirt to ease it away from his wounded shoulder. The fabric whispered under her fingertips, impossibly smooth shalisse—far too elegant for a churl. And his buckskin breeches had been tanned to a butter-softness that molded around him. No common slave, not even one who served in the household, merited such finery. And yet, slave he was, as his collar garishly proclaimed.

What had he said? The lord's wife's bedroom. Oh, Dendra, a handsome-man. She couldn't help herself, she took a step backward.

"So," he gritted. "You know what I am."

"I don't judge."

"Liar." He glared at her. "You can't get away from me fast enough."

"You startled me...I hadn't known..." That much was true, at least. She'd heard of such doings but hadn't credited the stories. That a man would allow himself to be thus used—a noble lady's carnal plaything.

He stared at her a moment more, his gaze boring into her. "Now that you do know, will you still help me?"

"Of course." She approached him again and slid the fabric of his shirt away from his wound. "This doesn't seem deep. You've lost some blood. And you'll need to rest for a time."

"Here?" He glanced around the room. "And where will you put me?"

"In the bed, of course."

He laughed, but the sound had little amusement in it. "In your bed, little mother?"

"I'll sleep elsewhere." She pushed his shirt off his shoulders. "As soon as I've cleaned the wound, I'll help you to bed."

He nodded and sighed, slumping in the chair again. Growing smaller, if that was possible for a man of his size. Like it or not, she'd have to heal him before she could again ask him to leave. Only, please Dendra, let him heal fast.

A groan awoke Kareth—for the third time. She rolled onto her back on the hard floor and stared up into darkness. Maybe the man was just muttering in his sleep this time. Maybe he'd fall silent, and she could rest for a few more hours before the sun came up. But no, he moaned again, louder this time. A cry of pain, of fever. He needed tending, again.

She threw back her makeshift bedding—his cape—and turned toward the hearth. The fire had dwindled down to embers, so she picked up a stick of wood and tossed it onto the top. It caught instantly, sending more heat and light into the room. That would have been enough for herself, but the man had had chills more than once after falling into a deep sleep. She sighed and added a few more logs. She'd have to gather firewood tomorrow.

He groaned again—a strangled, helpless sound. He'd robbed her of her bed and then her rest. Now he'd used up her fuel, too. And she had no choice but to go to him.

She scrambled to her feet and approached the bed. He'd thrown back the blanket and lay curled up on the side of his good shoulder. A sheen of sweat coated his naked shoulders and back. She'd helped him take off his boots and stockings, but his breeches would have to stay on, no matter what.

Poor fellow. He'd come to her for help, and all she could see in him was danger—a threat to what little inner peace she had managed to find here. She had feared him so much, in fact, for what he was she hadn't bothered to find out who he was.

But enough of fearing him, or pitying him, either. She took a deep breath and focused her mind on her goal—getting him well so he could go. At least his sweat promised healing. Perhaps his fever had broken.

She sat on the edge of the bed and checked the bandage on his shoulder. It appeared secure, still holding the herbal poultice tightly against his wound. Now she need only make him comfortable and trust in Dendra.

She reached to the basin of cold water she'd placed on the bedside table earlier. Keeping her gaze on the man, she swished the cloth around and then wrung it out. His face twisted into a grimace, and one leg lashed out, almost sending her flying to the floor. She resumed her seat and pressed the cloth to the back of his neck where his collar rested just below the nape. He arched, and a hiss escaped his clenched teeth.

"Hush," she crooned to him, all the while dabbing at his neck with the cool cloth. "Hush."

He sighed, and some of the tension seemed to ease out of him. She continued down his spine. He had a beautiful back—broad and smoothly muscled. The sort of back that would offer shelter, warmth—an anchor. But his scent didn't comfort, no matter how pleasant it might be. She could just make it out now—a spicy perfume that tickled her nostrils and haunted the back of her mind. But she couldn't mistake it, not after spending the night wrapped in his cape and surrounded by the smell of him.

Dendra guide her, she had to rid herself of such thoughts. She reached again to the basin and replenished the cloth. With her free hand, she brushed stray hairs from his eyes. As delicate as the shalisse of his shirt, the strands slipped through her fingers and back over his forehead. Odd how they could be so soft when the rest of the man was so hard. She placed the cloth against his cheek and dabbed at his temple.

He let out a soft "ahhhhh," and rolled onto his back, revealing his chest. The broad expanse glistened with moisture, outlining sinew and muscle, two tawny male nipples, and a furrow down the middle. Sleek and hard it was, naked and vulnerable, with not a hair to mar its beauty.

But that was what he was, after all—a man cultivated for beauty, kept for a woman's pleasure. She ought not to expect the scars of hard work on the chest of a man who crept in and out of his lady's bedroom window. She ought to expect exactly what lay before her, a man so flawless her breath froze in her chest at the sight of him. A man whose perfection caught the fire's light and held it in shining glory.

She let her fingers trail over the length of his throat to his shoulders and then along his collar bone. The man was a test—one that would be all to easy to fail. No intellectual challenge this, no bookish debate of good versus evil, but far more dangerous than that. The goddess knew her, had searched out the weakest part of her soul and had sent this man to undo all her cool contemplation. And if she let down her guard for an instant, she'd be lost.

She moistened her cloth and brought it to his chest. She stroked him quickly, trying to give no heed to the smoothness of his skin where her fingers brushed it accidentally. Forcing herself not to notice the heat of his flesh that penetrated through the cloth as she worked. She'd be finished soon. Her duty performed, she could get away from him. Even if she did have to sleep in his cape, cloaked in his scent, she'd be rid of the vision he made in the glow of the fire.

Finished, she put the cloth back into the basin and lifted the blanket to cover him. One glance downward, and she dropped it again, a tiny cry escaping her lips.

There, straining at the front of his breeches—a bulge, long and thick. He was hard in that animal way of men. Impossible but true. And large, so large.

Dendra, give me strength. She couldn't be tempted by this man, a stranger, as she had been by Jahn. She wouldn't let herself be. No matter how sleek he was...how beautiful...how...

He grabbed her then. His hand came up, and his fingers curled around her arm, pulling her down. Down until she rested against the width of his chest, her face inches from his, his breath burning against her cheek.

"No," she cried. And she struggled against him. But he held her fast, his fingers like iron bands around her flesh. "No," she said again, a plea this time.

His eyes opened, and the light of the fire played in their emerald depths. He studied her as if he'd never seen her before. Then his gaze focused, and his features softened. "You," he whispered.

She swallowed hard and nodded.

His grip loosened, but he still held her. His fingers played over her skin, soothing now where they had crushed before. He lifted his head slowly, as if the movement cost him.

"Thank you," he said, his voice as soft as a spring breeze.

She nodded again, helpless to do anything else. He closed his eyes and parted his lips as if to kiss her. She couldn't allow that, didn't dare let his mouth touch hers. But, as strong as he was, how could she prevent it without struggling so hard she'd open the wound in his shoulder again? Breath of the Beast, she'd have to find some other way to free herself.

She pulled back, firmly but cautiously. "Let me go."

He gave a twist with his hips, and suddenly she found herself flat on her back, looking up at him. His eyes were open, flashing sparks of firelight at her. The hardness she had seen before now pressed into her thigh—more tempting that she could have believed possible. This wasn't Jahn, wasn't the man she had loved. Why did the feel of him make her so weak and fluttery inside?

"Please, let me go."

His lips curled into a seductive smile as he gazed down at her. "Not until I've thanked you properly."

"I don't need any..."

His mouth came down on hers, stealing away her words and dismantling any protest. His lips moved slowly, softly along hers, in a gentle exploration that pleaded for an answer rather than demanded it. And answer she did, helpless creature of the flesh that she was. She took the urgings from his mouth, amplified them, and gave them back until the kiss burned hot and sweet enough to singe the edges of her heart.

"That's it, my little one," he murmured against her lips. "That's it."

"You can't do this," she whispered.

He raised his head and gazed into her eyes. "Do what?"

"Make me feel like this."

"How do you feel?"

She couldn't answer. Didn't dare answer. Had not the words. She shut her eyes and turned her head on the pillow.

He laughed softly. "Does it feel good?"

She said nothing but lay as still as she could, counting her heartbeats, measuring out her breaths.

His lips slid along her jaw and then down the length of her neck—nipping, teasing, setting fire to her skin. His hand brushed aside the light fabric of her shift and reached inside to cup her breast. Her breath caught on a gasp.

"Does that feel good?" His mouth followed along the path his fingers had taken. "Does this?"

His lips closed over her breast, and he sucked gently, as his tongue flicked at the nipple. She cried aloud, and her back arched. He didn't stop but continued the pressure, on and on until she ran her fingers into his hair, catching handfuls of it in her fists.

"Please," she gasped.

His hand trailed over her hip, bunching up her shift and then dipping beneath to stroke the outside of her leg. A fire kindled inside her—the forbidden flame that had burned at her as she had lain so many nights alone and dreamed of Jahn. As she had imagined his caress until the need grew past her control and she had to touch herself to find peace.

No — more. Those nights, that fire, that hunger paled next to this. Even the final reality of Jahn's loving came nowhere near this. Feather soft, his hand slipped over her leg—now over her calf, now inside her knee, and then between her thighs. Close to the throbbing, so close.

"Please."

"Please? Please what, little one?" he repeated. "Please stop? Please more?"

"Please." The word was all she had, all she could hold onto in a world gone mad with throbbing.

"Please here?" he asked finally. Then his fingers found her most feminine spot, parted the petals, and slipped inside to rub her.

She cried aloud, all language gone.

"Yes, here," he whispered. "You're burning."

He stroked her firmly and then gently, until she floated, hovering outside of reality, ready to explode. Then he hesitated just long enough for her to take a gasp of air. And he started again. A maddening rhythm that took her to the brink over and over. She cried out, pressing herself against his fingers, begging with her body for release.

He granted it. His touch quickened, pushed her steadily toward ecstasy and then past it. She rode the crest, her body convulsing. Violent spasms of pure delight. One wave on top of another until she fell, weak and trembling, back onto the mattress — a mere mortal again.

He sighed and rested on top of her. "And now, my little one," he murmured into her ear, "now you have been properly thanked."

Chapter Two

A cold breeze woke Kareth. It grazed her cheeks and blew stray hairs into her face. She opened her eyes and found herself on the floor next to her hearth. The previous night flooded back to her in one humiliating, cheek-burning, stomach-churning wave. What she'd seen. What she'd done. What she'd let the man do to her.

Dendra forgive her, she'd succumbed again, and this time to a man she'd just met. A man who didn't have a name — only smooth muscle, shining eyes, and persuasive lips. And fingers. Oh Dendra, his fingers.

The cool air floated to her again. She clutched his cape around her and glanced across the room. No wonder she was shivering. The cottage door hung open, and tendrils of mist curled inside, incited by early morning light that made the fog shiver like fingers of ice. She looked toward the bed and found it empty, the sheets turned back. The man himself was gone.

She heaved an enormous sigh of relief and hated herself for it. As a healer, she ought to care about him and his wound. He was hurt, perhaps delirious again. And she had his cape, so he couldn't keep himself warm. But instead she only wanted to be rid of him and his temptation. Better he leave her in peace. She wished him well.

He appeared then — filling the threshold, backlit by the mist. The fog touched him only tentatively, brushing against the shalisse of his shirt and then retreating as if frozen. But the light—that was another matter — the morning light shone on him as though the distant sun recognized him as one of its own.

A smile warmed his features, amused and indecent and breathtaking. "Did you sleep well?"

She sat and looked at him, near blinded by the light. Her heart danced a few steps in her chest—turning her earlier relief at his absence into excitement at finding him still here. Traitorous heart.

He stepped fully into the room. In his hand he held the ax, shaft in hand, and he leaned on it for support. "Why is it so blasted cold in here?" he demanded.

She found her voice finally. "Because you left the door open, for one thing."

He grunted and closed the door behind him. Then he walked slowly, haltingly toward the bed, using the ax to anchor his movements. He reached the bed and sank onto it, letting out a deep sigh as he did.

So, back he was. And injured. And still in need of her help. She couldn't turn him away. But she could take charge of things in her own cottage, and she would. She threw back the cape, rose, and walked to him. "Where have you been?"

"I had to go out." He set the ax on the bed beside him.

"If you had awakened me I could have helped you," she answered.

He smiled again, mischief now crinkling the corners of his eyes. "There are some things a man doesn't want help with."

She glared back at him. "Open your shirt."

He laughed but did as he was told. Kareth pushed the shalisse away from his shoulder and lifted the bandage carefully. The redness and swelling of the joint had eased, and the wound itself had lost its angry look.

"Why did you leave me last night?" he asked, his voice soft in her ear.

"You needed your rest."

"I needed your warmth."

She held the cloth of the bandage tightly in her fingers and took a steadying breath.

He moved his lips closer to her face. "Didn't you like what I did?"

Strict obedience forbade lying. But her faith did not demand that she answer him. So she continued her inspection of his shoulder and remained silent.

"I can do much more," he added. "If you'll let me."

"That won't be necessary," she said. "This will heal completely in a few days, and then you can leave."

"Ah, no. Then I'll cut you some firewood, and we can make this cottage warm, you and I."

"I can gather my own firewood, thank you."

"I would have done so today, but I found I wasn't quite up to hard work."

As if he ever had been. "That's very kind of you, Sir..."

"Sir?" he repeated. Then he laughed again, heartily this time. "No one calls a churl 'sir.'"

She replaced the bandage and put her hands on her hips, looking down into his face. "Then, what is your name?"

"Thiele."

"Only Thiele? No sa-name?"

"A churl takes his sa-name from his master. When my lady made a gift of me to Rabal on the occasion of their marriage, I became Thiele sa-Rabal to the world. To myself, I'm Thiele."

"Very well, Thiele. I'm Kareth sa-Damil."

He put his hands over her own, circling her waist with his long fingers. "As soon as I'm well, Kareth sa-Damil, I'll chop you enough wood to build a hot fire—one that will let you go naked in here."

"Why would I want to do that?"

He shrugged. "To amuse me?"

She pushed his hands away from her. "I'll heal you and that only. Then you can leave."

The gleam in his eye grew cold, his mouth tense. "But I can't."

"Of course you can. The border's not far. You can make good your escape."

He slipped his fingers under his collar and gripped the metal in his fist. "With this I'll never get across the border. My lord's magician has conjured up a barrier. No one wearing Rabal's collar of ownership can cross the border undetected."

"That's nonsense. Faith can't be used that way—to throw up a pen to hold people inside like animals."

"Rabal's man has done it somehow." He released the collar and dropped his hand to his lap. "The news went through the churl quarters like wildfire."

"Put out by someone in Rabal's pocket, no doubt," she replied. "To keep you all under control by fear."

"It's true, I tell you."

"And I tell you it's impossible."

He glowered at her, and his hand clenched into a fist again, this time against his thigh. "I can't take the chance. I'd be caught at the border."

"Listen to me. I know something of spells, and the one you describe doesn't exist. Nor would Dendra allow such a perversion of her powers to exist."

His eyes widened again. "You? You know magic?"

"I know something of it, and that only a little."

"Then you're my solution." He took her hands in his. "You'll work the spell to get this collar off me."

"I know nothing of such spells. You must remove the collar yourself."

"I can't. I've tried everything—files, saws, even prayers."

"I can't help you. You have to leave. You have to leave me in peace."

He gripped her fingers, now so tightly the pressure hurt. "Kareth sa-Damil, you will get this collar off me. I won't leave here until you do. Do you understand?"

She looked down into his eyes, into the fire of determination there. Determination and something more. Stay he would, and she would confront that something more. Over and over.

Dendra, give me strength.

"Sun."

Kareth turned and found Thiele standing, looking skyward with his hands shading his eyes. Ferns that came up to her own waist barely reached the middle of his thighs. But the large basket he carried, nearly full now of firewood, still disappeared among the leafy, green fronds. "Finally, some warmth," he added.

"The sun's been out since morning."

"Not so that you'd notice."

She crossed her arms over her chest. "What's wrong with you, anyway? You've done nothing but complain about the fog and the cool air since you got here."

"The spinner's dream," he said.

"Ah, yes," she replied. "For roast meat, a hot fire, and..."

"...and an even hotter lover to warm her bed," he finished.

"I know the proverb. What has that to do with you?"

He looked at her, his gaze even but definitely not tranquil. "My mother was a spinner."

"Spinning is done in mills, with waterwheels to do the work."

"Perhaps in towns where you lived before you became a slave to your goddess," he said.

"A priestess of Dendra," she corrected.

"In grand houses churls still do the work," he went on, "women with long, agile fingers."

"Why?"

He lifted his arm from his side, and the shalisse of his shirt billowed around him, catching the sun's rays and fracturing them into sparks of light and shade, highlights of different hues. "The thread is finer if spun by hand."

She turned and proceeded down the path. "So," she said over her shoulder, "your mother was a spinner."

"A churl like myself."

She pushed aside a fern frond and found a good bit of wood—a branch nearly as thick around as her wrist and yet not too long to fit into the basket. She picked it up, walked back to him, and tossed it onto the pile they had already gathered. Then she raised her eyes and looked into his face. "What has that to do with your complaints about the climate?"

"I spent my time with my mother when I was small," he answered, gazing back down at her. "I understand the spinner's dream."

"Of meat, of fire, and lover?"

"Of warmth." He stared at her in silence for a moment. "And I think you do, too."

"Dendra, how could I?" She turned to search for fuel. "I don't know what you're talking about."

"Shalisse fibers have an oiliness to them."

She pushed aside another fern but found nothing of import underneath. "So I've heard."

"They must be kept cold until they're woven into cloth and the cloth is cured, or they'll go rancid. The churls who work the fibers—the spinners—are kept cold, too."

"How?"

"Unheated rooms in winter. Underground chambers in summer. Sixteen hours a day, seven days a week."

She straightened and turned toward him. "All that time in the cold?"

He stood there and looked straight at her. "In winter, their quarters are underheated, too. To save fuel."

"That's cruel."

He shrugged. "A churl expects no better."

"I always thought the spinner's dream was..." She let her voice trail off, not sure exactly what she had thought. All those women going cold. And all their children, like the one standing before her. Grown now, but once a little boy shivering with cold.

"I thought it was just a saying," she said. "A warning about caring too dearly for the comforts of the flesh."

"Easy enough to rail against the comforts of the flesh when you have enough of them. Harder when you're always wanting."

"I'm sorry."

He smiled, a cockeyed sort of expression that might charm but didn't reassure. "It isn't your fault. You've never worn that sort of shalisse, I'm sure."

"But you have." She raised her hand to point toward his shirt. "You're wearing it now. When you know what it cost the women who spun the fibers."

"This is what I was given to wear," he snapped. "My lady Eria always wanted me in shalisse. She said it felt good against her naked skin."

"I see." Kareth turned away from him, facing down the path into the forest.

"Especially in her most sensitive places—her throat, her breasts, her..."

"I see," she repeated. She strode off, leaving their little pool of sunlight to step into the shade of an ancient emperor tree.

Soft laughter followed her. "There's no disgrace in taking pleasure where it's offered. Not even your Dendra condemns what goes on between men and women."

"I know that."

"And yet you're ashamed of what I did for you last night, aren't you?"

She didn't look at him but continued around the massive trunk of the tree, her attention fixed on the ground.

"Aren't you?" He grasped her elbow and turned her around to face him.

She couldn't avoid his gaze. But instead of mockery, anger, or even a seductive smile, all she found was puzzlement in his deep, green eyes. He didn't understand her confusion over what had happened between them the night before. After all, touching was a simple act for him—something he did because he was supposed to do it. Something he did as an uncomplicated thank-you. But for her, intimacy was a very complicated thing, indeed. It had driven her here, to solitude where she had hoped to arrive at some understanding of herself. She had never expected a man like Thiele to appear and tempt her back into the hunger, the madness.

He set the basket onto the ground and lifted his hand to her face. "You've done nothing wrong, little mother," he murmured, caressing her cheek with his thumb. "You did me a kindness by saving me from the catchers. I paid you back the best way I knew."

"I don't require payment," she whispered. "I'm supposed to help the afflicted. I don't want anything in return."

"But you did." He lowered his hand to her throat and stroked its length, feather-light pressure that set her skin on fire. "You wanted the touching very much. I've never seen a woman respond like that."

"Please don't..."

"Your body came alive in my hands."

She took a step backward, but he followed, his fingers still brushing the length of her neck. She took another step and another until her back met the trunk of the tree and there was no more escape. He stayed with her—so close he towered over her and his chest pressed against her bosom. Her heart raced, and her breath came in a labored, erratic rhythm, crushing her breasts against the rock hardness of him in bondage too sweet to resist. "Thiele, you mustn't," she gasped. "I can't."

"Yes, you can. And yes, I must," he murmured. "Your fire excites me. That doesn't happen often to a man whose business is loving."

"No," she sighed. But the sound came out as a plea, not a command. A plea for him to continue—not to stop, but to press himself against her harder. And he did until the rough bark scratched against her back and her face buried itself into the crook of his neck and she had to taste him.

She pressed her mouth to the base of his throat and felt his pulse beating under her lips. His skin gave off that wonderful perfume of spices and wood smoke she had slept in the night before, and she sipped at him greedily.

He groaned and bent to take her mouth in a searing kiss—hot and honeyed and intoxicating. His tongue opened her lips and entered her, at the same moment that his knee parted her legs and slid between them. He moved his body against hers, the hard ridge of his manhood rubbing her hip—beseeching and commanding, inciting and demanding her response.

She wound her arms around his neck and pulled herself against him, plundering his mouth with her tongue, taking his breath to feed her hunger. He caught her buttocks in his hands and kneaded them. The action brought her even harder against the thick ridge of his arousal, and she answered with her own movements, until her body measured every inch of him. Until she knew exactly how it would feel to have him inside her, rocking, thrusting, pushing her to the edge of herself.

She was going to have him. Now. Here among the ferns, with

leaves clinging to her hair and the breeze playing over their bodies. She was going to open the front of his breeches and take out his sex and stroke it until he growled and roared and yanked up her skirts so that he could take her like the animal she was.

Animal. A blind, groping, hungry animal. And she didn't care. She had to have him now, and she didn't care.

Overhead a loud, shrieking cackle sounded. He pulled back from her and lifted his head, scanning the branches. She rested her fists against his chest for support and felt his breast rising and falling in a struggle for air.

An answering call came, every bit as ear-splitting as the first, and Kareth finally recognized it.

"What is that?" he demanded.

"Curo-curas," she answered.

"What?"

"Birds." She took an unsteady breath. "One seldom hears their call so close."

With a fluttering of wings, the curo-curas flew into view. The large cock settled on a branch twenty feet above them and smoothed an errant scarlet feather with his curved beak. His smaller, less colorful hen swooped down next to him and studied her mate with an adoring eye.

"Birds?" Thiele ran his fingers through his hair. "I was distracted from you by a pair of birds?"

"Very loud birds," she answered. And very welcome ones. One more minute and...Dendra, that didn't bear thinking about. "I've seen these two often. They're almost pets."

"Then they won't mind if we resume." He reached for her.

She caught his hands and pushed them away. "But I'll mind."

"Kareth," he chided.

"There's something between us, I'll admit."

"Something?" he repeated. "Something?"

"There's a madness between us."

"Why must you call it madness? It's normal for a man and woman to make love to each other."

Not for me. She leaned against the tree and closed her eyes, digging her fingertips into the cracks in the bark. The touching, the kisses, the sighs had never been normal for her. Her drive was too strong. It robbed her of all reason, made her want people she couldn't have. It made her do things she shouldn't do.

His fingers brushed her shoulder. She jumped and pushed them away. "I can't," she cried. "I can't make love to you. I can't."

"Very well." He sighed. "I won't make love to you. But I will stay until we've found a way to rid me of this collar, and I will give you comfort while I'm here."

She turned and stared at him. The indecent smile had returned to his face. With the sunlight forming a golden halo around his head and sandy brows lifted in amusement, he looked for all the world like a naughty little boy. But the heat in his eyes belied any resemblance to innocence. Comfort her, would he? How would he do that without raising the fire again in her blood? He couldn't, of course, which he knew very well.

Somehow she'd have to convince him to leave. And until he did, she'd have to keep him at arm's length. But how? Dendra, how?

The moon was high in the sky by the time Kareth led Thiele to the pool to bathe. She held a lantern in front of her, although she'd already memorized the path. If Thiele tripped and fell, he might re-injure his shoulder, which would delay his leaving. She hadn't yet arrived at how she would convince him to leave when he was healed. He truly seemed to believe the story about the magic barrier at the border. But convince him she would, and then she'd be rid of him.

He crashed behind her now, just as he had when running through the woods the day before with the catchers after him. Everything about the man was an intrusion, from his power and his size to his scent and his wicked smile. She would have given him the lantern and sent him out alone, but he might have ended up lost, blundering through the forest bringing grief to ferns and wildlife alike.

No matter. She'd sit by while he bathed, looking safely off into the darkness until he finished. Then she'd take him back to the cottage. She'd have her bath after he had fallen asleep.

They turned a corner in the path, and a small shape scurried past her and disappeared into the undergrowth. Behind her Thiele gasped and stopped in his tracks. "What was that?"

She laughed softly. "No need for secrecy. There's no one here."

"Then what was that?"

"Only an animal."

"But what type?"

She turned back to face him. He glanced around, his eyes darting from one shadow to the next. For such a big man, he frightened at very small things. "A woodlar, perhaps, or a scimp. Little creatures. They won't hurt you."

"Little, eh?" he answered. "The vermin that lived in the grand house walls were little enough, and pest-ridden."

"There's no pest here. The forest is a healing place."

He looked down at her, skepticism clear in his gaze.

She reached out and took his hand. "Come."

She turned and led him down the path again, the lantern held before them. "Why did we wait until dark to bathe?" he asked.

Why, indeed? Because she couldn't bear to look at him naked, and yet she wanted to be nearby. Wanted to hear his body enter the water. Wanted to smell him when he'd finished rinsing the saarflowers from his hair.

"We spent most of the day gathering wood so the fire would be big enough for you," she answered. "Then I was hungry and wanted supper after all that work."

"Gave you an appetite, did it?"

She glanced at him out of the corner of her eye and found that smile again. The one he'd teased her with all afternoon. "I was hungry for my supper and that only."

Now it was his turn to laugh softly. "Of course."

"We're here now, and you'll thank me when you've done."

"For plunging me into frigid water?" he grumbled. "I don't think so."

"Did I say the water would be cold?"

"What else could it be?"

She lifted the lantern high, showing him the pool and the clouds of steam rising from it.

"Mercy, woman," he gasped. "How did you do this?"

"I didn't. It's only an underground hot spring."

"It looks like a saint's afterlife." He charged toward the pool, stripping off his shirt, dropping it beside the path as he went. She set the lantern down and turned to look into the forest. Behind her more clothing dropped into the undergrowth. Then water splashed, and he let out a loud "Ahhhh."

She put her fingers over her mouth and giggled. More splashing sounded and more animal noises of contentment. "Ah, little one. Of all the kindnesses you've done me, this must be the greatest."

"I'm glad you like it."

"The water's perfect, as though you heated it for me. Are you sure it isn't magic?"

"Absolutely certain."

"Thank you, anyway." Splash, splash, splash. "Thank you a hundred times."

"You're very welcome. Now I'll pick you some saarflowers for you to wash with." She walked to a spot a few yards away where a saarbush grew, draped in rays of moonlight that had managed to slip between two emperor trees. She picked a few branches and walked back with them to the pool. Keeping her eyes averted from Thiele, she reached down to hand him the herbs.

"What's this?" he asked, taking them.

"Saarflowers. Moisten them and rub them into a lather to wash your hair."

"I know this scent. The potion I used on my lady's hair smelled like this."

"The essence is made into a soap."

"Yes." He splashed some more and crushed the flowers between his palms, releasing the fragrance of saar into the night. "Aren't you coming in?" he asked after a moment.

"I'll bathe later."

"Please, Kareth, there's plenty of room."

"I don't think..."

"Let me wash your hair, as I did for Eria," he said. "You have very beautiful hair."

She tugged at her braid, and the gentle pulling let her imagine how it would feel to have his fingers in her hair, pressing against her scalp. It would feel wonderful to have him wash her hair, to sit in that deliciously hot water with Thiele and let him minister to her.

"Please," he entreated. "Let me do that for you."

"All right." She unlaced the bodice of her gown and lifted it over her head. Her shift went next, dropping beside the gown. She stood for a moment, naked except for her crystal amulet, and the cool night air washed over her, warring with the steam from the pool to raise little bumps on her flesh. She looked directly at Thiele. He smiled an innocent invitation and extended his hand. She took it and lowered herself into the pool, finding her favorite rock and sitting on it.

"That's better," he declared. He rubbed some flowers between his palms, making a thick lather. "Eria loved for me to wash her hair."

She unplaited her braid and turned her head, offering her hair to him. He massaged the herbs into it in a hot, soapy balm.

"She had nice hair," he continued. "Bright red and curly. But yours is much softer."

"How did she..." She hesitated, searching for the right word. Find you? Get you? Buy you? "How did you come into your lady's service?"

"I was fourteen and working in her father's granary. She saw me and felt stirrings." His fingers made lazy circles over her scalp, soothing and invigorating all at once. "Eria called me a pretty child, even though she was only sixteen herself. She asked her father, and he gave me to her. He gave her everything she wanted."

"How terrible," Kareth said. "To be chosen like a prize animal."

"Not at all. She took me into the house, found a position for my mother so that she could be warm in her last years, at least. Rinse."

Kareth dipped her head back, bringing the hot water up over her ears. He stroked her hair, pulling it back and spreading it out between his fingers. Then he guided her back to a sitting position and lathered his hands again.

"Eria was a stunning young woman—all elegance and bright colors." His fingers slipped into her hair for a second time. "Copper hair, sapphire eyes, alabaster skin. After I first saw her in the granary, I couldn't take my eyes off her. The first sight of her naked, waiting for me in her bed almost unmanned me."

"Did you love her?" Kareth whispered.

He sighed. "At first I did. We had a game of our own—if I were in love with you, we called it. We made up stories of how we'd run away and live together, just the two of us. I half believed them...then."

"What happened?"

His fingers stopped their motion through her hair. "One night she sent me to pleasure a friend of hers who was visiting. I was to share our intimacies with a stranger."

"Did you...that is...could you?" Dendra, how could she even ask such a question? It was certainly not her concern.

"Was my manhood up to the job?" He laughed and resumed his massage of her scalp. "Not really. But I still had my hands and my tongue. She was satisfied."

"Thiele, I didn't mean..."

"I've schooled my cohort since then. He performs when I want him to."

"What about your pleasure?"

"My pleasure? Who would care about my pleasure?"

"Why, you, of course."

He laughed again. "What odd ideas you have, little one. You've lived alone in this forest too long."

"Still..."

"Rinse."

She ducked her head into the water. He smoothed his fingers through her hair, rinsing away the flowers and their fragrant oil. She pushed back up, and he caught her around the waist and pulled her into his lap. She ought to object, to move away. But it felt so right to float in his arms, looking into the moonlight, listening to the breeze rustle through the emperors, smelling saarflowers and warm, clean man.

He moved his hips and, unhindered by clothing or any other barrier, his hardness pressed into her back.

"Have you commanded your cohort to perform now?" she whispered.

"You're different, my little sorceress. He has a mind of his own where you're concerned."

"I've told you—I'm no sorceress. I know no magic."

"You've worked your charms on me. I've never been so continually, so maddeningly hard and ready."

At that she did try to pull away. But he held her firmly. "Let me show you how it feels," he murmured into her ear.

His hands moved from her waist, up and over her ribs, finally catching her breasts in his palms. Her breath came hard on a gasp, as he kneaded and tugged softly—using just the right pressure to heat her blood to the same temperature as the currents of water that lapped at her collar bone and slid between her thighs.

"Yes," he whispered, his thumbs now playing over her nipples, making them hard. Achingly hard. She bit her lip, but a cry escaped from between them before she could stop it.

"Yes," he repeated, as his hands moved lower. Back over her ribs in a slow caress. To her hips and down to her buttocks. He smoothed his palms over the outside of her thighs and pulled her against his hardness. She melted inside, tipped her head back against his shoulder and sighed and rubbed herself against him. If she made just the right move—it wouldn't take much—she could rise up and lower herself onto him. She could take him inside her. And he would...he would...he would...

He rose abruptly, setting up waves of hot water around her and leaving her bereft. She glanced up to find him beside the pool, moonlight spilling over his shoulders and reflecting out of his eyes, his manhood standing erect. He reached his hand down to her. "Come, Kareth sa-Damil. It's time."

Chapter Three

Kareth stood in her little cottage and looked around her as though seeing everything for the first time. And indeed, this was the first time the room had been so brightly lit by a fire. The first time a man had stood by that fire, piling wood onto it until the flames jumped high, their tops disappearing up the chimney. The first time in this place that she would lose herself in a man's embrace. The night before had been only a sample, that she knew. Tonight her body would reveal how deep her passions ran, and this man—Thiele—would know how to play them.

He finished building the fire and turned to her, stretching out his arms. "Come, little one, let me make you warm."

She went to him. No point in resisting—he'd only bring her to the hearth if he had to. She stood only a foot away from him, staring up into his face. The light of the fire captured his beauty as the moonlight had before. The long shadow of eyelashes against his cheek, the angle of his jaw, the seductive curve of his lips. Those lips could move softly over hers, or they could burn against her skin. They pursed now, as he took her face in his hands. He tipped it upward and planted a soft kiss on her forehead.

How did one resist such tenderness, even knowing the madness that would follow? Kareth had not the strength, so she leaned into him and sighed. He lowered his mouth to hers and took her lips, softly again. He lingered at her mouth, his lips and tongue tasting her, tempting her, daring her to come to him for more honey, more heat. She tried to embrace him, but he held her away, drawing out the kiss for heartbeat after thundering heartbeat.

His hands moved to the closure of her bodice and unlaced it. One last little voice of sanity sounded in her brain. This hadn't gone too far yet. She could still stop. "Thiele, no," she whispered.

"Yes." He moved his mouth to her ear and nibbled at the lobe.

"You promised," she breathed. "You said you wouldn't make love to me."

He lowered his head further and kissed her neck. "I lie sometimes."

She caught his arms, digging her fingertips into his flesh.

He straightened and looked down into her face, his own expression drugged with passion. His eyes hung sleepily half-open, his lips moist and parted. "You want this, Kareth. You need this."

"Thiele..."

"If this were only for me, I'd resist. As hot as you've made me, I'd still hold back. But you—you're trembling, vibrating in my hands."

"The cold," she tried.

"It's not cold in here." He pulled her into his arms and buried his face into her neck. "And you're hot, too. You're burning. Let me put the fire out."

He held her against him, and she felt his hardness again. He crushed her to him, and a moan escaped his throat. He wanted her, and, Dendra help her, she wanted him. She would have him before he left. So, why not now?

"Yes," she whispered. "Yes, Thiele, take me."

He swept her up in his arms and spun her around, letting out a triumphant whoop. When he stopped, the room continued to swirl around her. Only his face stayed in focus—beautiful and radiant with passion. "Ah, woman. How you make me work to have you. I'll have my revenge. Wait and see."

"Take it now. Please, take it now."

He headed toward the bed. He laid her down softly and reached for her gown. She offered no resistance but instead lifted herself to allow him to slip it and then her shift over her shoulders and head. When she lay back again, her crystal slipped smoothly into the valley between her breasts.

Thiele sat back on his heels on top of the coverlet and gazed at her, his eyes wide.

"Mercy, woman. You're beautiful."

She brought her hands up and over her nakedness. But he reached out and pushed them away. "I want to look at you," he said.

"You've seen me."

"It was dark last night and again tonight when we bathed. I never would have believed that under your loose clothes I'd find a form so perfect."

"Don't flatter me."

"It's not flattery." He reached out to run his fingertips over the length of her throat and then along her shoulder. "You don't have a glass here. You have no idea how you look."

Perhaps not, but she knew how she felt. And right now the gentle pressure of his fingers made her skin come alive. She lay perfectly still, watching him. Watching his gaze follow the progress of his hand, along her side down to her breast.

"And these," he sighed, covering one globe with his palm. "So full and round."

He flicked his thumb over the nipple, and it grew hard, standing erect for him. A charge of pure pleasure shot through her, from the point of contact to her core. The restlessness started in her belly and below. Soon it would be a throbbing, and she would have to use her all the air she could fit into her lungs to beg him to take her. For now, his fingers trailed along her ribs to the flare of her hip.

"And your thighs." He stroked the outside of her leg. "So soft, so warm. So vulnerable I'm tempted to nibble on them."

His hand moved to the inside of her leg and slid up and down slowly. Up and down. Until the throbbing started and built.

"I think I will nibble on you here," he murmured, his voice growing dark and husky. "I'll start here." He touched a spot just inside her knee. "And move along here." His fingers slid up her thigh. "Until I get here."

He touched her at her most sensitive spot, where her legs came together, and her hips began to move. He rubbed her, and the pleasure grew into a hot flame, its center at her core.

"Ah, yes. I like this part of you best. Your sex, so hot and sweet. So little, it's bound to grip me tightly. I swear I could come just thinking of it."

"Take me," she whispered.

"In a moment. First—while I still have some control—I'll do what I promised." He lowered himself to the mattress and slid his arms under her hips, lifting them and pulling them toward his mouth. Dendra, he meant to do it, he meant to kiss her there. He pressed his lips to her inner thigh. Then he stroked her with his tongue and nipped at her with his teeth. Heavenly and gentle. Incendiary and irresistible. If he did that at the juncture of her thighs, at the center of her femininity, she'd splinter into so many fragments she'd never put herself back together. She'd die with the joy.

But she didn't.

He buried his nose into the curling hairs of her sex and breathed hotly on her. She gasped, and her hips rose, but she didn't die. He gripped her tightly, even though she moaned and tossed about. But she didn't die. When his lips closed over the throbbing nub and sucked, she was very much alive. She cried his name and dug her fingers into his hair, holding his face against her.

"Thiele! Oh, Thiele. I'm going to...it's on me. I can't stop it."

He rose above her, taking away the pressure. The caresses that had her ready to burst. She whimpered in disappointment and moved her hips again. Searching, searching for something to ease the ache.

"Not yet, little one. I can take you still higher."

"Now, please. Now."

"Undress me."

She took a shuddering breath and tried to slow her heart. The fire still raged in her loins, but she did as he asked, tugging the tails of his shirt out of his breeches, pulling the shalisse over his head, and tossing it to the floor. She reached to the buttons of his breeches and fumbled with them. Just under the ruckskin, his sex strained to be free. As she twisted first one button and then another, he moved his hardness against her hands. She curled her fingers over the thick ridge of flesh, and he took a sharp inward breath.

"Hurry, little one. I want to feel your fingers around me."

The fury of his passion helped her bank her own need—to keep her own lust at the simmer, demanding and hot. Ready to run free the moment he could join her. She worked at the buttons more calmly now, savoring his every moan, his every movement. Finally, she had the ruckskin open, and she could reach inside and take his sex into her hands. It was heavy and swollen into an impossible hardness, smooth and hot. She curled her fingers around the shaft and stroked its length.

He gritted his teeth in an expression of desire that approached pain. "Ah, Kareth...I never...ah, Kareth...stop now. You have to stop."

She dropped her hands to her sides and looked up at him, waiting. She didn't have to wait long. He stripped out of the breeches, nearly ripping them at the seams in his haste. Then he parted her legs and positioned himself between them.

She slipped her arms around his neck and pulled him down to her. He moved his hips, and the tip of his sex touched her own. She jerked up to rub herself against him, and in an instant she was lost again. The fire, the hunger, the need came over her again, stealing her breath. The universe centered at the point where his hardness pressed against her throbbing. She dug her fingertips into his back and held on as he moved against her. She couldn't hold out much longer. She was going to shatter, any moment now. Just one more movement. Just one.

She shifted, only a few inches, but enough to bring him to the entrance of her core. She took the tip of him inside her, and a shout tore from her chest. He thrust—deep, so deep inside her. She did die then, after only one thrust. She shuddered and convulsed. She grasped at him, over and over. Pulling at his manhood, milking him with her spasms.

He held absolutely still as she floated back onto the coverlet, her hands still clutching his back. He bent his lips to her ear. "Was it good, little one?"

She took a few gasping breaths. "Yes," she finally managed.

"I nearly came, too. Feeling you around me like that was almost more than I could bear."

She opened her eyes and found him smiling down at her. Not with mockery but tenderly. "Truly?" she whispered.

"Truly." He kissed her gently. "We'll just wait now until you're ready again."

She moved her hips and felt him inside her—still so big and hard. "Now," she said.

"Now?"

She lifted her hips, sliding herself over the length of him. "Now."

"Mercy, woman." He let out a strangled laugh and moved inside her. "I won't last."

"Now," she said for a third time.

He obeyed, pulling himself almost out of her and then surging forward to fill her. He did it again, growling as he did. Again and again, stretching her. The passion flared in her belly. The same inexorable climb to bliss.

He thrust deeply now, savagely, out of control. She joined him in his hunger, reality slipping away until she was left with nothing but him—his breath in her hair, his back under her palms, his manhood inside her. She reached the precipice again and flew over, taking him with her. He shuddered in her arms, cried out in his release, and collapsed on top of her.

She stroked his hair, raising the perfume of saar to her nostrils, and sighed.

After a moment, he rolled onto his side and slipped his arm around her waist, pulling her to him—her back to his front—and cradling her head in the crook of his elbow. "Ah, Kareth," he murmured into her ear. "You are a sorceress. I haven't felt like that since I was a lad whose breeches filled with lust at the mere thought of a woman."

Not any woman, though—Kareth knew that. Only his lady Eria. She of the copper hair, the sapphire eyes, and the alabaster skin.

"No," he said, as though contradicting her very thoughts. "I've never felt like that. Even with Eria."

"Then why did you continue to sneak into her bedroom after she was married?" Dendra, forgive her for asking that question, loaded with envy as it was. Already she was slipping from her faith. Lovemaking was one thing—the hideous emotion jealousy another.

Still, she lay holding her breath for his answer.

"I didn't sneak into her bedroom."

"But you said yesterday that Lord Rabal stabbed you as you were climbing out of her bedroom window."

"He stabbed me not because I was in her room, but because I was escaping from it."

"I don't understand."

He pulled her closer and kissed her shoulder. "I was still welcome in my lady's bed. I was even expected to keep her occupied while Rabal toured the countryside inspecting his holdings and finding his own amusements. What I wasn't allowed to do was drug Eria and run away."

"You did that?" she asked. "Even though you'd been happy with her?"

"Content, not happy. Until she married that stupid oaf. The two of them deserved each other, so I decided to leave them alone together." He smoothed a hand up her ribs and cupped her breast. "And I ended up here."

His fingers played over her bosom, making nonsensical patterns on her skin. Now on one breast, now on the other, now in the valley between. What would have set her on fire only moments before now comforted—so quiet, so tender, so intimate. She sighed again and snuggled back against him.

"How did you end up here?" he asked.

"I came of my own choice," she answered, lying. The order had given her a choice between the desert, a mountaintop, and the forest. But the decision to use solitude to search out her heart and soul had not been a voluntary one. Jahn had been allowed to seek his own solution to what had happened between them, and he had chosen to stay with the people who loved him. No—adored him, worshipped him. All that had been left for her was to leave.

"Who was he?" Thiele asked, reading her mind again. How did he do that?

"Who?"

He nuzzled her ear. "The man. You've been with a man before."

"A priestess of Dendra isn't required to be a virgin."

"Who was he?" he repeated.

"My teacher," she admitted. "We became involved."

"And for that you had to be banished to the wilderness?"

"I wasn't banished."

"That's what this looks like."

She stroked the back of his hand in silence for a moment. In the hearth a log split, sending out a hiss and shooting sparks up into the chimney. "I was very privileged to study with Jahn. He took only the best, most promising students. I took advantage of our closeness. I tempted him."

"You tempt me," he said, hugging her ribs. "Where's the sin in that?"

"It's not supposed to be that way between teacher and student." She closed her eyes, trying to block out the memories. Being with Jahn in his study—rapture on his face, twining her arms around his neck, their lips meeting. Then their bodies falling back together onto the thick carpets in front of the fire. "It's supposed to be a spiritual bond, the most important one of the student's life."

"And who do you suppose is responsible for keeping the bond spiritual? The student or the teacher?"

"You don't understand," she whispered.

"Then explain it to me."

"Jahn didn't normally take women as students. I had to beg him even to consider me. I felt that I could learn more from him than the others, and I so wanted to serve."

"You served him well enough, I'm sure."

She rolled over to face Thiele. "He wasn't like that. He was a great teacher. If I hadn't given in to my urges, if I hadn't pressed him so hard to love me, I could have found enlightenment through his teaching."

Thiele stroked his thumb over her cheek. "He used you."

"No."

"Believe me, I know. I've been used my entire life. At least with churls and their masters, the using is done honestly."

"Jahn loved me," she said, not looking Thiele in the eye but staring at his chest. "He told me so."

Thiele slipped a finger under her chin and raised her face to his. "Then why didn't he marry you?"

"He had a wife," she whispered. "And children."

"The bastard," he cursed softly.

"You don't understand."

"I understand this. He took your innocence, didn't he?"

"I gave it freely."

"He didn't push you away when he realized what was happening between you, did he? Send you to another teacher?"

She lowered her gaze again.

"I thought not," he muttered. "I'll wager he wasn't even much of a lover. Was he?"

She looked back up at him. "How could you know that?" she gasped.

"Oh, Kareth." He kissed her gently. "Men who don't care about women don't learn how to pleasure them."

Dendra, yes, that made sense. The pain she had felt the first time with Jahn. How quickly he had finished each time after that. It hadn't been anything like what she'd shared this night with Thiele.

"And so you were sent away where you couldn't do any harm to his reputation or his marriage," he continued. "And so he won't take any more female students. At least not until some young, earnest innocent begs him to. Then he'll do it—oh so reluctantly. He'll have his pleasure with her, and she'll end up here or somewhere worse."

She rolled over, presenting him with her back. She couldn't contradict him, so she turned away from him. But he wouldn't let her get far. His arm snaked around her again, tugging her across the coverlet until she snuggled against him whether she wanted to or not.

"It's not your fault, little one," he murmured into her ear. "The men in charge—the Rabals and the Jahns—they get what they want, and there's precious little you and I can do about it."

"That sounds so hard."

"It's true. All we can do is protect ourselves as best as we can." His fingers moved again to her breast, and her breath caught as he toyed with the nipple. "And comfort each other."

His hand dipped lower, over her ribs to her belly, pulling her firmly against him, against the hardness that pressed into her backside. Dendra, he was ready again, and she caught fire inside—wanting him instantly. He lifted her leg up and over him and entered her from behind. Then his fingers parted the petals of her sex and dipped between them to stroke her. She gasped and rocked against him and forgot all about the universe outside.

Cammite had two properties that made it of value. First, it took on the hues of other elements, combining them with its own particular luminescence to produce an astonishing range of colors. Second, despite cammite's porosity, or perhaps because of it, its alloys were possessed of a hardness such that only special cutters studded with ground-up gems could scratch the surface. Perfect material for gaudy jewelry and for churl's collars.

Kareth had no special cutter and so had only her faith to remove Thiele's collar. Unfortunately, she didn't have his cooperation, and the afternoon had turned into a battle of wills. One that was rapidly getting out of her control.

She glanced at him now where he stood by the window, tapping his foot against the floor boards. "Come sit back down," she said. "We'll try again."

He looked over at her, and an eyebrow shot up. "That same gibberish? I'd rather not, thank you."

"They're prayers," she corrected.

"Gibberish," he muttered.

"Gibberish or prayers, they won't do you any good standing over there," she snapped.

He huffed and stood where he was for a moment. Then he crossed the room and sat back on the bed.

She took his hands and curled her fingers around his, interweaving them over his collar. "Now, concentrate," she ordered for at least the fifth time.

He glared up at her, his eyes gone bright emerald with impatience. "This won't work."

"Thiele..."

"You don't want this to work."

"Don't be ridiculous."

"If you get the collar off me, I can escape over the border. And you don't want me to leave."

She took a deep breath and stared at him. Dendra forgive her, as much as she wanted to give him his freedom, she couldn't deny that she didn't want him to leave. In the past few days that he had spent with her, she'd had more touching from him, more tenderness, than she'd had in the whole rest of her life. She might have mistaken what went on between them for true love, if she hadn't known that such was his profession, what he'd been trained to do.

"I'm doing my best," she answered, still holding tightly on to his fingers. "You might try to help me."

"Help with what?" he grumbled. "I'm no magician."

"Neither am I."

"You said you knew magic," he said.

"I said I knew something of it. I can't recite some charm to remove your collar. I need your faith, too."

He pushed her from him and rose. Hands clenched in fists by his side, he strode away again—this time to the hearth—and then turned back to glower at her. "I have no faith."

"But you must have faith."

"In your Dendra?"

"Not mine. The goddess belongs to everyone."

He snorted at that. "And so I thought, too, when I was a babe. Dendra would make everything right. If only I had faith in her. And where did my faith get me? Whoredom."

"You're not a whore," she answered.

"What would you call it?" he demanded. He rested his arm against the mantle and stared into the fire. "And the irony of it all, the merciless, crushing cruelty is that I made out better than the others. The ones who worked the fields until their backs were permanently stooped. The ones in the mines, coughing out blood with their last breaths."

"Dendra has nothing to do with that."

He glared back at her. "Dendra has nothing to do with anything. She's a figment of your imagination."

"No."

"And a tool the masters use to keep their chattel under their control."

"You must believe in something greater than yourself," she said. "You have to, or you're not fully alive."

"I believe in magic," he answered. "I've seen that with my own eyes. I've seen Rabal's magician bend cammite rods with his bare hands, turn water into blood."

"Mere tricks," she countered. "Magic without faith is a perversion of Dendra and the power she's given to all of us."

He snorted again and turned away from her, back to the hearth. "She hasn't given me any power."

"But she has. If only you'll look inside yourself to find it."

He stood, staring into the fire, his fist clenching and unclenching over the mantel. "Get this collar off me," he said finally. "Please, Kareth."

"I can't. Not by myself."

He left the fireplace to come to stand beside her. He towered over her, enveloping her in his scent, his warmth. "I'll do whatever you want," he murmured into her ear. "I know how to satisfy you. In these days together I've learned how to make your body sing."

"Thiele, don't."

He touched her breast, not roughly but without his usual tenderness. "This is what you want, isn't it?" he whispered.

"No, it isn't," she answered.

He straightened and glared down at her. "Don't deny it, Kareth. I've been with you. I know what you want. You want a handsomeman of your own, someone you can keep enslaved to pleasure you."

"That's not true," she gasped. And it wasn't. Dendra help her, it wasn't.

"You're no better than Eria," he gritted. "Worse, maybe. At least she dealt with me honestly."

"Curse you, Thiele, I am dealing with you honestly. I want to help you. I want you to be free."

"No, you don't. This is what you want." He gripped her breast more tightly, rubbing his thumb over the cloth of her bodice until the nipple beneath grew hard to the point of pain.

"Stop that," she ordered.

"And this," he growled, moving his hand to the place where her legs met. He groped her roughly through her gown, pulling at her sex in a cruel parody of their usual intimacy.

She slapped him, hard. The sound of the blow rang out, echoing off the walls of the tiny cottage. He reeled under it, taking a few steps backwards. His eyes filled with emotion, first surprise and then rage and finally pain.

She brought her fingers to her mouth and stared back at him, pleading with her eyes for him to understand. She hadn't meant to hurt him. But she couldn't let him do that to her, touch her in anger that way.

His stared back, and his jaw clenched, as if holding words inside him that he didn't dare let out. After a moment he turned and strode toward the door.

"Don't go," she cried. "We can get your collar off—together—if only you'll believe we can."

"I believe nothing," he snarled. He yanked the door open, slamming it against the wall. Then he stepped outside and walked down the path until he disappeared among the trees and ferns.

Chapter Four

He came back a few hours later, looking subdued and thoroughly ashamed of himself. He stood on the threshold, his hand still on the doorknob, and gazed at her out of little-boy eyes. As though he didn't know whether she'd welcome him in or slap him again.

She ought to slap him, of course. She ought to let him know beyond any doubt how boorishly he had acted. But the look of him took her breath away, as usual. And he actually had managed a blush of contrition. How could she stay angry with him?

"I'm sorry," he said finally. "You'll forgive me?"

"I already have."

"I have to trust you, after all you've done for me. I do trust you."

She smiled and nodded.

"It's just so hard sometimes..." He gripped his collar in his fist. "This thing..."

"I know."

"Perhaps you do. You care so much, perhaps you do." He cleared his throat and shifted his weight from one foot to the other. "I've made you a present."

"In the short time you've been gone?"

He smiled shyly. "Actually, I've been working on them for days now. They're not much." He reached inside his shirt and pulled out two tiny figurines—wood carvings. Of birds.

"The curo-curas," she exclaimed.

He closed the door, walked to her, and put the little figures in her hand. "I know how you love that loud pair."

Almost as much as I love you. No, please, no. She couldn't love him. He had to leave her, and she didn't dare love him. "Thank you, Thiele," she whispered.

"They're crude, I'm afraid. And I couldn't capture the colors at all."

She stared at the figures in her hand. He'd done an wonderful job—smoothing the wood to a fine texture and depicting the curo-curas in a life-like pose. He even had the crests right, the male's more prominent than the female's. "They're beautiful. But I don't have a gift for you."

"No matter." His smile grew into a grin, and the light of mischief she adored entered his eyes. "Now that I'm forgiven, maybe you'll sit with me for a while."

"Of course."

He took her hand and led her to the chair. Once there, he dropped into it and pulled her down into his lap. She half expected to feel the familiar hardness against her hip. She usually did when she sat with him this way. But it wasn't there this afternoon. Instead he nuzzled his face into her hair and hugged her close, seemingly content simply to hold her.

"I will have to leave, little one," he murmured. "Whether we get this collar off me or not."

And he would, she knew that. Thiele would never be safe anywhere near Rabal's domain, no matter where he hid. And she would have to go back to her contemplative life. But a tiny voice inside her cried out to know why. Why couldn't he just stay? Why couldn't they live together, sharing kisses and heartbeats, until they died in each other's arms?

"If the catchers find me with you, they'll take you, too," he said. "They're not much easier on people who help escaped churls than they are on the churls themselves."

She set the bird carvings in her lap and slipped her arms around Thiele's neck. "I don't care about that."

"But I do. I didn't when I arrived here, much to my shame. But I do now." He sighed against her skin. "Kareth, Kareth, you make me feel things...want things. Impossible things."

She pulled back and stroked his face. "Like what?"

He gazed at her, the green of his eyes so deep she could drown in it. "Like taking you with me."

"I couldn't go." She couldn't. She hadn't even begun to explore her inner life, the hungers and the failings that had brought her here. If she didn't know herself, how could she give herself to anyone else? Even to Thiele?

"And I couldn't take you to the outside," he said. "It's a wild place. People live in mud huts and slit each other's throats for no reason at all."

"So I've heard. Do you suppose the stories are true?"

"That doesn't matter. With no wealth, I couldn't offer you anything, not even protection."

She trailed her fingers along his jaw. "And if you were wealthy?"

"But I'm not."

"Pretend," she murmured. "Pretend you had taken all of Lady Eria's jewels with you when you ran away."

"Ah, pretend is it?"

She shrugged. "You know, a game."

"Well, then..." He tipped back his head and studied the ceiling. "If I had all of Lady Eria's jewels...let me see...I'd give them to you."

"No," she said, nudging him in the ribs. "That isn't very creative."

"I'll try again." He squeezed his eyes tightly closed, as though the effort taxed his brain. "I know. I'd use the jewels to start up a smuggling operation—liquors from the outside into Rabal's domain and churls from the inside out." He opened his eyes and grinned at her. "Very profitable business, smuggling."

"And very daring," she said. "Very like you."

"Then I'd set myself up as a border lord. I'd build the most fantastical castle for you, with huge banners flying from the turrets and with sharp-toothed rudwurms."

"And what would I do while you were accomplishing all this?"

"Nothing but satisfy my lust," he answered, his eyes sparkling. "I wouldn't have anyone in the castle with us—not even servants—until I'd ravished you in every one of its rooms."

"Dendra," she exclaimed. "How may rooms would it have?"

"Dozens," he answered. "Hundreds."

"And you'd have your way with me in each of them? Even the kitchen?"

"Especially the kitchen. I'd bend you over the work table and take you with the smell of baking bread in my nostrils."

She shoved his shoulder. "And who'd bake that bread, I'd like to know? And feed the livestock and wash the floors? And all the other chores?"

"I hadn't thought of that."

She harumphed. "Just like a man. You work your women near to death all the while insisting you keep us in the lap of luxury."

His slipped his fingers around her waist and rocked her gently. "We'd have servants, then. But they'd have to stay out of sight. And I couldn't let them see you."

"Why in Dendra's name not?"

His grin broadened and a gleam entered his eyes that was absolutely evil. "Because I'd keep you half-naked all the time. That's why. So I could always look at you."

Her cheeks flamed, and she squirmed in his lap. "Thiele..."

"No more than ribbons and scraps of shalisse." He slid his hand over her shoulder. "Hanging from here, over your breasts, your beautiful breasts." His fingers trailed down the valley between her breasts to her belly. "Covering your hips but loosely so that the smallest draft would lift the material and expose you to me."

"You'd like that, would you?" she said.

He smiled and parted his lips. She kissed them, using the moves he had taught her in their days together. Breathing into his mouth in exactly the way she knew would arouse him. It worked. He rubbed himself against her, and his swelling manhood pressed into her hip.

"You'd like to have me naked?" she murmured against his mouth. "Even if I got cold?"

"I'd keep you hot," he answered, his voice husky with desire. "Always and forever hot."

"Then I do have a present for you, after all." She picked up the carved birds in her lap and rose. "Close your eyes, and don't open them until I tell you to."

He squeezed his eyes shut, and Kareth walked to the wardrobe. She placed his presents carefully on top, opened the door, and leaned inside to rummage around in the bottom. After a moment her fingers found the parcel where she had hidden it on her first day in the forest. She'd bought the thing in a dark little shop, meaning to wear it for Jahn. But in the end, she hadn't had the chance. She'd never thought to put it on for anyone else, hadn't really understood why she kept it. But now she had a reason, and Jahn no longer mattered. Only Thiele mattered.

She set the parcel on the floor while she stripped out of her gown and shift, letting them fall wherever they cared to. Then she bent, untied the string that held the plain brown sacking together, and removed the flimsy under-gown from inside.

"What are you doing over there?" Thiele demanded.

"You'll see soon," she answered. "Keep your eyes closed."

He crossed his arms over his chest and smiled.

She shook out the immodest garment and studied it. With its filmy, transparent material and its ribbons and bows, it fit Thiele's description perfectly. No doubt he'd seen such things—they weren't truly forbidden, only naughty. Except between a teacher and novice. For her and Thiele, it was perfect. She slipped it over her head, leaving her amulet underneath, and arranged the ribbons so that they highlighted her nipples and the curls between her legs, not hiding them at all.

Then she turned to face him full on. "You can open your eyes now."

He did, and he shot out of his chair, toppling it behind him. "Mercy, woman," he gasped. "Where did you get that?"

"Does it matter?"

"No." He swallowed. "I only...I've never seen...it shows everything."

"Isn't that what you wanted?"

He crossed the room in two strides and took her into his arms. He lifted her right off her feet as he pressed her to him everywhere. He bent his head and took her mouth in a bruising kiss.

She dug her fingers into his shoulders and answered him, opening her lips under his and sliding her tongue into his mouth. He growled in the back of his throat and pulled her hard against him. Her breasts crushed into the muscles of his chest, setting up a delicious friction that coursed through her veins to heat her sex. She extended her toes down to the tops of his feet to gain them some purchase so that she could move against his hardness. He lowered his face into the crook of her neck and whimpered, kneading her back in his fists.

She pushed her hand between their bodies and stroked him, and his whimpers swelled to cries as his hips began to rock. Back and forth, back and forth, bringing the thick ridge of flesh against her hand in a rhythm older than the forest. She squeezed him and felt him shudder.

Suddenly he pushed himself away from her, holding her by her shoulders, his chest heaving as he worked for breath. "I can't," he gasped. "Dendra, I can't."

She touched his chest, and he jumped nearly out of his skin. "It's too much, Kareth," he cried.

"But our castle, you said you'd take me in all the rooms. In the kitchen with the bread baking."

"That was fantasy. We'll never have that."

"Thiele..."

"Understand, little one. It's too much," he said, gazing down into her face. "Every time I love you, you get further inside me. I'm afraid the next time I'll lose myself completely."

"You're supposed to lose yourself," she answered. "My soul comes undone every time we make love."

"That's right for you. You can trust." He clenched his teeth and sucked in a breath between them. "For me...I can't...it's total surrender."

"Then surrender."

"No," he said.

She took his face in her hands and gazed into his eyes. "Do it. Give yourself to me. All of you."

"No."

"Trust me. Trust Dendra. Lose yourself. We'll bring you back."

"I can't."

She rose to her full height, calling up the goddess from deep inside her. Summoning everything she had—the wisdom of the trees, the tenacity of the fog, the power of her love. She opened her eyes wide and stared at him, straight on, eye to eye, mastering him. "You will surrender to me, Thiele. You will do exactly as I say, and we will merge until nothing separates us—not flesh, not blood, not breath. We will give each other life."

He looked back at her, unblinking, silent. Another moment and she'd own him. Just the right combination of words, the right entreaty.

"This is why you came here," she went on, chanting to him. "This is why you were born. For me—here and now. Do you understand?"

He nodded slowly. "Take me, school me," he whispered, reciting the ancient prayer. "I am yours."

She took his hand and led him to the bed. He sat on it, never taking his eyes off her, as though under her spell. She pulled off his shirt and threw it to the floor. Then she guided him backward, down until he rested on his back, still staring at her.

She climbed on top of him and captured his mouth, darting her tongue in and out, tasting him. She slid her body over his and teased his chest with the ribbons of her under-gown. Then she lowered herself, took one of his nipples into her mouth, and sucked.

He cried out at that, his voice rupturing the air around them. "Ah, woman, you'll kill me."

She lifted her head and found his eyes closed, his jaw clenched. Fighting for control, no doubt. And losing, losing badly. "You'll be reborn," she answered.

Then she pressed her lips to the other nipple and claimed it, too. Beneath her, his hips began to move, and she shifted so that she could press her palm to his manhood. He gasped, and she squeezed him, running her fingers along the entire length of him.

Slowly, slowly she slid herself even lower, until her head rested against his belly and she was face to face with the bulge in his breeches. She unfastened one button and then another, taking her time with him, drawing out the agony of waiting. Finally, she had them open, and his sex came free. She caught the shaft in her fingers and guided the head into her mouth.

He nearly floated off the bed then, and a roar tore out of a place deep in his chest. "Woman, stop," he shouted. "You don't know what you're doing to me."

But she did know. She knew exactly what she did as she sucked on the tip of him and stroked the length of his shaft, dipping her fingers into his breeches and between his legs to caress the soft sac there. His member throbbed in her hand, a thing with its own life. And she knew that he would come soon, no matter how hard he tried to fight it. He'd spill his seed, and when he did, she would take it deep inside her.

She rose and swung her leg over him, still holding his sex and positioning herself over it. She guided herself onto him and surrendered her own sanity to the pleasure. He filled her so completely, so perfectly. She howled with the joy as she pressed her hands into his ribs and moved herself. Up and down, bringing herself to him, over and over, stroking his length.

He matched her movements. He circled her waist with his fingers and held her while he pounded into her, pumping wildly and sending her to the edge. She closed her eyes and let the madness have her. The universe shifted, sensation crashing over her. Impossible, but real. Scents from childhood, music, blinding lights, and distant thunder. One loud clap nearby—Thiele's cry of release—and she dissolved with him into bliss. She slumped onto his chest and basked in the shuddering of her womanhood where she was still joined to him.

Slowly the world settled back into place. Her fingertips registered the smoothness of his skin underneath them, her palms measured his warmth. She pressed her lips into the furrow that ran down the center of his chest and sighed. His fingers slipped into her hair.

Thiele, beloved Thiele. He had surrendered to her, but so had she to him. The priestess' spell had turned itself back on her, and she would never be the same.

She ran her hands up his body, touching him everywhere, memorizing his arms, his shoulders, his throat. She found her beloved everywhere, and something more. No, not something more—rather something less. No metal. She opened her eyes and looked up at him.

His collar was gone. "Thiele," she whispered.

His hand pushed her head back against his chest, his fingers still making slow circles in her hair. "Not now, little one. Let me rest."

She sat up and searched again. Not a sign of cammite anywhere. Not even broken pieces lying beside him. The atrocity had disappeared completely. "Thiele," she said more loudly. "Open your eyes. Your collar's off. You're free."

He came alert at that, his eyes flying open. He sat up so suddenly he threw Kareth off him, and he ran his hands along his neck. A sobbing shout escaped him, and he twisted to search the bed, running his palms over it as though the hated collar had merely become invisible but still might lie somewhere on the coverlet. After a moment, he stopped and turned to her, his eyes wide with wonder.

"You did it," he whispered.

"We did it," she corrected.

The next morning Kareth lay in bed, eyes closed, listening to Thiele move about the cottage. The sounds he made weren't random, rather they cried out with purpose—the cabinet opening and closing, then the wardrobe. And always coming back to the table. She heard him move away, toward the door, and she cracked an eye open. Just as she had suspected—a bundle lay on the table top, and he was fully dressed, complete with cape and boots. He was packing, getting ready to leave.

She sat up, pulling the coverlet over her. "What are you doing?"

He turned and looked at her, surprise registering in his eyes. "Awake so early? I thought after last night you'd be exhausted."

As well she should have been. Freedom from his collar had released them both in so many ways. They'd spent the hours before dawn exploring that freedom and each other. Wonderful and intimate. But she'd known, too, that this was the last. That in the morning he would leave.

"What are you doing?" she repeated.

He walked back to the table, a water flask in his hand. "I think that's obvious."

"Weren't you even going to say good-bye?" she demanded.

He didn't answer, but raised an eyebrow and stared at her for a moment. Then he went back to packing, slipping the flask into the bundle and bringing the ends of the rough material up into a knot.

Curse him, he hadn't intended to say good-bye. He had meant to pack up her things and slip away while she slept. She climbed out of bed, walked to the wardrobe, and found her shift and gown where they still lay on the floor. She slipped them over her head and turned on him. "Let me help you," she snapped. "I wouldn't want you to forget anything."

"Kareth..."

"No, truly," she said, charging to the cabinet. "Let's see. You'll need meal." She opened the door and peered inside. "But it appears you've already taken it."

"Of course."

She crossed her arms over her chest and glared at him, fuming. "And knives. Have you taken them, too?"

"Only the big one," he answered.

How could he? After all they'd shared, he was simply going to steal what he wanted from her and disappear without a word. "Take the bird carvings, too. If you're not here, I don't want them."

She walked to the wardrobe again. She looked on top and found nothing there. "No," she cried, spinning back to face him. "You were taking them, without even asking. Give them back."

"You just said you don't want them."

"Give them back," she repeated. Breath of the Beast, those birds were hers. She crossed to the table, grabbed his bundle, and tore the knots open.

"Is this the priestess who taught me about trust yesterday?" he demanded. "I let you touch my core, and today you won't trust me with some possessions."

She got the cloth open and searched through the contents—food-stuffs, tools, but no carvings. "Where are they?" she shouted, tears threatening to choke her voice. "What have you done with them?"

He put his hands on his hips and glared at her. "I put them in your pack."

"My pack?" she echoed.

"Over there." He nodded toward the hearth. "If you'd asked, I would have told you."

She glanced over and found another bundle just where he had indicated. A smaller one, made out of her shawl. "You packed for me?"

"Just a few things," he answered. "Some clothes, the carvings, that under-gown."

"You planned to take me with you."

He put his hands on her shoulders and turned her to him. "You disappoint me, little one. Do you really think that I'd steal everything you have and leave without even saying good-bye?"

"But we agreed," she said. "I couldn't go over the border with you."

"I wanted to do the noble thing, leave you where you'd be safe, despite how much I loved you. You took that choice away from me yesterday."

She rested against his chest and sighed. "You love me?"

"Can you doubt it?" he rumbled from his chest.

She ran her arms around him and hugged him. He slipped a finger under her chin and lifted her face to his. "I planned to leave you, but you became part of me yesterday. If I lost that part, I'd bleed inside until I died."

"Truly?" she asked, her voice suddenly tiny.

"Truly," he answered.

"But I can't go," she said. "I haven't completed my work here. I haven't yet discovered Dendra's design for me."

"Can't you find that on the outside?"

"No." She pushed away from his chest and looked around her at her haven. "I belong here. This is where I've been sent to find the truth in me."

"Then I'll have to stay here with you," he said. "Unpack and stay and hope the catchers don't find us."

She twisted her hands together and tried to think. "That won't work, either."

"You'll have to decide. Here or the outside. But either way together, both of us."

"Dendra, I don't know."

He spread his arms wide. "Which will it be, priestess? Stay or cross the border?"

She studied him, the gleam of mischief, of triumph in his eyes. The sandy hair that fell into his face. His broad shoulders, muscled legs. Her haven lay in him, inside the circle of his embrace. That decided, the rest was easy, after all. "The border," she said.

His smile broadened as he walked to the threshold and opened the door. "Get your pack."

She flew to the hearth and picked up the bundle he'd prepared for her. Then she headed back to his outstretched hand. A few feet away she stopped, suddenly remembering. She walked to the far wall, took down the ax, and slid the handle through the knots of her pack.

His eyes widened. "For you, priestess?" he said. "A weapon?"

She walked back to him, gazing up into his face. "To chop firewood. To keep us warm."

He laughed heartily at that, still holding out his hand to her. She took it, and they crossed the threshold together.

About the author:

Alice Gaines has a Ph.D. in personality psychology from a large west coast university. She lives in the hills of Oakland, California with her husband of 16 years, 50 or 60 orchids, and one neurotic cat.

Alice recently sold a historical romance to Leisure Books. Currently titled **Waitangi Nights**, *the story is set in 19th century New Zealand and features spirits from Maori folklore*

The Gift

Jeanie LeGendre

To my reader:
The Gift tells the tale of a woman who dared everything to find love and the man who challenged the boundaries of culture to cherish her. While the characters and their romance are very much fictional, their world is drawn from historical fact. With that in mind… Alessandra and Solimon's love story really might have happened.

The Ottoman Empire

"Behave, my lady," the Kislar Agha ordered, "or the Sultan will be greatly insulted. Calm yourself."

Alessandra de Got tugged the edges of the guimlik over her bare breasts, aghast at the command. Calm herself? When the very idea of bondage as the Sultan's concubine nearly made her faint!

The chief eunuch glared at her, black eyes peering from his face. "You are the Gift, and the Sultan has called you to him this eve. He wants to see how Ibrahim Pasha honors him. This is a chance to distinguish yourself, to earn a place as his favorite." His thick-set fingers gripped her chin, tilting her face upward, preventing escape. "The Sultan is young. His energies have been devoted to fighting and strengthening the boundaries of our beloved land. His haremlik is virtually empty. He has taken no wife. Do you understand what this means?"

Alessandra didn't care. But the words stuck in the back of her throat, and no sound passed her lips.

His mouth thinned into a tight smile. "His mother, the Sultan Valide, is dead. The women are his father's slaves with no one to rule them. The Sultan has called you to him this eve, my lady, and you alone have a chance to catch his eye."

"I am no concubine. I am a French woman—"

"You are the Gift!" He released her chin abruptly. "Your fate lies within the haremlik of the Sultan's Palace. You can live life as a lowly slave, or you can attract the Sultan and claim a position of honor in his household."

Alessandra's mind raced. A lifetime as a concubine! Sheer panic swept through her. She could not live her life imprisoned within the walls of the haremlik, her every action dictated by the lustful whim of a man. Slaves had no freedom. Every tale she had ever heard of the haremlik—and she had heard many—described a place rife with debauchery, mystery, and intrigue. She must persuade the Sultan to free her. Once he discovered she was the French Ambassador's niece, surely he would return her. He wouldn't risk diplomatic problems with France, would he?

Taking a deep, steadying breath, Alessandra straightened her shoulders, preparing herself for what was to come. She glanced up at the Kislar Agha and nodded.

He sighed in obvious relief. "All will be well. Just smile and remember what I've taught you." The sleeve of his emerald satin robe swept against her neck, and she trembled as he brushed strands of hair from her face. "There, there, you are exquisite. Your silver-gilt hair is as fine as spun silk, and your skin glows like a pearl. The Sultan will be enchanted." He reached for the corded bell pull. Instantly, the doors to the chamber opened, and she followed him past the gilded columns of the entrance into the Royal Salon.

Braziers glowed from all corners, and the melodious strains of the lyre filled the air. The Kislar Agha led her past silent rows of black eunuchs prostrated along the path to the throne. His words echoed in her memory instructing, "Never utter a sound and always keep your eyes lowered."

She focused on the silver rosettes of her slippers, willing herself not to stumble, to walk gracefully. Her heart pounded wildly in her breast, and she was keenly aware of her nakedness through the gauze garments that swirled with her every step. She fought the urge to cover herself, feeling shockingly vulnerable in the presence of so many.

In one fluid motion that belied his size, the Kislar Agha fell to his knees, stretching his wide chest flat to the carpet and pressing his turbaned brow to the Sultan's feet. "Grand Seigneur, I beg permission to humbly present the Gift."

He moved aside, and Alessandra slipped to the floor, conscious of appearing awkward in the wake of the Kislar Agha's more experienced bow.

"Rise, fair one. Let me view you," the Sultan demanded in a rich, smooth voice that sent a wave of trepidation through her.

Alessandra rose before him. The silk-bordered edges of the guimlik slid from her grasp with the movement, and she hastily drew the garment closed. At the intensity of his gaze, she bit her lip until it throbbed in time with her pulse.

"You hide your loveliness from me." The words were more a statement than a question. His long fingers brushed against hers, but Alessandra clutched the blouse over her breasts even tighter. "Clear the chamber," he commanded, the imperious tone of his voice slicing through her.

Sweet Mother in Heaven, she had offended him. The Sultan's power was absolute. With the mere snap of his fingers, he could have her killed, and no one would utter a syllable in her defense. A spark of resentment leapt to life deep inside. He commanded her to attend him garbed like a whore, then wanted, nay expected, her to acquiesce to his touch. But no matter what the punishment, she would not submit. She stiffened, only no reprimand came—just the shuffling sounds of the departing assemblage, and after what seemed to be an eternity, even those sounds faded away.

"Why do you resist?" he asked.

Although he had not spoken harshly, his question shattered the last vestiges of her composure. She had never been so frightened... so outraged in all her life. No matter how she willed it otherwise, hot angry tears slid from her eyes.

"Look at me."

With the greatest effort, Alessandra lifted her gaze. He stood before his throne, darkly beautiful and strong, just as she would have envisioned a proud Ottoman king. His expression was carved in stone, yet the fury she anticipated was not evident in the bold lines of his face. He was not angry, but curious. Her turbulent emotions eased slightly while the force of his unwavering gaze surged through her.

He was a tall man. A diamond-studded dagger flashed from the jewelled girdle around his waist. The scarlet robes flowing from his broad shoulders emphasized the sheer power of his frame. A white egret feather was fastened to his turban by a starburst of diamonds and rubies, but the exotic beauty of his dark face took her breath away. His features were so perfect, so full of strength, he appeared cast in gold.

The powerful Solimon.

As his eyes met hers, a foreboding shiver ran the full length of her spine. His hand shot out, catching hers in an iron grip, forcing her to relinquish hold of the silken blouse. The guimlik fell open to her waist, exposing her breasts to the warm, scented air.

His gaze raked boldly over her, the heat of his touch searing her flesh. She fought the desire to break away, to run from him. With unnaturally heightened awareness, she heard the thin warbling of the finches in the aviary, the soft patter of droplets from the fountain. The slightest trace of moisture hung in the air. She could see its sheen on the diamond-paned windows and the ornately-carved columns lining the walls, feel its misty shimmer on her skin.

"You are magnificent." He stepped toward her, so close, she smelled the spicy citrus scent of him. "Your eyes are the color of the richest amethyst. Not cold like the stone, but vibrant, alive, like the dew-kissed petals of a violet."

His deep-velvet voice poured over her, sending the blood rushing through her veins. She stared at him, pinned beneath his relentless gaze.

"Ibrahim Pasha honors me with your loveliness, fair one."

"My name is Alessandra," she said in a ragged whisper.

His expression did not change. But when his brow lifted ever so slightly, her courage faltered. The silence between them grew heavy, tense, and she could barely catch her breath, knowing he awaited some word of explanation to pass her suddenly dry lips. "I am not a slave."

"I agree, fair one. You are not a slave, but my slave, and there is a vast difference."

At his words, her hopes plummeted, but Alessandra was determined to make him understand. She shook her head. "I was taken . . . abducted from the Pasha's palace. I am a member of the diplomatic delegation. My uncle is the French Ambassador." She paused, waiting for his surprise, some sign of outrage at her cruel treatment, but the Sultan just stood there, seemingly unaffected by her news.

"And," he prompted her to continue as if they discussed nothing more important than the latest bloom in the garden.

"And I was abducted from the bedchamber where I slept, bound, gagged, thrown over some miscreant's shoulder, and brought to the Palace."

So the fair beauty had spirit. Solimon admired the flush of color that raced like a shadow from her rounded breasts to her heart-shaped face. The willowy outline of her legs through the diaphanous folds of the trousers caught his attention, and the thought of her pale buttocks poised over anyone's shoulder captivated him.

Abductions were fairly common, although an emotional and precarious way to fill one's harem. Even though he had never pursued that particular course, he knew of many who had, but couldn't imagine Ibrahim Pasha making a gift of an unwilling slave. There was more to this girl's abduction than she knew. He would send men to delve into the matter immediately.

"What is it you would have me do, fair one?"

"I want to go home!"

"You do not wish to serve me?" He could see by the expression flitting across her delicate features that the idea terrified her. She shook her head, sending silken tresses of pale-blonde hair tumbling around her shoulders. Her hair shimmered like shifting moonbeams, and the urge to feel the cool strands brushing against his bare flesh suddenly seized him.

The women he cared for in the Palace, the women who had never caught his father's eye, all ran toward his sire's tastes, golden-skinned and lush-bodied. Solimon could not recall one who rivaled the fair beauty of the exquisite creature before him. Perhaps the Kislar Agha was right—he had neglected his own harem too long.

He could not deny the spark of excitement that flared inside him. To introduce her to passion, to tempt her with his touch until all inhibitions melted away, praise Allah!—the very idea fired his imagination. "What do you think I would have you do as my slave?"

Her flush deepened like the lingering hues of sunrise on sand, but she remained silent.

He waited.

She lowered her gaze, the dark smudge of her lashes shadowing her fair skin. "Satisfy your . . . desires."

"And you find that thought distasteful?"

Her teeth tugged at the flesh of her bottom lip. Fascinated, his gaze travelled from the inviting fullness of her mouth, down the slender column of her neck, to the creamy white skin that peeked from beneath the loose edges of the sapphire guimlik. The blood pounded hotly in his veins.

Solimon reached out, his fingers enveloping the velvet curve of her breast. She inhaled sharply, startled, and her hand lashed out to strike his away. He caught her wrist with his free hand and held it firmly within his grasp.

"Do not fight me."

The jewel-like eyes, shocked and angry, clashed with his. He ran his thumb across her nipple, feeling it harden like marble in response to his touch. A gasp slipped from her lips, and a tremor visibly rippled through her lithe frame, revealing the passion that simmered beneath her reluctant surface. Was this fair beauty worth the time and energy it would take to coax away her resistance? As he gazed upon the sweetness of her body, he knew the answer.

He withdrew his hand, the warmth of her flesh lingering on his fingertips. She immediately folded her arms over her breasts, shielding herself from his view.

"I risk war if I insult Ibrahim Pasha by refusing his gift. Why would I do this?"

"I do not belong here. I'll die in captivity, Grand Seigneur." Her words came in breathless bursts. "I am an educated woman, respected for my intelligence, an asset to my uncle in business." Her plea grew more impassioned, her voice stronger and clearer, making him desire her all the more for such a spirited plea. "I must be free to learn, to think, to speak my mind."

"I hold my slaves in the highest regard. They have the freedom to think and to speak their minds."

Her hands clenched into fists at her sides, and her chin rose a notch. "A slave has no freedom."

"A slave has no freedom but what her master allows." Solimon stifled a grin. "Ah, fair one, you simply do not understand our ways. I respect my women above all else! They are Allah's most precious gifts, the life-givers, the pleasure-givers."

"You do not speak of wisdom or honor. I am more than a... a pleasure-giver."

"Is there anything more important than bearing life?"

"But there is so much more a woman can do."

Solimon took a step back and sat on his throne, regarding her curiously. The delicate angle of her jaw bespoke defiance, the seriousness of her argument. Should he be intrigued or offended? Women who dwelled in the seraglio could be manipulative and greedy, like those he had grown up with in his father's haremlik. He had neither the time nor the patience right now for those tricks.

She was a rare beauty, though. Slender and graceful, she had firm, uptilted breasts and skin like ivory satin. Her straight hair shimmered like sunlight on the Marmara, falling in a silver-white wave to her waist. Despite her defiant stance, she tensed at his continued silence. The need to tame her, to harness that gentle spirit for his own, overcame him. "For your disobedience, I could banish you to the farthest corner of the haremlik, where neither life-giving nor pleasure-giving would occupy your thoughts, but only how to fill your lonely days."

"I will perish in such a place," she said simply.

"You've no choice but to submit."

"I fear death less than losing my soul."

His admiration for her grew when she didn't back down at his threat. "Then, fair one, we are at an impasse. I have no desire for war or an unwilling slave."

She stamped her slipper-clad foot on the thick carpet. "There must be some other way. I simply cannot be a slave. If you knew anything about me, you would understand." Her voice quavered, rising like the chiming of bells. "Please. Give me a chance to prove how unsuited I am to such a life."

"You challenge me?" he asked, not sure whether to be annoyed or amused. But she would have to share his bed to prove herself unsuitable, and as he was struck by the possibilities, all thoughts of annoyance fled.

Surprise flitted across her finely-drawn features. "Yes. Yes, I do," she whispered in a rush of breath. "Give me three nights, Grand Seigneur, three nights to convince you how unsuited I am for a life of slavery. If I fail, I'll enter your haremlik willingly. But if I succeed, you'll send me back to my uncle."

He watched her for a long moment. Perhaps he had misjudged her. Such a challenge bespoke more boldness than intelligence, for insolence could earn her a trip to the bottom of the Bosphorus in a weighted sack. But then, she had said she would prefer death—and a quick death would be preferable to languishing in some remote corner of his haremlik.

The tremor that visibly rocked her willowy frame revealed the tremendous effort it took her to oppose him. So, this was no display of hysterical emotions. Was she like the majestic bird of the summer wind, unable to be tamed? He wanted to know. He respected strength and honor—even in a woman. "How do you plan to prove yourself?"

She hesitated only a moment, long enough for him to recognize that she had no clear idea of what she intended, but like the summer bird trapped in a net, grasped for any chance at freedom.

"I am schooled in diplomacy. I could help you better relations with any of the European countries, most certainly with France."

He could just imagine her sitting in the reception room, unveiled, chatting with the many rulers and diplomats he entertained. One glimpse of those lush rose-colored lips and amethyst eyes would likely incite a riot right within the Palace walls. But her challenge presented some intriguing possibilities. He could easily envision long, moonlit nights spent bettering relations with her, melting the barriers of her innocence and stoking the fire he sensed within. Solimon decided to play the game and smiled. "Each morning I will send you a scholarly present, a book or some such treasure, for discussion that eve. You'll have from sunset to sunrise to prove why you're a poor choice to be my slave."

"And you'll allow me the freedom to speak my thoughts and make my points?"

He nodded, growing more charmed with the game as each moment passed. "And you vow not to resist my touch?"

That took her off guard, and her eyes widened. She obviously wanted to refuse, evidence of her struggle sweeping across her exquisite features. She finally shrugged in resignation.

"Then so be it," he said. "The boundaries are drawn. Is there anything else you wish to add?"

"No, Grand Seigneur, you have been most generous." She slipped to her knees, pressing her brow to his slippers.

Pleased with her show of manners, he tugged the bell pull, and a page arrived to escort her from the Salon. "Prepare yourself well, fair one. You will attend me tomorrow evening at nightfall."

She flew down the carpeted walkway, and Solimon eyed her retreat in appreciation. The light of the sconces revealed her gently-curved silhouette through the silk gauze of her garments. So fair of form and feature, she should pique his ardor rather than his patience.

One person in particular would be delighted by this twist of fate. The Kislar Agha paraded harem slaves before him like ripe fruits in a quest to ensure the succession. Solimon could only imagine the chief eunuch's delight that he had committed to this bedchamber game.

"Three nights, Grand Seigneur?" the Kislar Agha squealed on an inrushing breath after hearing an explanation of the challenge. "Praise Allah."

"I am pleased my actions meet with your approval."

The florid rise of color that crept up the chief eunuch's neck revealed his embarrassment over such a vulgar display of emotion. "Forgive me such rudeness." He prostrated himself at Solimon's feet, kissing the hem of his master's robe in a grandiose plea for clemency.

Solimon resisted the urge to roll his eyes. "Never fear, my loyal servant. I did not doubt your response for an instant. You have been quite free with your complaints about how I neglect my haremlik."

The Kislar Agha stood, smoothing the folds of his embroidered robes and drawing his round frame up with impressive hauteur. "Forgive me for mentioning this, Grand Seigneur, but you have no haremlik. The women who inhabit the Seraglio passed to you through your father. All of them."

"I have had much to accomplish in the six years since I became Sultan. Even you must realize that establishing my strength as ruler takes precedence above all else. And that task has left me precious little time for anything more."

The Kislar Agha's plump features sharpened with determination. "And you have achieved your goal a thousandfold, mighty one. Now you need a wife. Yet every woman I bring you is cast into obscurity after only one night in your bed." He threw his hands up in despair. "You had me marry off the last three who claimed your attention."

"They were troublemakers." He waved his hand impatiently. "You cannot deny that. They caused dissension in the household."

"Any change will cause dissension. The women lived together before you brought them from your father's palace. They are too comfortable, too complacent. You need a wife to establish your household, to create order."

Solimon suppressed a sigh. Quite simply, he had yet to encounter a woman who came close to the standard he had set long ago. A wife should be more than a slave. She should be a partner, a lover, a friend. Was he foolishly searching for the perfect woman—a woman who didn't exist? Perhaps. But some unfamiliar emotion gathered inside when he thought of the violet-eyed beauty, his latest gift. He could not fathom why, but she intrigued him.

In all fairness, Solimon could not resent the Kislar Agha his opinion. His job was to manage the haremlik, to keep peace among the women—no mean feat. Yet despite his skill and competence, he would never understand Solimon's wish for a wife who would be his mate in all ways.

"I will send the fair one a book of romance for the first night." He came to his feet, standing before the throne in a gesture of dismissal. "Wrap it in a lavender silk handkerchief, bordered with amethysts."

"Lavender silk… amethysts? You do her great honor." The strained expression left the chief eunuch's face. He beamed, his full lips curving into a smile. In a rustle of satin robes, he bowed low, prostrating himself easily. "It will be as you wish, Grand Seigneur."

The Sultan's present arrived with the dawn, and Alessandra unwrapped the rich packaging to reveal the first of her scholarly tools— a book. She had learned enough during her short stay in the Palace to know that the Sultan honored her with such a costly handkerchief. The women who had witnessed the arrival of his present whispered excitedly among themselves while inspecting the quality of the jewels.

She opened the book. The blood pounded hotly in her temples as she studied the pages, finding the tales between the gilded leather bindings so erotic she could not help but blush. The women chided her for such a maidenly display, reminding her that she was a concubine, subject to the whim and will of her master. Alessandra fought down the hurt, well aware of their surprise at the Sultan's interest… and their envy.

However would she win the challenge if he turned her own game to his advantage? Yet she admired his cleverness and vowed not to underestimate him again. He had maneuvered her into a corner. She could not bemoan the nature of his gift without protesting the boundaries of their challenge, the very boundaries she had agreed upon.

Through the long hours while eunuchs plunged her into hot baths, massaged her with fragrant oils, then garbed her in delicate silks, Alessandra searched for some way to make the Sultan view her as a person and not simply a pleasure-giver. By sunset, she had formulated a simple plan—he must come to know her, know her history, her desires, her dreams—only then would he realize how unsuited she was to a life of slavery.

As the sun went down, she clutched the book against her breasts and followed the Kislar Agha down the beautifully-tiled corridor connecting the haremlik to the Royal Apartments. Alessandra thought she had reconciled herself to the upcoming confrontation, but the memory of the Sultan's bold eyes raking over her undermined her courage. As the carved doors to the Royal Chamber loomed ahead, her chest grew tight and panic mounted with every step. The Kislar Agha guided her into the room, whispering, "Make him burn to possess you. Allah will guide your path." He departed, the heavy doors echoing shut behind him.

The Sultan's private quarters were richly furnished. The paneled walls were inlaid with ivory and intricate pieces of coral, and patterned rugs decorated the floor. The Sultan lounged upon a reclining chair with a brocaded mattress, silken pillows scattered beneath him.

Alessandra barely recognized his long, powerful form without the adornment of royal robes. His gaze captured hers, then travelled slowly over her scantily-clad body while she sank to her knees in a bow. Conscious of his eyes upon her, she resisted the urge to snatch the embroidered coverlet from the back of his chair and cover herself with it.

"Come, fair one. Be seated." He motioned to the thick pillows around him.

Alessandra took a deep breath and rose to her feet, holding the book like a shield before her. His strength and will were legend throughout Europe. How in Heaven's name could she persuade him to release her? He would never convince her of the merit of carnal bondage, and she clung to that thought while positioning herself on the floor by his feet.

Sprawled across the chair, he wore only white silk trousers which contrasted sharply against his deep golden skin. Candles flickered lazily in ornate holders, casting a burnished glow along the lines of his muscular frame, and she was again struck by his incredible beauty.

"Pour us fruit nectar," he said.

Forced to set aside the book, her bare breasts were revealed to his perusal while she performed the task. Alessandra quickly realized the nature of his game. He knew she was embarrassed to the core of her soul at having to run around in various degrees of undress, and he planned to use that fact to disarm her. Somehow she had to conquer her modesty. Although how she would overcome a lifetime of propriety, she had no idea. Taking a deep breath, Alessandra handed him an etched-crystal cup, trembling slightly as his long, straight fingers brushed hers.

"Were you pleased with my present, fair one?"

He smiled, a slow, knowing smile that gleamed brightly against his handsome face. A ripple of awareness fluttered through her. What could she say? She would not let him see how his gift unsettled her—she would turn his own present to her advantage. After all, there was more to intelligence than simply knowing how to read. Crossing her arms over her breasts, she forced her voice to remain casual. "Your gift is most generous, Grand Seigneur."

He propped himself on an elbow to drink, motioning to the cup which still sat on the table. "Enjoy."

She eyed the drink with suspicion, wondering if he'd resort to aphrodisiacs in an attempt to win the day. He drained the contents of his own. "I drink with you, fair one. I have no need of potions to increase my ardor. Or yours."

Alessandra did not doubt his words. His presence was so confident, so male that the very air seemed charged and alive. After sipping the fruity liquid, she returned the cup to the table and opened the book before her. "Am I to believe these stories are scholarly treasures?"

"They are tales of romance, valued as treasures by my people, little jewels of an ancient art honoring the glory of sensual pleasure." Amusement twitched at the corners of his full mouth. "I can see by the color creeping into your cheeks this writing is new to you, so I shall read the first tale." He took the book from her, turning the pages until he found the one he sought. "'When young Ciclazade first lay eyes upon the fair Safiye, it was most surely an accident destined by Allah himself. He would never have been near the women's bath house had it not been for the Pasha's lust of sweetmeats and the cat-sized rat who fled with a pouch of Turkish delights between his sharp little teeth.

"'Mourning the loss of the Pasha's attention since he had grown so fat, Safiye languished around the pool, her thick hair tumbling in ebon waves to the floor, the soft lines of her naked body sparkling beneath the spray of the fountain. Water droplets rolled over her heavy breasts, their sable tips gleaming, taunting him with their dusky beauty. With slender fingers she traced a path down her stomach, over the gentle swell of her abdomen, to the place of her most secret desire. As Ciclazade gazed upon her loveliness and realized her need, honor demanded he save the alluring Safiye from the ravishings of the sugar-crazed rat....'"

The Sultan's deep-velvet voice flowed through her like warm honey, conjuring up images of entwined limbs gliding over cool marble benches, of steamy caresses beneath the moisture-laden air. Her body grew heavy, as though she was drifting on a cloud, and a strange anticipation built inside her to hear what happened next to the beautiful heroine and her bold lover. The Sultan slid from his seat, taking a place beside her. He rested back against the lounging chair, the warmth of his flesh softly branding her own. Remembering her promise not to resist his touch, she forced herself not to pull away.

His voice never wavered as he lifted a strand of her hair, stroking it between thumb and forefinger. But he did nothing more threatening than touch her hair, his fingers twining in the tresses almost absent-mindedly. She gazed up at him, his profile outlined against the golden glow of the candle light. Her heart fluttered softly within her breast. His rich voice, low and melodic, penetrated her senses, the steady motion of his full lips mesmerizing her. Her limbs prickled in pleasant awareness of his touch, warm and liquid, his words summoning a curious sensation in the pit of her stomach.

Was this seduction?

His voice trailed off at the end of Ciclazade and Safiye's adventure in the bath. "What do you think of Turkish romance, fair one?" He turned the book around and placed it across her lap, his hand lingering along her silk-clad thigh.

Her flesh tingled where he touched her, and she tried to push aside the feeling, intent upon responding to his question with intelligence. "Written with the Turkish flair for drama, but humorous as well. Delightful. Sensual."

He propped an elbow on the chair and leaned toward her. "Definitely sensual. Do you enjoy this kind of literature in your country?"

"Oh, yes," Alessandra responded. "The French are great romantics. But I've never read any. Erotic literature is considered quite inappropriate for someone of my youth and status."

"Your status?"

"I… I'm a maiden."

His dark brow rose. "So I guessed."

Heat rushed to her cheeks. He brought his hand to her face, traced her lower lip with his thumb, then trailed a path to her jaw. Fire raced along her flesh to the places he touched. "In France," she said in a rush of breath, "in most of Europe in fact, it is considered improper for a woman to be anything but a maiden when she weds."

"Do you think it fair for a woman to go into marriage unschooled in lovemaking?"

"It is a husband's job to teach his wife of desire. And European women have many other duties. Like managing entire chateaus—"

"Duties." The Sultan cringed in mock horror. "Lovemaking is no duty. Lovemaking is a gift of pleasure; the ultimate intimacy between a man and woman. There are slaves to market and prepare food, slaves to launder garments and polish floors."

Alessandra rested her arm on the chair and faced him, intent upon making her point. "But as wives, European women share much more than lovemaking with their husbands. They become partners and friends." She peered at him intently, adding, "And they most certainly do not share their place with other women."

The Sultan chuckled. His fingertips caressed the arch of her brow, then ran softly over her ear. "Ah, your Christian ways. Where is the dishonor in sharing?"

She met his laughing gaze straight on, ignoring the tiny starbursts of heat that prickled her skin where he touched her. "I see where sharing affords you wondrous variety, but what is the benefit to your women?"

He hesitated momentarily, his dark eyes growing wide, and she experienced a small surge of triumph. He obviously had not considered that question before.

"Companionship… and luxury," he began. "Sharing the responsibilities of raising children and making a comfortable and inviting home for me. Those are clear benefits."

"But you don't live in the haremlik. You only visit your women when the mood strikes. They do not in truth create a home for you."

"But they do." He squared his jaw for battle. "They live there with my children, caring for each other in my absence. With whom does a lady of the chateau share her responsibilities?"

"Her ladies-in-waiting."

He raked a hand through his dark hair, sending a glossy black wave tumbling over his brow. He looked boyish. No, he looked roguish, she decided, then forced her concentration back to his words.

"They are not her equals. She cannot reveal herself as she would with another noblewoman, a friend of similar rank."

Now it was Alessandra's turn to consider his words. France was a hodgepodge of connecting baronies and duchies with many miles between one city and the next. Noblewomen commonly moved away from sisters and friends of similar station with marriage and did not see them again except during infrequent gatherings and celebrations. Did a noble lady of the chateau find herself alone on a lofty perch?

"What of your own mother, fair one?"

A wave of sadness washed through her. She squelched the familiar sorrow and let out an audible sigh. "My parents died when I was a young child. I barely remember them."

"Who is this uncle you would return to?"

"He raised me. He's my mother's oldest brother, the French Ambassador. I have travelled with him since my parents' deaths."

The Sultan's gaze swept over her gently. "I have made you relive your anguish, fair one, and that was not my intent." He uncrossed his legs and gathered her into the strong circle of his arms. "Do not be frightened. Relax against me. Let us lighten our hearts with Ciclazade and Safiye's adventures in the Chamber of Robes."

Something in his manner soothed her, and Alessandra did as he bade, resting against the iron-thewed wall of his chest, enveloped in the heady warmth of him. His nearness made her senses spin. With the greatest effort, she focused on the page before her. His hand caressed the curve of her shoulder, and she tried to steady her racing pulse.

At first, Alessandra's nervousness caused her to stumble over the words. Wedged between the Sultan's hard thighs, she heard the steady beat of his heart where her head rested against his chest. That she could not see his face helped ease her tension, and soon her voice settled into a rhythmic cadence.

The Chamber of Robes was one of the few rooms in the Pasha's palace that could be accessed by both the selamlik, where the men resided, and the haremlik, where the women were quartered. This, of course, lured the lovers to conduct their second tryst within its veiled walls.

Alessandra kept her voice steady while relating the beautiful Safiye's emergence from the racks of fabric. "'Safiye twirled and swayed in a silent dance, whispers of silk against satin skin the only sounds to announce their presence behind the rows of brilliantly-hued garments. With filmy gauze ties, she bound Ciclazade's arms to a rack, then moved seductively, just out of reach, while revealing tantalizing glimpses of rounded thighs and full breasts as she peeled away one veil after another.'"

As she described Ciclazade's growing anticipation, the desire that flared through his veins, her voice grew raspy, breathless. To her amazement and shock, an indolent warmth permeated her senses. The Sultan did nothing more than trail a fingertip along the inside of her arm, but his touch ignited flames along her skin.

While Safiye teased her lover's senses to life, whipping her heavy midnight tresses across his cheek and brushing a curved hip against his bare shoulder, the Sultan's strong hands enveloped Alessandra's waist, his fingers dipping into the waistline of her trousers then travelling upward to encircle her breasts. She inhaled sharply, but the Sultan urged, "Do not stop."

He did nothing more than cup her breasts within his palms. She focused her gaze on the tale, but as the sensual words rolled from her tongue, she grew preoccupied with his skillful hands upon her. Her blood pulsed defiantly, distracting her, agitating her. She longed for… sweet God in Heaven, she wanted him to touch her. Arching against him ever so slightly, Alessandra pressed her breasts more fully into his hands, a silent plea for something she had no name for.

His thumbs flicked lightly across the rosy nubs, sending a bolt of fire straight through her. She pressed her eyes tightly shut, losing her place on the page, the yearning so deep, so unlike anything she'd ever imagined. What magic did the Sultan cast upon her with his fiery touch?

His hands roamed from her breasts to her shoulders, and a sigh almost escaped her at the loss of that breathtaking sensation. But rallying her scattered thoughts, she opened her eyes and located her place on the page spread before her. Slightly embarrassed at having responded so strongly, so noticeably to his touch, she resumed the tale, trying to keep her voice as level as possible. If he noticed her struggle, he made no comment, only continued to stroke that sensitive place between her shoulder and the curve of her neck.

Safiye's seduction diverted Alessandra's wayward feelings for a time. "'The sultry heroine roused both her own passions and her lover's as she bared her lovely flesh in a tantalizing dance. But someone heard Ciclazade's heavy breathing. The soft patter of silken slippers on the tiled floor alerted them to the Mistress of the Robe's approach, and Safiye dove on top of her lover, pulling a mountain of fabric over their heads to conceal them.

"'The danger of discovery inflamed their already raging desires. Ciclazade strained against his bonds while Safiye unleashed his sword of arousal, stroking the rigid flesh with experienced fingers. Barely able to draw air through the diaphanous pile of silk that enveloped them, their breathing grew heated, their bodies slick with passion. Safiye refused to free her lover, instead she traced light kisses along his muscled chest and over his taut stomach, then down toward his pulsing—'" Alessandra sputtered, the breath catching in her throat.

The Sultan's gentle laughter rippled through the air. "Do not be embarrassed, fair one. You did quite well... for a maiden." Sliding his arms around her to grasp the book, he tilted it toward him. He rested his chin on her shoulder and read from the place she left off, relating the tale of Safiye's seduction with enthusiasm.

Alessandra had accomplished her goals of giving the Sultan cause to reflect upon her questions and of learning something about her life and work. But as his deep voice sent swirls of newly-discovered pleasure through her, she wondered how many of his own goals he had met this night.

Solimon stepped from the terrace and strode the path across the tulip gardens with an eagerness he had not experienced since youth. The fair beauty intrigued him like no other. A tantalizing enigma, her mystery drifted just out of his reach, promising untold pleasures when he learned her secrets. Yet with the thought came another, one that sobered him instantly: her uncle had sold her to Ibrahim Pasha.

Even if Solimon was inclined to grant her request for freedom, he could not in good conscience return her to someone who cared so little for her best interests. The man would probably sell her again, and who knew if another master would see her gentle spirit and care for her with love. He would not take that chance.

The entire situation made him unaccountably angry. How dare a family member, entrusted to care for such a beautiful, tender creature, betray that trust for profit? Feelings of fierce protectiveness awoke in him, feelings he was unfamiliar and uncomfortable with.

A sultry breeze floated up from the Marmara, tugging at the loose fabric of his trousers and filling the air with the moist tang of the sea. He did not know yet how best to handle the situation, but he could not reveal her uncle's perfidy. Knowledge of such betrayal would surely squelch her proud spirit, and that he would not do.

He entered the Moonlight Kiosk through silver-filigreed doors and quickly toured the palace, pleased to see the chamber awaited him in all readiness. Adorned with no furnishings save several low tables, the round room boasted an array of fat silk pillows in all shapes and sizes. Through windows which ran from the carpeted floor to the domed ceiling, the view of moon-bathed waters beneath a star-filled sky never failed to take his breath away.

Untying the robe, he slid the garment from his shoulders then kicked the slippers from his feet. The shifting flames of cinnamon-scented candles twinkled in the edges of his view. He gazed out over the silver water, wondering what his fair one thought of his second present. At the knock on the door, he contained his impatience. He'd find out what she thought of the latest "scholarly device" soon enough.

The Kislar Agha entered. "Grand Seigneur, I humbly present the Gift," he announced, waving his charge forward.

Solimon could not help but stare. The light of the tapers played along the amethysts and diamonds sparkling in her hair, and the blood rushed to his loins at the sight of her, so ethereal and delicate. The Kislar Agha slipped silently back into the vestibule, closing the door behind him. The fair one simply stood there, uncertain, then bowed low. Solimon admired the gentle curves of her body outlined by the sheer violet silk of her garments. Her shimmering hair fanned out around her, and he yearned to catch soft fistfuls in his hands, to pull her into his arms and feel her warm against him. "Good evening, fair one. Come. Share this magnificent view with me."

Clutching the latest present to her chest, she hid her glorious breasts from sight, and Solimon vowed not to send her another book. Yet despite her modesty, she came to stand beside him, appearing much more at ease in his presence than the previous eve. He was satisfied. "Do you like my gift?"

Her bright eyes rested upon him, and a soft smile played at the corners of her mouth. "Many thanks, Grand Seigneur. If at all possible, it is even more beautiful than the first. But this one does not contain Turkish romance. What do you call this—Turkish art, perhaps?"

Solimon nodded. "Each painting shows how the heavens govern different forms of pleasure." He took the book from her, enjoying a quick glimpse of her breasts, before opening to the first tissue-covered page. "This constellation suggests an embrace." Running his finger along the replication of stars, he then traced the silhouette of the naked young couple entwined below the night sky.

"Like finding imaginary animals in the clouds," she said, excitement evident in her clear voice. "What a wondrous book, for all its sensual intent."

Despite the gentle reprimand that edged her words, he was pleased by her graciousness. His choice of presents was rather calculated, clearly not what she intended, yet not forbidden either. He admired how she accepted each gift in stride then tried to turn it to her advantage. "Let's try this one," he said, flipping back to a page where the lovers stood embracing each other. Uncertainty flitted across her heart-shaped face. "Do not be frightened."

She inclined her head demurely in consent. Wrapping an arm around her slim waist, he pulled her against him. The edges of her guimlik fell open with the motion, and her breasts pressed full against his chest. She caught her breath sharply and stiffened. Loosening his hold slightly, he whispered against her ear, "I will release you if that is your desire, but I would much rather hold you. There is much pleasure to be had in a simple embrace."

His whole being filled with waiting. Would she pull away or melt against him? She leaned toward him slightly, so slightly he thought he'd imagined it until her straight hair cascaded across his arm in a cool wave.

Pulling her closer, he rested his cheek atop her head, inhaling deeply of her sweet lavender scent. He dared not move lest he break the spell and reveled in her pliant curves molding the contours of his body. She tilted her head back and studied him. "You are surprised," he said, watching her.

"You are so gentle. You are renowned throughout Christendom as the mightiest of warriors, yet you coax me like a frightened bird to your hand. Yes, I am surprised. By you. By your tenderness and understanding."

"A tender warrior." He chuckled. "Be careful where you tread, fair one. I may never let you leave the seraglio lest you spread tales that damage my fiercely-won reputation."

Her eyes widened for an instant, then she shrugged. "I only hope you learn as much of me as I am learning of you."

Hearing the seriousness in her tone, he drew her down to the floor. "Come, lay beside me." He stretched out full length, positioning the book before him. She unfolded her slender form over the pillows, careful not to touch him, and propped up on her elbows, chin in hand.

"As a child in summertime, I watched the ships sail over the Marmara," he told her. "Look, there's one now. Only just visible beneath the light of the moon." He pointed to a pearly streak gliding over the silver-black water. Lifting himself up on one elbow, he studied the elegant curves and angles of her face, watching her expression soften in thoughtful interest. "Tell me, fair one, what would you have me learn of you."

"I would have you see the woman who is respected enough to be asked for advice in business. The woman who is an asset to the French consulate."

Solimon rolled on his side to face her, sliding his legs against hers. His hand explored the hollows of her back, and to his delight, she did not shy away. "You speak much of business, but what of love? Was your uncle a loving guardian? Was there someone you had in mind for a husband?"

She cringed. "My uncle... provided for me. He is not a rich man," she said in way of explanation. "He devoted his life to serving the crown, and my parents' estate dwindled during my upbringing. I have no dowry, nor any lands to offer a husband, so I work as my uncle's aide." She fixed her gaze on the sea, her pink tongue darting out to moisten her lips.

Solimon realized the admission embarrassed her. That newly-discovered feeling of protectiveness flared inside him again. He grew infuriated at her uncle, a man he had never met, while envisioning the jewel-eyed child who never knew the love of her parents. Or the love of her guardian, it would seem. And along with these feelings came the realization that his fair one wanted to fill this gap in her life, that she searched unknowingly for love.

"The Moonlight Kiosk," she whispered. "It is aptly named."

Sliding his fingertips beneath the silk blouse, he trailed a path up the slim line of her waist to the contour of her ribs. Her skin was so pale against his own, like orchids in the moonlight. She shivered, and the blood tingled in his veins. "I could call this tiny palace nothing else," he said. Sliding the sheer garment from her shoulders, he revealed her bare flesh to his gaze.

She sat up instantly, burying her luscious breasts in a red silk pillow. "You twist the rules," she accused, violet eyes flashing fire.

"You did not expect me to try to turn your challenge to my advantage?" He sat up and faced her.

Her brilliant eyes deepened like the sky on a stormy night. She sat straight-backed and defiant, staring at him with ill-concealed fury. She was so close, so delectable, a bolt of desire shot straight through him. He could not tear his gaze from the lush moistness of her lips— so ripe they beckoned to be kissed.

Before another moment was spent, the red silk pillow sailed across the chamber and she was coiled within his arms. In a swift movement, he dragged her back into the cushions with him, breasts rasping his chest as he fitted one hand in the small of her back while burying the other in the sleek tangle of her silvery hair. Capturing her mouth with his own, he kissed her.

A silken sigh slipped from her lips, and the warmth of her sweet breath made him burn. As he explored every inch of that tantalizing mouth, delighting in the way she trembled against him, his ardor flared. He devoured her softness, demanding a response, and she raised herself to meet his kiss, the full length of her body nestling into his. The gentle caress of her hands on his shoulders sent his senses soaring. She was passion. He had known it from the first moment he laid eyes upon her. As her hips arched upward, enveloping the very core of his desire in her yielding flesh, an urgent need rushed through him.

He yearned to possess her, to pleasure her, to love her. His own excitement had never before leapt to life so quickly, so fiercely. Her hesitant touch was intoxicating. A tender ache tightened his loins, an ache so great he grew breathless, and he was forced to abandon his exploration of her lest he lose the last shreds of his control and make love to her where they lay. But he desired more than her impassioned surrender. He wanted her to come to him willingly, to hunger for him like he hungered for her. Dragging his lips from hers, Solimon cradled her against him, listening to the sounds of their ragged breathing, the thundering of their hearts, stunned by their passion as she appeared to be.

His arousal cooled by slow degrees. The magic of the moment passed, and he could feel the subtle change in her body as she slowly drew away. Once again in control of his all-too-easily inflamed lust, he decided to guide her further down the path of ecstasy. "There is a constellation called Capricorn. Let us try to find it," he said, his voice sounding unaccustomedly hoarse to his ears.

Sliding the book toward her, Solimon exhaled sharply when she rolled onto her stomach, leaving him bereft of her velvety warmth. He reached out to bring her back, but realized the moment was gone. Tucking an oblong blue pillow beneath his chest, he propped himself up on his elbows, and turned his attention to the sky. He easily spotted the pattern of stars he sought, while the pages she turned rustled gently in the moonlit silence.

"Here it is." She kept her gaze shyly averted.

His humor returned with her modesty, and he again cautioned himself to tread carefully. "Can you identify that constellation among the stars?"

She gazed into the night for a long moment while he admired the finely-drawn outline of her profile. A strand of hair tumbled over her shoulder, and she swept it behind a perfectly-formed ear, leaving him fighting the urge to weave his fingers through the silken tresses.

"There." She pointed toward the heavens. "A bit north of the Eagle."

"You are familiar with astronomy?" Solimon asked, more than mildly surprised.

She faced him, a grin tipping the corners of her rosy mouth. "You didn't believe me when I claimed to be educated?"

"No... yes. I didn't doubt your claim, but I wouldn't have thought astronomy of much interest to a woman."

The lights in her deep violet eyes twinkled. "Aside from enjoying the beauty of the night sky, a lady uses her knowledge of constellations to determine the planting and harvesting schedules."

"Well defended, fair one." He chuckled. "I concede the point. Now, let me show you another way we use the constellations."

He guided her into his arms, her bare back full against his chest, rounded buttocks cradling the very heart of his desire. She relaxed in his embrace, and he rested his hand upon the gentle slope of her hip, inhaling deeply of her sweet fragrance while staring out into the black-velvet sky.

This delicious woman he held in his arms intrigued him as had no other. She denied her suitability as a love slave, yet responded to his touch with a vibrancy that promised extraordinary passion. Gentle-natured and innocent, she was unlike the women of his haremlik who were skilled in the art of pleasure. Her every thought was not to satisfy or manipulate him. Instead, she challenged him to coax her undiscovered desires to life. Was she the woman he had yet to meet, the woman who would be not only lover, but friend—his soulmate?

He played upon her responses like a musician. His hands trailed along the arc of her waist, and her shuddering intake of breath rippled through the tranquil air. He found her breast. Weighing their velvet heaviness in his hands, his fingers teased the rosy peaks of those pale mounds, and a silken moan escaped her. He pressed light kisses against the line of her cheek, the curve of her neck, the slope of her shoulder until she gasped in shallow draughts. Caressing her breasts with his hands, he gently tugged at their tight tips until her hips arched upward, seeking fulfillment.

He cradled her against him, flesh against flesh, sinking deep into the pillows. But before too much time had passed, the fluid lines of her body grew taut. "You choose now," he whispered as distraction. He was not willing to give up the newfound intimacy they shared and was eager to see if she would match his choice with courage or retreat with a faint heart.

She obviously understood the underlying challenge of his request. The tissue of the turning pages crinkled softly as she slowly scrutinized each and every position before finally settling on one—the Swan.

He met her gaze. Uncertainty was written clearly across her face, her pink mouth deepening in a frown. Solimon smiled, encouraging her choice while excitement seared his blood. Did she understand what glorious part of her anatomy she was offering him? "Shall I find it in the stars for you, fair one?"

She nodded, rolling onto her stomach and out of his arms. Solimon breathed a sigh of relief for this brief reprieve, a chance to check his own passion. His unbridled responses amazed him, and there was no doubt he would need every ounce of his usually-formidable control to survive this next position without the promise of easing his own desire. But he would not make love to her this night. They did not yet share the most precious of intimacies, and he would not risk their progress by behaving like an untried youth when he was a man of thirty and learned in the ways of pleasure. He would restrain himself no matter how he longed to do otherwise.

Gazing up at the tiny pinpricks of silver that flickered and glowed against the obsidian sky, he said, "There it is, nestled between the Dragon and the Dolphin. Do you see it?"

She tilted her head back and looked into the night. Her gilt hair, studded with jewels, shimmered as it fell in a heavy wave over her bare shoulders and back. "I see it," she said breathlessly.

Solimon bade her roll over and pressed her into the pillows. She lifted her arms as though to shield her breasts, but managed to resist the urge. Her slender white fingers curled into fists, revealing her struggle, and her whole being seemed to tense with expectation.

Did she think he would bite her? Stifling a grin at the thought, he rolled over, wedging his hips between her thighs and bracing himself above her. Her eyes flew open in astonishment. He held her gaze while sliding down, his chest raking across her nipples, his hips forcing her legs to part as she drew her knees upward to accommodate him.

"Oooh," she gasped aloud when he buried his face in her lush breasts.

He could not help but smile as her whole body tightened in response to his touch. "Do you like this?" He gently tugged at the rosy tips with his teeth.

She arched against him, her black lashes flying upward as she stared at him wide-eyed. He chuckled, resting his weight on one elbow and freeing his hand to join in the sensual game. "You look so surprised," he murmured against her gleaming flesh. "You were made for love, my fair one, made to share these pleasures." His tongue swirled lazily around first one nipple, then the other. He blew softly against the moist flesh, delighting when they hardened in response. Her lips parted and a sigh escaped. She lifted her hands to stroke his shoulders, and a surge of desire shot through him at the mere touch of her cool hands. He traced the curve of her waist, then his fingers plucked apart the silken knot that held her trousers together.

"Grand Seigneur!"

He did not need to see her face to know of her shocked resistance. As she tried to pull away, her hips rocked within the limited confines of his body's embrace. "Do not be frightened, fair one. I would never harm you." He brushed the silk-gauze trousers from her hips and eased them down the length of her, revealing pale, shapely limbs to his appreciative gaze. "You have the power. Simply tell me to stop and I shall." His mouth trailed over her breast and down the soft skin of her stomach. "Would you like me to stop?" Her violet eyes glowed with a sultry inner light. He pressed languid kisses along the rounded line of her hip. "And now?"

"No."

His mouth found the place where her thighs met, his lips moving over the mound of her arousal. Her low moan echoed through his entire body. She was so sweet. His tongue traced her honeyed warmth, passion making her unfold like the dew-kissed petals of a blossom. His own need rose to frenzied heights as he found the center of her woman's desire and nipped at the turgid little bud. "Should I stop yet, fair one?"

Her thighs trembled, the soft flesh caressing his cheeks. He could feel her desire mounting, cresting as he drew on the tiny jewel. Her fingers twined into his hair, urging him on, and she gasped. "Don't stop."

With a surge of triumph, he abandoned himself fully to his tender ministrations, feeling every ripple, every shimmer that pulsed through her. He caressed her moist cleft with his thumb, drawing her to the edge and back, guiding her to even greater heights until she melted against him in ecstasy, crying out her rapture. A bolt of unleashed passion rocked him. He rested his face against her thigh until he found some relief from the turbulence of his own raging emotions.

He finally rolled onto his side and pulled her into his embrace, marveling at how quickly she scaled the heights of pleasure and at the intensity of his own response. She had risen valiantly to his challenge, but he would retreat to the safety of a position named Libra, giving the blood a chance to cool in his veins.

Solimon stood unseen behind the stone-worked wall of the harem bath. Below him, several of the women strolled through the bathing chamber, pausing at wall fountains or grooming themselves, while others frolicked in the pool. His fair one appeared in the doorway, draped in a flowing caftan. The sapphire blue fabric swirled and shimmered around her slender frame like a waterfall. He could not drive the memory of the past night from his mind. Visions of her, soft and yielding, distracted him so he could think of nothing else.

At her appearance, the women's chattering quieted before resuming in an agitated fervor. The fair one straightened her back and entered the chamber, but as she passed by the edge of the pool, the women made unkind comments, laughing and splashing water at her. With her head held high, she ignored them and walked past, sitting on a low stone bench to comb the tangles from her glorious hair.

"It has been thus since her first night with you," the Kislar Agha explained. His voice betrayed no hint of emotion, but his obsidian eyes glowed accusingly.

Solimon ignored the pointed glare, unwilling to debate the topic again. The chief eunuch had warned him repeatedly about neglecting the haremlik. But that choice had been made long ago and he could only look to the future now. He had a favorite, and the women would adjust.

Yet he could not contain his disappointment as the scene unfolded below. The women could be kind and gracious. He had brought only the best behaved from his father's palace, and any troublemakers were quickly sent to plague some other man's household. Their jealous behavior was unforgivable, especially since his fair one already struggled to understand their way of life that was so different from her own. Even more unsettling was the possessiveness he felt toward her. He wanted to protect her from this hurt, wanted her to find acceptance and companionship in the haremlik.

"Her uncle sold her to Ibrahim Pasha," Solimon said. The blast of rage that seared him was a physical explosion, like the fury that overtook him in battle. Stunned by the intensity of the emotion, he could no longer deny the truth to himself. The fair one was more than a favorite—he had lost his heart to the violet-eyed beauty.

The Kislar Agha watched with a knowing expression. "I've heard, Grand Seigneur."

"Is there a breath of air I draw without your knowledge?"

"No, Grand Seigneur."

Solimon could not help but laugh, and his spirits lightened considerably. He gazed down again at the fair beauty whose fate he held so precariously within his grasp. Allah had brought her to him for a reason. They were fated to be together. No matter that their backgrounds and expectations differed, they could learn from each other. Above all she wanted love, and he had that in abundance for her.

She stood, sweeping the glimmering-gilt tresses behind her shoulders while unfastening the ties of the caftan. As the garment slipped from her shoulders, falling into a silken puddle at her feet, the blood surged through his veins. She was ravishing. The graceful lines of her body were still love-flushed from their night of passion.

"Bring her to me at sunset," he told the Kislar Agha, then strode from the room, suddenly certain of what he must do.

Alessandra's emotions were in a wild swirl. Was she frightened or excited to spend another night with the Sultan? He was not at all what she had expected, and after the past night, she realized just how badly she was losing the battle—and just how much she didn't mind. For the first time in her memory, she felt special. The Sultan would bind her to him as slave for a lifetime, yet he made her feel so…cherished, desired, as if being his slave was more than she had ever aspired to be. He was a legend throughout Christendom, a mighty warrior and lusty ruler with an insatiable appetite for women. But when he encircled her in his powerful arms, he was a gentle teacher, a tender lover, a man honorbound by his word.

Her emotions swung like a pendulum between excitement for the unknown future and fear of the very same. The Sultan wielded her own innocence as a weapon against her, but instead of resenting him, she found herself yearning for the glorious sensations his touch evoked. He had discovered some wild, impulsive fire smoldering inside her and had expertly stoked it until every inch of her flesh burned for him. Even the passing hours of daylight had not doused the flames.

And Alessandra faced yet another night of his ardor. Pleasure, hunger, desire suffused her. But most disturbing was that all fears paled in the swirling memories of his lips upon hers and his strong hands caressing her bare flesh. She wanted him, wanted him to make love to her. To love her. Did she love the Sultan?

The idea jolted her from her thoughts. No matter how thoughtful and considerate he had been, he still considered her no more than a pleasure-giver. She only had one more night. One night to convince him she was much more than a slave. Retrieving the amethyst-encrusted bottle, which had arrived that morning, Alessandra told the Kislar Agha, "I am ready."

She was led through the corridor to the Sultan's private bathing chamber. The chief eunuch prodded her into the disrobing room. "Your arrival needs no introduction this eve. Go to him, my lady, and may Allah be with you." He slipped out the door, and the clink of a key turning the lock sent a shudder through her. The final night of the challenge—there would be no turning back.

Passing through the finely-wrought gilt door, Alessandra stopped short in the entry, stunned by the luxuriance of the chamber. The entire room was paved in white marble, from the endless expanse of floor to the smooth dome of the ceiling and every narrow column in between. A beautiful cascade fountain bubbled and splashed like a waterfall on an opposite wall. The square pool in the center of the room caught her attention, for it was there the Sultan sat, in the midst of all this bright opulence, evidently so deep in thought he had not heard her enter.

He ran a hand through his hair, tousling the glossy black waves into dishevelment. Alessandra was suddenly struck by how solitary, how alone he seemed in the vast chamber. She remembered their conversation during the first night when he pointed out how isolated a lady could be with no one to share her responsibilities. Was he lonely sometimes? Even with a palace full of servants and a harem full of slaves, he was a man. And not just any man, but one with the weight of an empire upon his shoulders. With that realization, a wave of tenderness flowed through her. "You would have me believe the contents of this bottle somehow resemble a scholarly device?"

Her softly-spoken words disturbed the bubbling quiet of the room, and the Sultan's head snapped up, recognition softening his features. He approached her so suddenly that she did not have time to pay him homage with a bow. But he did not seem to notice as he grasped her hand firmly and seated her on the wide ledge of the pool. He took the bottle. "I can only plead for tolerance, fair one." The warmth of his smile echoed in his voice. "I wanted to tempt you with something truly special on our third night together."

His long fingers worked the amethyst-topped stopper from the bottle. Kneeling beside her, he poured its contents into the steady stream of water propelled into the pool by some hidden pump. The scent of lavender filled the air, and to her surprise, a froth of white bubbles spread along the surface in an ever-widening circle. She could not hold back the squeal of delight that slipped from her lips, and he watched her, clearly amused. "It's beautiful. What is it?" she asked.

He skimmed a handful from the pool and blew it at her. "Bubbles."

"Mmm. Smells wonderful." She wiped the foam from her nose and blew it back at him.

He brushed his own face clean, bowing his head deeply. "Lavender. In your honor."

Alessandra smiled, captivated by the boyishness of his gesture. "Another ancient form of Turkish art?"

"No. But only a person of true intelligence can appreciate relaxation and enjoyment."

"Like Ciclazade and Safiye perhaps?"

"No... well, yes." The Sultan laughed, a rich, deep sound that sent tingles through her. He came to his feet, strode to the disrobing chamber, and disappeared. "Since you so graciously indulge me, fair one, I will allow you to choose our topic of debate this eve," he called from the other room. "What would you like to discuss?"

She ran her fingers through the frothy confection swirling along the pool's surface, then blew the bubbles from her fingertips. "You. Tell me about yourself and your upbringing."

He reappeared in the entry, and the breath solidified in her throat. He was naked. Like a Greek statue of a god come to life, he strode toward her, muscles shifting with each step, bronzed skin in sharp relief against the stark whiteness of the chamber. She could not tear her eyes away and admired the set of his powerful shoulders and the smattering of black fur across the stony ridges of his chest. His flat stomach and trim hips brought memories of his flesh beneath her hands, the feel of his rigid arousal nudging her. Her gaze riveted to the very spot where his manhood nestled against the dark thatch of hair between his legs.

"Sweet Mother in Heaven," Alessandra choked, pressing her hand to her temple and closing her eyes.

"Of all the worldly subjects, you would discuss me?" he asked.

She could hear the ill-concealed laughter in his voice and did not chance a peek until the telltale splash of water resounded through the chamber. He leaned against the wall of the pool, only his face visible above the bubbles. "Join me, fair one, and I shall tell you all my secrets."

A passionate fluttering began deep in her stomach. She tried to push aside her shocked impropriety over his request, but failed miserably. His voice was a silken lure, urging her to the water, but a flicker of pride held her rooted to the spot. This was her heart, her entire life at stake. She must earn his respect before yielding the game. "I... I cannot."

"Why ever not? Can't you swim?" He stood to show her the water reached to only the middle of his broad chest. "It's not deep. I won't let you drown."

The scoundrel! She cast a quick glance at the locked door, the only exit to the chamber. Her gaze darted to his, her cheeks warming at the thought of swimming with him. She shook her head.

"Oh," he said. "I forgot. You're a maiden. What if I move over there, where I can't touch you?" He swam the length of the pool with swift powerful strokes. The water splashed against the gleaming tiles, bubbles separating in his wake. "Not good enough yet?" He turned his back to her. "What if I promise not to look while you disrobe?"

Alessandra simply sat there, frozen.

"If you don't come in willingly, I shall come get you, and then, fair one, I vow to touch every luscious inch of your delicious self."

Sheer panic swept through her. She stood then sat down abruptly, uncertain of what to do. She could not swim with a naked man!

"If you still don't trust me, I'll go under water. But please be quick. I can only hold my breath for so long."

To Alessandra's horror, his dark head disappeared below the surface. She glanced around frantically, seeing no escape. Leaping to her feet, she kicked off her slippers and fumbled with the corded sash that held the pink-spangled trousers at her waist. The garment fell to the floor in a silken heap, and she kicked it away, dropping the guimlik as well. Feeling every inch of her bare flesh, she slid into the luxuriant water and sank down to her chin.

Several long moments passed, and yet he still did not appear. She couldn't see beneath the bubbles. Had he drowned? Just as she grew truly concerned, he erupted from the water in a forceful burst, his wet flesh gliding full against her. She screamed, startled, instinctively pulling away. His strong arms caught her, saving her from going under. "I'm sorry." He flashed a wet grin. "I didn't mean to frighten you."

Alessandra just stared at him, stunned by the feel of his sleek, hard body.

"What would you know of me?" He swept the damp strands of hair from her cheeks then traced the curve of her jaw. "Do you know I find you delectable, that I yearn to feast on your sumptuous flesh?"

His mouth slowly descended to meet hers. He rained tender kisses around her parted lips, nibbling her flesh, sending waves of pleasure spiralling through her. Alessandra wanted to respond with some semblance of reason, but turning their conversation into an intellectual debate was far beyond her ability at the moment. She had promised herself not to surrender, yet here she stood in his arms, quivering and naked, the smooth shaft of his desire pressed boldly against her.

"Do you want to know that I was raised in my father's palace, beloved by my mother and adored by my father's women, not one of whom ever came close to matching your exquisite beauty."

The heat of his body seared the entire length of her, and his breath came sweet and warm on her lips. Drowning in a tide of desire, she wanted to abandon herself to him, but was firmly caught in a trap of her own making. She could not yield, nor could she push him away. Her mind swirled with doubt. She wanted his respect. She wanted his love. And in that moment, Alessandra knew if she could not have both, she might have to choose only one.

"Do you want to know that even among the flowers in my haremlik, I have yet to know a woman who awakens such a powerful longing in me. Share this passion, fair one. Let us explore it together."

If she gave in to him, she gave him everything, her virtue, her life. And in return he would cherish her. Not as a wife, but as one of his women. A lifetime of slavery. The words echoed in her memory. Yet could she possibly live without this tantalizing love he offered?

As though he understood her struggle, he forged ahead with increasing vigor, determined to coax her over the precipice of her control. His hands stroked her every curve, the scented water enhancing the sleek feel of his fingers on her flesh.

"Discover this pleasure with me." His teeth tugged on the fullness of her lower lip. He found her breasts, his hands curling around them gently, teasing each nipple between his thumb and forefinger until she grew breathless and pliant beneath his caresses.

Perhaps she could survive without being loved, but living without this man who made her heart dance with excitement wasn't much of a future. Her head spun with his kisses, and she couldn't think of any way to win both his love and his respect.

As his tongue ravaged the soft recesses of her mouth, Alessandra slid her arms around his waist, abandoning all pretense of resistance. What was his magic that her will dissolved at his slightest touch?

She gave in to the urge to caress him, to explore the hard planes of his body. Her hands roamed freely over his tight buttocks and narrow hips. A savage groan escaped him when she found his hard shaft and stroked its throbbing length, gently, then more daring as he moved against her. She experienced an unfamiliar feeling of power as she recognized his need, his tightly-bridled restraint, knowing instinctively that only she could slake his thirst.

A tremor rocked his sinewy frame. Uncertain, she brought her hands to rest lightly around his waist and searched his darkly-beautiful face. He opened his eyes and peered intently at her, his breathing ragged, his black eyes smoldering with unfulfilled passion. Her heart fluttered wildly in her chest. Did she really want freedom when it meant giving up his love?

His mouth covered hers hungrily, and he brought her hard against him. Caressing her body in bold strokes, he shattered her composure with the fierceness of his touch. He aroused such exquisite feelings in her, feelings she couldn't resist. He slid his hot, pulsing length between her thighs. The throaty groan that tumbled from his lips sent the last of her will scattering like the tiny bubbles that converged and popped along the surface of the pool. She moved her hands over the sleek, plated lines of his chest, up the corded muscles of his neck, and finally cradled his square jaw in her palms, returning his kisses with abandon.

She flexed the muscles of her thighs around his rigid flesh. He grasped her buttocks and pulled her close, the water flowing between them, creating a slick tunnel where his pulsing desire glided silkily against her. The breath caught in her throat at the intensity of these awakening sensations and she held his face firmly in her hands, tasting his sweet tongue, knowing she would give herself to him if he would ease this ache in the very core of her being.

"Let us love, my fair one," he whispered hoarsely against her lips.

Her life for his love. Her freedom for his passion. She would have to choose. He willingly offered all that he had to give, and she would have to accept or deny him.

"Share this love with me."

His simple request eroded the very last of her control, draining the strength from her limbs, forcing surrender. She loved him. The realization flowed through her mind and body with such strength that she would have fallen had he not held her so tightly. If she had to choose between his respect and his love, Alessandra chose love. If she had to give up her world to be with him, then so be it. She loved. The word slid from her parted lips, an emphatic whisper. "Yes."

The Sultan's black eyes flashed in victory. Before another moment spent itself, he spun her around in the warm water, his mouth never relinquishing its hold upon hers. A heated languor spread through her, her legs heavy as they drifted through the water. He pulled her toward him and leaned back against the pool's edge.

"You are mine, fair one." Lifting her into his arms, he helped her wrap her legs around his hips, leaving the core of her woman's desire revealed to his probing hardness.

Suddenly he was filling her, stretching her open in a slow, silken thrust. "Seigneur," she gasped, arching against him when he met the resistance of her maidenhead.

"I am Solimon. Say it," he commanded, impaling her with his depthless gaze.

She could not suppress a shiver at the rough tone of his voice. And as his name slid from her lips, he drove into her. A bolt of pleasure-pain pierced her, and she cried out, only to find his mouth back upon hers, drawing the very sound from her. He swelled inside, and her flesh yielded to accommodate his thickness. She clung to him, only half aware of his tenseness, the passion he held barely in check.

Gripping her buttocks in strong hands, he drew her slowly upward, withdrawing almost completely, then plunging into her in one controlled stroke. She gasped aloud, a tide of liquid fire flooding her tender loins. Trailing her fingers down the shifting muscles of his back, she filled her senses with him. His tongue demanded a response, and his surging maleness awakened an unimagined need deep within. She crushed her breasts to his ridged chest, rasping her nipples across the springy curls, even as he thrust back into her again, and yet again.

His husky moan rose over the lapping water and the gentle bubbling of the fountains. His mouth slid from hers, leaving behind only the spicy warm taste of his rough-velvet tongue. Wrapping his arms around her waist and hips, he locked her against him, embedded deep inside, then slowly moved away from the wall. She clung to him, lips pressed into his glossy black hair, gasping as each long stride pushed his hot flesh into her and sent waves of sheer rapture pounding through her.

When they reached the stair, he was forced to relinquish his possession of her and withdraw. A sound passed his lips as they parted, half-groan and half-gasp, and he swung her into his arms. They emerged from the pool, the coolness of the air sending a shiver through her body. With one broad sweep of his arm, he sent the neatly-folded piles of linens toppling off a marble bench. His eyes were heavy-lidded with passion as he pressed her back into the soft white mountain of fabric.

The spray of the fountain veiled them in its shimmering mist. His dark skin gleamed like molten gold, and Alessandra could not ever remember seeing such a magnificent sight. Bringing her hand to his face, she caressed the square line of his jaw in wonder. "Solimon, love me," she murmured, experiencing a rush of excitement at the look of raw desire on his face. She was his, and there was no where else in the world she would rather be.

"Ah, fairest one, you are perfection." He lowered himself into her tender embrace.

He thrust into her. He filled her body, her very senses. He was rapture and love. She molded to his hard form, overwhelmed by the fullness inside her, by the completeness she felt. His mouth found hers, and she yielded to his demanding mastery, swaying against him and meeting each thrust with a longing of her own.

"Love me," she gasped, the intensity of her need draining every thought from her mind. Their bodies met in exquisite harmony—

surging, receding, plunging into awesome depths she had never before imagined. She was drowning in a golden wave of pleasure, diving into an eddy of sensation. A mighty shudder rocked his frame, and he took her with him, riding on the crest of ecstasy until breaker after breaker crashed along the fine-spun shore of their emotions.

Slowly Alessandra became aware of her heart hammering against her ribs and the feeling of their slick limbs entwined. The Sultan shifted his weight, carrying her onto her side, so they faced each other. He held her tightly, brushing damp tendrils from her cheeks, and rocked her back and forth, burying his face in her hair. "You are precious to me, fair one."

At the tenderness in his voice, a wave of sadness poured through her. Mingled with the awe of the moment was the understanding that she had not only given this man her virtue, but her heart, and with those gifts, her consent to enter his haremlik. She loved him, would give her life to him. But no matter how much he wanted her, no matter how gentle he was, the Sultan still viewed her as a slave. Alessandra could not suppress a sob—she had found love, but lost the game.

"What troubles you, fair one?" He pressed a light kiss on her brow. "Have I hurt you?"

Swallowing hard, she met his gaze. "I have gambled and lost."

"No one has lost. We have both won. We are bound together." His arms tightened around her, and she could not suppress the slight shudder, the ripple of confusion that ran through her.

His dark gaze searched her face. "Is what I offer you so distasteful?" he asked, his expression serious, without a trace of humor.

"What exactly do you offer me, Grand Seigneur?"

The Sultan watched her for a long moment. He loosened his hold on her and swept his arm around in a half circle. "All that I am. A place of honor in my haremlik."

Her tumultuous emotions rose to the surface. No matter how she willed it otherwise, tears welled in her eyes and spilled over.

He frowned, the flickering muscle at his jaw betraying deep frustration. "Is a lifetime spent laboring at your uncle's side truly more desirable than what I offer you here?"

She wanted to say something to magically erase the troubled edge to his voice, but could do no more than wipe the tears from her cheeks. He stared at her, and when she didn't respond, his face transformed into an inscrutable, kingly mask. In that instant, Alessandra no longer recognized her handsome lover.

"Once again we are at an impasse," he said. "The three nights have passed—whom shall we call victor?"

"You may approach," the Sultan said from his seat upon the throne.

Alessandra thought him an imposing figure in his royal finery. Unlike her tender lover of the three nights past, he barely resembled the man who had captured her heart. A wave of apprehension coursed through her. He had triumphed. Forcing herself to leave the Kislar Agha's side, she crossed the Royal Salon, past the rows of silent eunuchs, then bowed low before the Sultan.

"It is sunset of the fourth night, fair one, and before we call an end to our game, I would ask you a question. Rise and face me."

Alessandra stood, pulse racing. She met his solemn gaze, hardly recognizing the man she had come to know so intimately, the man who had unlocked her heart and soul.

"I have learned there is strife within my haremlik, that my women have welcomed you in a manner that brings shame upon me. Is this true?"

She cast an accusing glance at the Kislar Agha, who scowled at her for such rudeness. What could she say? Upon her arrival at the Palace, the women had welcomed her graciously, helped ease her fear of an unfamiliar world. But they had turned just as quickly when the Sultan committed to spending three nights with her. They had been both kind and unkind. Finding no words to adequately explain the situation, she fixed her gaze on the far corner of the room, where finches bobbed from perch to perch in a wrought iron aviary, and shrugged.

"I have witnessed their cruelty, fair one, and now must deal with it."

Alessandra cringed. Did the very walls of this Palace have eyes? She was more than mildly embarrassed that he, a man who bore the responsibilities of an empire, felt the need to concern himself with troubles so trivial in comparison. If she was going to spend her life in his haremlik, she would have to make a place for herself. "Grand Seigneur, I appreciate your concern—"

"I would ask your counsel on the matter." He leaned back on the high-backed throne and steepled his fingers before him. "How would you deal with this jealousy?"

He wanted her counsel? Alessandra stared at him, unsure if she had heard correctly. Despite a momentary flash of panic, she could do no less than tell the truth—whether it pleased him or not. "The women simply follow your lead. You do not spend time with them, so they lose all desire to make the haremlik an inviting place. With nothing more constructive to do with their days, they aspire to tasks loftier than those they now possess and scheme for your meager attentions. When you committed to spending so much time with me, I became a threat."

Some unrecognizable emotion glimmered in the depths of his eyes, and she swallowed hard before continuing. "If you would have them behave differently, you must treat them differently—like you have me."

He did not respond, and the silence grew heavy between them. Barely daring to breath, Alessandra forced herself to hold his gaze, back straight and head high, knowing full well the next moments would decide the rest of her life.

His voice shattered the tense quiet. "Clear the chamber."

She flinched, but resisted the urge to look away. Studying him intently while the occupants of the room departed, she wondered at his thoughts, wanted so badly to erase that distant expression from his face and see him smile. The realization led to another—he was right when he said there was no loser in this game, no winner either. If she left the haremlik, they would be apart; if he did not respect her, she would lose respect for herself.

As though he read his thoughts, he said, "You are wise as well as beautiful. You understand that neither of us can claim victory?"

She had been holding her breath without realizing it and slowly exhaled at his words. "I know."

He extended his hand, and without hesitation she placed her own within it. He looked down, silent, his dark fingers tracing her pale ones. "You have given me a gift beyond price, fair one. The gift of yourself." His gaze lifted to hers again. "I would give you a gift as precious in return."

She listened, bewildered. What could possibly compare to entering his haremlik? Her chest grew tight, and time seemed to hang on the edge of his words. Her fingers tingled where they twined within his.

His expression never wavered, but his grip tightened ever so slightly, so slightly, she might have imagined it. "I have learned there is a part of you which I cannot command or take, a part you must offer freely. I would have that part of you as well."

He rose from his throne. Still holding her hand firmly in his, he took a step toward her, the ceremonial robe swirling from the powerful set of his shoulders. "I will free you if you wish, but I ask that you stay."

He would disregard their bargain to make her happy. The knowledge filled her with tenderness. But Alessandra no longer wanted freedom. She wanted him—all of him. And that he asked her to stay willingly proved he could respect her as more than a slave.

The white turban covered his head, hiding all but his dark features from her view. His expression softened, the cold mask melting away to reveal his heart's desire. "Stay with me, Alessandra. You already have my heart, I would give you my loyalty as well." He peered down at her, his sparkling gaze reaching into her very soul. "Be my wife in the eyes of Allah and your Christian God. Be the mother of my children, if we are so blessed. I don't offer you a lifetime of slavery, but a lifetime of love."

He spoke of love… and marriage. A haze of surprised emotions assailed her, and she could do no more than gape at him.

"I love you." Bringing her hand to his lips, he pressed a gentle kiss into her palm. "I will marry you in your Christian way and devote my life to your happiness. Will it be enough?"

Marriage! It was more than she dared hope. The shadows fled her heart. She felt fully alive, blissfully complete. Tears of joy prickled at the backs of her lids, and a sound, half-sigh and half-laugh, bubbled from her lips. "You offer me everything you are, and it is more than I ever imagined."

His dark eyes caressed her, promising to fulfill her dreams. She stepped into the strong circle of his arms and raised her face to him.

He smiled, a smile that brightened the strong lines of his face, a smile filled with love. "Come with me, my beloved. We have the entire night before us." His mouth slowly descended on hers. "And our entire lives."

About the author:

Jeanie LeGendre lives in Florida with her romance-hero husband, her two darling little girls, a feisty five-pound Maltese, and two stray tabby cats who adopted the family as their own. Born into a big Italian brood, she simply adores family — her mom and sister live close by, her various aunties, uncles and cousins are all near and dear to her heart, and she considers herself blessed with the most precious friends on the planet.

*She has had a head full of romance for as long as anyone can remember — no one was surprised when she named her daughters after her favorite heroines — and believes the stories in **Secrets** really can happen. After all, she and her husband are living proof.*

The Proposal

by Ivy Landon

To my reader:
Sex of an unconventional kind for those who seek the hard to find.

"I have an important proposal I need to run by you tonight." Craig's husky voice came through Tracey Vennet's speaker phone, and the anticipation of seeing him sent a thrill down her spine.

Tracey made a note to have her secretary cancel her dinner engagement with the Japanese trade group and reschedule for next week. It was uncharacteristic of Craig not to give her more warning of his sudden arrival in town. Usually their meetings were set weeks in advance.

She kept her tone smooth and business like. "Is anything wrong?"

As president of Acton Industries, she was responsible to Craig Logan, CEO and owner of Acton, and his demands on her time took top priority. She tapped her pencil on her desk. In her mind, Craig Logan would always be first.

She'd fallen in love with him the first time they'd met during the Tinker Truck advertising campaign. While the other executives sat around the enormous conference table, Craig had taken off his jacket, rolled up his sleeves, and kneeled on the floor. With childish pleasure and intuitive genius, he'd pushed the Tinker Trucks across the carpet, scooping up imaginary piles of sand. Afterward, he'd quickly sketched his suggested design changes and diverted the necessary funding to the appropriate department.

His maverick design and her hard work on the ad campaign led to the most successful new toy on the market. When she convinced a major film company to use Tinker Trucks in their movie, sales skyrocketed, and Craig promoted Tracey to the presidency. Oddly, he left her alone to run Acton as she wished, only rarely flying in to check on his company.

Tracey looked forward to the intimate dinners in the private company dining room where she had Craig to herself. On several occasions he'd taken her to his penthouse apartment, and they'd made love on his bed overlooking the city's skyline. Their sex life might not set her ablaze with passion, but she'd always believed torrid lust a romance writer's invention. For months now, she'd hoped for a proposal that would make their arrangement more permanent.

"Nothing's wrong," Craig's voice reassured her. She could almost see the corners of his lips twitching into a teasing smile. "At least nothing we can't fix over the weekend. Are you free?"

For him, she would always be free. "I'll give my theater tickets to my mom. Unless you'd like to go?"

"Let's keep this weekend private. I don't want to see anyone but you." At his sensual tone, her heart beat accelerated a notch. She imagined him looking lazily across his desk though half-closed lids that disguised the most brilliant intellect she'd ever matched wits with. Many a businessman had been taken in by his enigmatic expression, unsuspecting of a mind that was equally comfortable reading Homer's Iliad in Greek, sketching pigeons in Central Park, or calculating the mathematical equations for high-tech computer chips.

Tracey worked through the afternoon, a special lurch of excitement urging her to clear her desk of the most pressing items. Making a short trip to the private restroom off her office three hours later, she took time to pat a few stray hairs back into her smooth jet chignon. She freshened her makeup, giving just a hint of eye shadow to blue eyes glowing with anticipation. After using her pinkie to dab on fresh lip gloss, Tracey straightened her white silk blouse and navy skirt. Not the ideal clothes for a romantic dinner, but then Craig knew she'd worked all day, and he usually seemed much more interested in what she had to say than the clothes she wore.

One of Craig's better qualities was his ability to look beneath the surface, to see more with just a glance than others saw with a telescope. And he had an uncanny knack for anticipating what might go wrong, delving straight to the heart of a problem, and fixing it before others recognized a difficulty existed. She'd trusted Craig's judgment implicitly and hoped he hadn't spotted any problems at Acton.

Craig's lighthearted hint that they could fix whatever he'd noticed cast a slight shadow of unease on Tracey's anticipation. As she walked down the staircase to the private dining room, her blood coursed through her veins in expectation.

She opened the heavy wooden doors and walked across the plush oriental carpet. She'd been in this room many times, but never before had the scent of fresh cut flowers wafted to her nostrils. Never before had the crystal chandelier been dimmed and replaced by candles on the dining table. Craig waited with a velvet jeweler's box next to gleaming silver, delicate china, and a crisp lace table cloth. A silver bucket holding a magnum of Dom Perignon on ice sat in the center of the table with two crystal flutes.

When she entered the room, Craig's face broke into a grin and he rose to his feet, his dark suit fitting his lean and tanned body to perfection. "Come in. You're early, darling. I've only been waiting fifteen minutes."

He held out his hand, and by the teasing glimmer in his dark eyes, she knew he wasn't angry. She gave his fingers a gentle squeeze and lightly brushed his cheek with her lips. "Sorry, I took a last minute phone call from our Paris office."

His eyes boldly raked her silk blouse and plain skirt. "You didn't have time to change into something more suitable for our date?"

"I was working. As it was I had to cancel the meeting with—"

He interrupted with light teasing. "Another woman would have gone shopping, ordered something delivered."

"Is it me you want?" Her eyes narrowed. "Or me in designer clothes."

His eyes twinkled. "I want you naked."

"Craig!"

He waved a hand dismissing her outrage and the sudden heat in her cheeks. "Forget it. We have more important things to discuss."

Pulling out a chair for her, he pushed the velvet box in her direction before taking a seat. When she started to open the box, his hand gently pressed down on hers, stopping her. Raising her gaze to meet his, she arched her brow in a questioning gesture.

"I'm going to ask you something important."

Her mouth went cottony dry. Were her dreams going to come true? Was Craig going to ask her to become his wife?

"Yes?" She'd never known him to be so hesitant before and thought it rather sweet.

"First, you must promise not to answer my question for at least twenty-four hours."

"But why?"

"Because the answer you give me in twenty-four hours may be different from the one you give me now."

"If this is a riddle, I don't understand."

Craig paused, then leaned forward placing both elbows on the table and resting his chin in his palms. "Do you trust me?"

At his hungry stare, her heart thumped against her ribs. "Of course, I do."

"Will you do anything I ask of you for the next twenty-four hours?"

She had absolutely no idea what he was asking her. And it was unlike him to be so vague. "Could you be more specific?"

"Will you marry me, Tracey?" As soon as the words popped out of his mouth, he pressed one finger to her lips. "Don't answer that. Not until tomorrow. Instead I'd like an answer to my first question, will you do anything I ask?"

A swell of confusion engulfed her. "Why?"

"Because our sex life is not all it should be. Because if we're going to spend the rest of our lives together, I want to do certain things for you. Please you in ways you have never imagined."

She stiffened, all her fears crashing on her in a stormy convergence of black clouds. Her hands turned to ice. He'd found her inadequate in bed. Swallowing the sudden lump in her throat, she forced the words past her lips. "You weren't satisfied when we made love?"

His eyes blazed. "That's part of it. How could I be satisfied when you didn't enjoy it?"

"But I did—"

"You enjoyed the holding, the cuddling, the talking." His tone hardened in a voice he used in the board room when he dared anyone to contradict him. "But as for the sex—you tolerated me." His hands reached across the table and gripped her shoulders. "I want to shatter your inhibitions and release your passion."

If his hands hadn't gripped her tightly, she would have slumped in her seat. At the moment she wished she could say, "Beam me up, Scotty," and a transporter would whisk her away so she didn't have to face him. She should have known he would realize she didn't enjoy sex. Not that she hated the act. Tracey just thought it was a whole lot of fuss over very little. Still she'd always felt deficient in the bedroom, and she'd been so sure love would solve her problems. Only it hadn't. She loved Craig with all her heart, but she hadn't seen stars, and if she was honest with herself, she hadn't felt much desire.

And now he wanted her to give him a blind promise—so he could crash through her inhibitions. She forced a breath of air into her starved lungs, barely realizing she'd stopped breathing. Suppose he discovered she had no passion? Suppose something was missing from her? No doubt he wanted to find out before he saddled himself to a wife.

"Think it over carefully. Once you give me your word, I'll expect total cooperation."

"You mean obedience," she snapped.

He inclined his head slightly but didn't deign to give a reply.

The pads of her fingers worried back and forth over the velvet nap of the jewelry box, too large for a ring. She wondered what it held, then realized her thoughts fluttered in indecision, preferring to dwell on anything but Craig's proposal. To allow him to order her about, to give him the power over her like a master over a slave terrified her. The thought of losing her freedom to anyone, even a man she trusted might be asking more than she could give.

Yet as she looked across the table and discerned his excitement, his exhilaration sparked her sense of adventure. If she could experience the pleasure of orgasm with this man, it would be worth any freedom she gave up. And submitting to him would only be temporary.

Taking another deep breath, she nodded. "I'll do anything you ask for twenty-four hours."

She expected a smile of triumph. Instead his eyes glittered with excitement, and his face softened, aiming a quiver of fear at her heart. Somehow she knew that after today their relationship would never again be the same. After today he might never want to see her again, and yet, she'd never forgive herself if she didn't try with everything she had to keep this man.

"This calls for a toast." Craig popped the cork of the champagne and poured her a glass.

Looking deeply into her eyes over the rim of the bubbling wine, he clinked her glass with his. "To passion."

"To love."

The fizzy drink quenched her parched throat. Uneasily she set down her glass, waiting for what he'd do next.

Craig nodded toward the velvet box. "Open it."

She lifted the lid and sucked in her breath. A golden choker at least two inches wide and set with sparkling diamonds and sapphires rested elegantly in the velvet box. "It's gorgeous."

"The blue stones reminded me of the dark cobalt in your eyes," he admitted. "Come here and I'll latch it for you."

She did as he asked, turning her back. The gold choker settled about her neck, and she raised her chin to prevent the diamonds from scratching her. The clasp snapped shut with a click, the necklace fitting her as if custom made.

"How does it look?" She turned around for him to admire.

"It's perfect. The necklace will remind you of your promise. There's only one problem."

She swallowed hard, realizing the beautiful necklace suddenly seemed too tight about her neck. And somehow she knew he'd make her wear the necklace for the next twenty-four hours as a constant reminder of their bargain. "What's the problem?"

"Your blouse is blocking my view. Would you remove it, please?"

Her pulse raced. Although the elegant dining room was private, anyone could enter at any time. "But the waiter—"

"Has been told to knock."

"He could forget."

Craig didn't say another word. He strode across the room and slid the bolt home with a loud metallic clunk, locking them in privacy. Then he folded his arms across his broad chest and waited in silence, the light of anticipation in his eyes.

She inwardly quailed at the idea of submitting to his request. Craig had never even seen her in a swim suit, and although they'd made love several times, the room had been pitch black; she'd insisted on it, and he'd gone along with her wishes.

Until now.

As her hand went to the first button, her fingers trembled. The gold collar forced her chin up, and as she undid one button after another then slipped off her blouse, she watched Craig's lips break into a grin of delight. The cool air on the bare flesh of her shoulders and midriff gave her goose bumps, or was it due to his hot look?

Standing before him clad only in her bra and skirt made her stomach clench. But when she realized how much he enjoyed looking at her, she forced herself not to squirm.

"In the candlelight, your skin has a pearly luminescence. Please remove your bra next."

Next? Her heart slammed into her ribs with the force of a freight train. Next, implied he might ask her to remove every stitch of clothing. Her knees felt like they might buckle at any moment and despite her promise she didn't know if she could continue.

If Craig sensed her hesitation, he gave no indication of it. He returned to his seat and poured them another glass of champagne. However the moment her hands went to undo the clasp his gaze pierced her with a fierce brilliance, and she had to remind herself she'd agreed to this. The air-conditioning cycled on, and the cool air from the overhead vent tingled on her bared breasts. She had the urge to raise her hands and cover herself to stop his bold gaze from raking her. But she refrained from such a childish gesture.

Nor did she dwell on how she wished her bosom was bigger. Watching Craig's face, she reminded herself this was the man she loved, the man she intended to marry. There was nothing wrong with him staring at her bare breasts. So why did her insides feel so tight?

"You're lovely. Later I'm going to explore every inch of you. I'm going to caress you, and nibble."

At his words, heat rose from her breasts, up her neck, over her shoulders.

"Place your clothes, there." He gestured to a basket. "And then come have dinner before it gets cold.

Relief washed over her when he didn't ask her to remove her skirt. Still, she'd never done anything more difficult than fulfilling his request of sitting across the table from him while she remained exposed.

His hands removed silver platter covers and the mouth-watering scents of conch-and-shrimp fritters, a West Indian soup, and stuffed Cornish game hen wafted to her nostrils. She snapped open her linen napkin and placed it over her lap while Craig filled her plate.

If he'd ignored her lack of attire, eating might have been easier. But his gaze slid from her eyes to her shoulders to her breasts repeatedly. Her stomach tightened, and she couldn't eat a bite.

Apparently the view whetted his appetite. And while she sipped her wine, he ate and ate. Finally he stopped his fork half-way to his mouth. "Short of returning your clothes, is there anything I can do to make you more comfortable?"

"You could remove your shirt," she suggested. At least maybe then she wouldn't feel so underdressed.

Lowering his fork, he grinned. "Ah, perhaps my plan is already working if you're so anxious for me to undress."

He unknotted his tie and unfastened the buttons of his shirt in a prolonged strip tease. Suddenly her hunger returned, and she placed a forkful of delicious shrimp into her mouth, chewed, and swallowed.

"Don't think I'm anxious to see your bare chest, Craig Logan. I merely thought that what's good for the goose is good for the gander."

Craig grinned nonchalantly. "Uh-huh. Do you feel less vulnerable now?"

She raised her gaze from her plate and took in the sight of his muscular torso. Like his face and hands, his torso sported a golden tan. Light swirls of hair decorated his chest in a v-shape, spreading from nipple to nipple, then tapering to his flat stomach. Tracey gave up all pretense at eating.

Instead she watched him, watched his shoulders flex as he cut his food, watched the muscles ripple, and remembered the feel of him in bed. His body was very different from hers. He'd been right in thinking she liked the cuddling and caressing, she'd thought she might have felt something when he held her, but it disappeared when they'd made love.

He wiped his mouth with his napkin, then dropped it into his lap. "I thought after we marry you would live with me. Give up your job."

"But I like it here."

"Acton Industries is only one part of the empire. You can travel from company to company with me. There's more than enough work for both of us."

"Your people would think I earned the position in bed."

He shot her a devilish grin. "That remains to be seen. Come here." He patted his lap.

She stood and took a step in his direction, suddenly very aware of her swaying breasts.

"It's time for dessert. You can remove the rest of your clothes."

Knowing he'd intended to ask it of her didn't make the doing any easier. "Why?"

"Because I asked it of you. Need I remind you of your promise or that we are totally alone? No one can enter. The door's locked."

She placed her hands on her hips. "What makes you think this is going to work?"

"Have you ever known one of my plans to fail?" A mocking glimmer of satisfaction crossed his arrogant expression.

"But—"

"Relax. There's no bed in this room. I'm hardly going to rape you. In fact, we aren't going to make love."

"We aren't?" Surprise and relief mingled with her confusion, the tension inside her easing a bit.

"Am I shocking you?" his husky voice rasped.

She nodded.

"Good. Then my plan is working. Take those off."

As she complied, the zipper's noise seemed unusually loud. Her heart thudded in her chest.

"The panties and hose too."

She hooked her fingers under the elastic and lowered the panties and hose over her hips. Tracey turned to sit and finish the job but a mischievous smile on his lips told her he wouldn't let her off so easily.

He pointed to a spot four feet from the table and well within the candlelight's glimmer. "Stand there."

His crisp order shot a sizzle of electricity through her. No one had ever spoken to her in that demanding tone, expecting complete obedience, and she suddenly wondered what he would do if she changed her mind.

One look at his face, and she didn't dare ask. He appeared more determined than she could ever recall, and a tiny spurt of fear mixed with a sudden agitation.

Slowly, she walked to the spot he'd indicated. He moved his chair back from the table slightly to have a better look. When she began to slip the garment past her hips, he helped himself to some coffee.

"Turn around."

Her face burned. "Excuse me?"

"I want to watch your bottom when you bend over."

"I don't think—"

"Do it."

She spun around, almost losing her balance and blinking back a tear. This wasn't her idea of a good time. For one thing, heat flushed over her face, and she thought she'd choke on the embarrassment. As she bent over to roll the hose down her legs, she imagined his stare, and her bottom felt hot.

"Come here," he repeated his voice soft now and sympathetic. She longed to run across the four feet separating them, fling herself against his chest, so he would stop staring.

As she neared, his nostrils flared, and beads of perspiration dotted his brow. She saw how her body aroused him, and the heady thought washed away her embarrassment, leaving a feeling of power in its wake. She might be the one standing without clothes, but obviously he was the one having difficulty mastering his desire.

She slipped onto his lap and wound her arms around his neck. His hand reached for a fresh strawberry, dipped it in melted chocolate and a dab of whipped cream before bringing it to her lips.

She opened her mouth and lapped off the cream, licked at the chocolate, then sank her teeth into the fresh berry. "Delicious."

"And you don't even have a smidgeon of sexual desire, do you?"

"No," she told him, ignoring the bevy of butterflies in her stomach. "Why do you think that is?"

"Perhaps you need an extra stimulus to get you started, to get you thinking in the right direction." He flipped her until she lay belly down across his lap. With the tips of his fingers, he traced light, circling motions across her elevated bottom.

She twisted back to look at him. "What are you doing?"

One powerful hand pushed the small of her back until her hands touched the floor. Blood rushed to her head, but suddenly all she could think of was her bottom, high in the air, and she wriggled in an attempt to get free.

In the struggle, her legs parted, and his hand slipped between her thighs. She gasped as his hand cupped her. Although he'd tried many times, saying he could please her, he'd only touched her there once before, and she'd been so miserable she'd begged him not to.

"You're dry," he commented as if she could be otherwise. "Haven't I been patient with you?"

"Yes."

"And it got us nowhere, don't you agree?"

"Yes."

"So now it's time to try something different." His hand slipped from between her legs and made tiny caressing circles with his palm over the crease of her bottom.

Fright made her voice rise. "What are you going to do?"

"Smack your bottom. Make the skin hot."

She squirmed in earnest, her buttocks clenched tight. "No, Craig. I'm not into pain."

"This won't hurt. Not a lot. Just lots of little slaps to stimulate you."

Her feet kicked, and she tried to twist off his lap. "Don't do this. I won't like it."

"Do you have any idea how the sight of your pert bottom turned up and struggling is making me feel?"

She didn't need him to answer. His arousal against her lower belly spoke volumes. "This won't work."

He smacked her. Her back arched in surprise more than pain. She'd been so sure she could talk him out of it.

His open hand smacked her in seven or eight lightly stinging blows. He hit her high across the crests, along her hips, down low on the curve of her buttocks.

She kicked wildly and then realized he'd stopped.

"Did I hurt you?" he asked. "Your skin is this delicate shade of pink."

"Of course you hurt me."

"What about now? Does it still hurt?"

She shoved on the floor with her hands, trying to get up, but he held her firm, forcing her to answer his question. She hated to admit it, but, probably because she had so much padding on her bottom, the area no longer stung.

"I feel hot," she admitted.

"Where?"

"Where you hit me," she snapped irritably.

Despite her efforts to clamp her thighs tight, his hand slipped between them. "And what about where I didn't hit you?"

Tracey couldn't believe it, couldn't deny the wetness his hand discovered between her legs. "Noooo!" she cried out, unwilling to believe she was so peculiar that pain could produce pleasure.

"Yes. Stand up," he ordered, giving her an extra smack on the bottom when she didn't scramble up fast enough to suit him. One light whack ignited her oh-so-sensitive nerve endings, sending molten lava coursing through her veins.

She stood as he'd asked of her, more stunned with her own reaction than by the fact he'd actually spanked her. He remained in his chair and pulled her onto his lap, settling her legs apart and dangling on either side of his hips. "Put your arms around my neck."

As soon as she placed her hands, he resettled her so her smarting bottom hung in the air between his spread thighs. Never in her life had she felt so open, vulnerable, hot. A mist of perspiration broke out on her brow. The air conditioner failed to keep up with the heat Craig aroused in her. She had no idea what he intended to do next, and the anticipation made her jumpy.

"Look at me."

She forced her gaze up to his face, afraid she might see disgust, but his warm eyes sparkled with amusement. His mouth twitched up at one corner. "Tell me how you feel right now."

"Ashamed. Embarrassed that you did this to me and are laughing at me."

"Wrong. First, there is nothing to be ashamed of. Any private behavior that is mutually pleasing by two consenting adults is acceptable behavior in my book. Second, there is nothing odd, peculiar, or strange about you. Pain didn't arouse you."

"Then what did?"

"A combination of two things." He reached up with his finger and tapped her head. "Your brain is the most sensitive sexual organ. And you love me."

He might be trying to make her feel better by explaining her odd reaction away with theories that were mere conjecture, but she knew differently. She'd loved Craig for a long time, and her body had never responded like this. Even now his hands traced tiny circles along the insides of her thighs, and she ached to rub her breasts against his chest. "But—"

"Heat from my slaps aroused you. The light smacks brought blood rushing to the area. And now that you're so sensitive, one or two whacks will bring the warmth back."

Craig leaned forward slightly, his arm reaching between her thighs to her exposed bottom. "And I now have your complete attention." He hit each cheek lightly.

Her lips parted in a gasp. She could think of nothing but what he was doing to her, what he would do next. The sting dissolved into waves of heat carried on a tide of excitement, swelling her breasts.

Tracey wriggled, attempting to press her nipples against Craig. His hands rested lightly on her hips, preventing her from attaining her goal of hugging him. "We aren't finished talking yet." Her eyes widened in surprise and alarm. Her nipples tightened into hard, aching little points. "You want to talk?"

He moved his fingers in ever-smaller circles up the insides of her thighs. "I am merely pleased by your excitement."

She would have dropped her head but the collar prevented that. Instead, somewhere past the vicinity of his left ear, she picked a spot on the wall to stare at.

"Don't look away. I want to see your eyes when I put my finger inside you."

His black stare bored into hers. And she waited for his finger to invade her body. And waited. Tensing. When she felt nothing, she began to drop her gaze to see where he'd put his hands.

With surprise, she discovered exactly where he'd put one hand. He gave her bottom four short whacks. "Look at me. Don't look away again."

Her bottom ached, searing hotter than before. And the heat spread, and suddenly she released a flow of wet, slick, heat between her thighs. She recognized the reaction for what it was—desire.

Arching her back, she thrust her breasts toward his mouth. Her hips gyrated seemingly on their own volition.

"Don't move. Tell me what you want."

"Please, Craig. I've never felt like this before. Make love to me before I lose this delicious feeling."

"You aren't ready."

Tracey choked back a sob of frustration. Delicious tingling sensations prickled her skin. Craig had kindled a fire in her belly and the sparks blew and caught, firing her imagination at new possibilities. He'd made her feel wanting, yearning, raw need.

Was there nothing this man couldn't do? A surge of love for him rose up in her throat so she wasn't expecting his tender gaze to turned decisive. The waiting was over. The tip of his finger slipped inside her, and her muscles clenched around him, silently asking for more.

"Kiss me, please," she whispered, knowing if he complied, she could press herself against his chest.

He didn't insert his fingertip farther, but his thumb parted her folds. "Not until you whimper. And don't think of faking it. I'll know the difference."

She opened her legs wider in encouragement. Why did he have to take so damn long? When his thumb flicked over her most sensitive spot, she almost leapt off his lap.

"Be still. Close your eyes now."

His fingers continued their magic, creating a hollowness inside her. She discovered the sensations seemed more intense without visual distractions. Without conscious thought, her hips gyrated in an attempt to take his finger deeper inside her.

Whack! Smack! She received two hard slaps on her bottom for her futile effort to hurry him. Either this time he'd hit her harder than previously, or her already stinging skin was becoming more sensitive.

She expected him to continue the fiery caresses between her legs but he didn't. With her eyes closed, she tensed, waiting to see what he would do. Longing to open them, she didn't dare, wanting to avoid any more spankings. Her bottom already felt hot enough to set her panties on fire—that is if Craig ever let her wear panties again. After the way she reacted to him, she wouldn't be surprised if he wanted ready access to her bottom at all times. One thing about Craig, when he found a method that worked, he—

"Oh my, God!" she gasped when his mouth found her breast.

"It's much too late for prayers." He chuckled, his breath teasing her erect nipple. His tongue circled her other breast, shooting quivers of liquid heat to her loins. "Do you like this?"

"Yes. No. I don't know."

He leaned back then, and pushed her thighs wider apart. "Would you care to explain your last three sentences." The amusement in his voice had ceased to make her blush. Her reactions had gone far beyond blushing, far beyond embarrassment, to discover a sweet, aching fire that needed to be doused.

"Every time you touch me, I want more. But no matter what you do, it isn't enough."

"Good."

Startled by the concept that he thought her frustration was good, her eyelids flew open. When she spied his cocked brow, she remembered she'd just forgotten the spanks she would pay for not following his orders. "Remember I owe you several pats on your bottom. I'll claim them at my leisure." And he always collected on debts. Clearly Craig didn't intend to discipline her now. He preferred to keep her guessing, off balance, aching for him to touch her.

"Please, stand up."

Her legs shook underneath her, but she did what he asked. When he stood and took her hand, leading her across the room, she breathed a sigh of relief. With the door locked, they could make love on the plush leather couch. She was positive it wasn't the first time the cozy room had been used for such purposes, although she doubted anyone else scented the room with fresh cut flowers and flooded it with candlelight.

Her heart skipped three beats when he led her to one end of the couch. Several boxes stood stacked by one side, and she turned to look up at him with some confusion. Didn't he know that right now she wanted him, not presents? Didn't he know she was doing everything in her power not tackle him onto that couch and tear off his clothes?

"I'd like you to put on everything you find in those boxes while I'm gone."

"You're leaving me!"

"I'm glad you'll miss me, but I'll only leave you for a few minutes. The last packages didn't arrive but a messenger promised to deliver them to the front desk." Craig scooped up her shoes and clothes. "You won't be needing these."

She sprinted across the room to him in a panic. "Wait! You can't leave me here without any clothes."

"Are you going back on your promise?" he asked softly, his eyes focused on her heaving breasts. "I'll lock you in. No one else has a key."

"But suppose there's a fire?" she wailed, unable to keep her unhappiness from her voice at the sudden turn of events. She'd expected to be on that couch with her legs wrapped around him, feelings sensations she'd never experienced. Instead he intended to lock her in the private dining room without a stitch to wear.

Craig shrugged into his shirt and fastened the buttons, then slung his jacket over his shoulder, refusing to even leave her that. "There's only going to be one fire. The one building inside you. While I'm gone, I'll expect certain things. One. Don't think of relieving your sexual frustration by your own hand. Two, I expect you to be wearing every item in those boxes, and Tracey—"

She swallowed hard. "Yes?"

He grinned, and his gaze boldly raked over her still-hard nipples. "When the lock clicks and the door opens, I expect you to be posing seductively."

"But aren't we going to make love?"

"I already told you, we wouldn't. Not here. Not now. Remember, when this door opens, you'd better—"

"I know, be posing seductively," she replied petulantly.

His hand smacked her bottom lightly. "Don't disappoint me."

Damn. Damn. Damn! As he locked her in the room, she swore silently, calling him every foul name she remembered. Why had he spoiled her mood? The precious feeling of arousal he'd worked so carefully to create vanished in smoke.

How dare he build up her expectations, then dash her hopes? Why was he even making her go through all this if he didn't intend to make love to her?

She kicked at the boxes in fury, toppling them over. One of the boxes opened and a pair of black stiletto-heeled shoes fell out. A rush of excitement filled her, replacing the anger. Perhaps he'd left her clothes after all. Unable to sit on her sore bottom without wincing, she knelt and opened the other packages. One-by-one, she withdrew luxurious, sensual garments, lace silk thigh-highs from France, a butter-soft black leather bustier, and thong leather panties.

Knowing she'd delayed too long, and Craig could return at any moment, she quickly rolled the silk hose over her calves, past her knees until they hugged her thighs. The thong-backed panties felt strange with the tiny piece of material clinging to the crease of her rear. As soon as she shrugged into the bustier, she realized what she hadn't seen in the dim light. The strapless cups didn't cover her nipples, but served to lift her breasts to beg for a man's attention. When she slipped into the elegant heels, her breasts lifted higher to compensate. The clothes Craig had picked out enhanced her nudity, and she understood that bare flesh was more modest than what he'd asked her to wear for him.

Tracey had delayed thinking about the inevitable but could put if off no longer. If Craig unlocked that door right now, she wouldn't be able to assume the seductive pose he'd asked for quickly enough to fool him that she'd been waiting. He wanted her seductively dressed, posed, and ready for him when he walked through that door.

Sitting on the couch or chair was out of the question. That left, kneeling—out of the question—standing, or draping herself upon the couch. If she chose the couch, she'd have to settle on her side or stomach. She considered the possibilities for a moment and wondered if he'd consider them sexy. She'd hate him looking down at her and decided to remain on her feet, facing the door.

Perhaps if she enticed him, she could even change his mind about making love. Tracey bent one knee, turned her hips, slightly and lifted her chin, wanting to see Craig's expression when he walked through the door. Odd how she didn't consider disobeying him, realizing she was having too much fun.

As she stood waiting in anticipation, her discovery that her feelings of arousal hadn't disappeared after all sent another flood of excitement washing over her. Since she hadn't been satisfied, the sensations surged back with surprising strength, and she wondered if she should have chosen the couch.

Too late to move. The soft tread of footsteps outside the door alerted her to Craig's presence. The lock clicked, and she stood straighter, tilting her chin to avoid the diamonds on the necklace.

The dancing light in Craig's eyes when he spotted her more than made up for her hesitancy, and a toasty thrill of exhilaration ricocheted from her breasts to her core. As he crossed the room toward her, his voice turned husky. "Don't move. You're gorgeous."

She trembled at his compliment, taking pleasure in his enjoyment of her newfound bravery. While wearing such exotic under garments, she couldn't help but think of where he'd touched her and how. Her exposed bottom, tilted high due to the heels, throbbed with a pleasurable tingle. As Craig walked around her slowly, her breasts ached for his caress.

His gaze stroked every inch of her, and her stomach tightened in expectation. What would he do next?

"Hold still," he ordered, at the same time taking her hand. From his pocket, he removed another velvet box, snapped open the lid and removed a bracelet to match the diamond and gold collar around her neck. This time when he clicked the clasp tight, she welcomed another symbol of his love.

"It's beautiful," she murmured.

"Not half as lovely as you. I'd like to sketch you like that. Then I'll never forget this moment."

Heat rose to her cheeks. Tracey didn't need a visual reminder to remember. She'd never forget the dark, dilated glimmer in Craig's eyes. Or the way the candlelight glinted off his high cheekbones, a tiny muscle twitching in his jaw. His jacket emphasized his squared shoulders, his proud carriage, his determination to sketch her.

Yet it was one thing to pose for his gaze alone but entirely another for him to commit what he saw to paper. And with the heat boiling inside her, she didn't know if she could remain still while he sent sizzling glances her way.

"I don't think—"

Opening his briefcase, he removed pad and pencil. "Don't argue. I have to sketch you. It'll just take a few minutes."

Pages rustled. He pulled up a chair in front of her, and she stiffened, suddenly uncomfortable with his nearness. He was close, so close she could feel the heat of his breath, hear him suck the pencil's eraser in deep concentration. Then she imagined his lips on her breasts and relaxed.

"That's better. Relax. Think of something besides sex," he teased.

If only she could. She watched his hands sketching in circles and recalled his fingers caressing the insides of her thighs. She'd wanted more. For the first time in her life, need, like grains of sand piled one atop another built a fragile castle of desire. Waves surged inside her, washing up more sand until she thought she would topple from the pressure. She shifted a bit, squirming at the realization that only Craig could satisfy her—and he had no intention of doing so.

From his position on the chair, Craig leaned forward and gripped the elastic panty band at her hips. He tugged her panties higher so the band no longer was horizonal but formed a deep V. As her flesh tingled, her lips parted in surprise. She could barely stand still with the exquisite sensations racing through her. Her breasts swelled. She wanted him—wanted him now.

"Yes. That expression is delightful. Don't move or I'll have to start over."

"Please Craig. Hurry."

"I'm almost done."

She no longer cared what he would do with his drawing. Her flesh had become so sensitive, his every glance darting a ripple of need through her until she almost writhed where she stood.

"All done." Craig's pleased smile drew her like a magnet, and she hurried to his side, pretending to want to look at her picture when she wanted him to touch her, take her. Every nerve ending screamed for release.

He turned the picture so she could see, stopping her forward progress before she reached him. "What do you think?"

It took a moment to recognize the sensual creature staring back at her. Craig drew only her face, with her eyes wide, her lips slightly parted. A raw sensuality dominated the drawing, making her more beautiful than any mirror. "Is that how you see me?"

"That's how you look."

He led her over to a mirror. She walked across the room and the panties slipped back and forth over sensitive areas. While she stared at the strange woman in the mirror, Craig came up behind her, and his hands cupped her breasts, flicking her nipples.

She squirmed, trying to face him. If she could have clawed off his clothes she would have done so. But when she attempted to turn, he tugged lightly on her nipples, effectively holding her in place.

"Look at your face, the full bloom of sexual excitement. I find your passion, your sexiness exciting."

She leaned her back to his chest and his arousal nestled against the crease of her rear. His face wore the expression of a hunter about to sight prey. And all the while his thumbs flicked her nipples, shooting tiny shocks inside her.

She had to have him. Knowing he found her so desirable set her hips wriggling against him. She received two light smacks on her bottom for her efforts. The sting brought back hot aching need.

"Please Craig, enough. Don't make me beg."

He took pity on her then, only not the way she wished for, gesturing to a chair by the door. "Put that on, and we'll go."

While he carefully put the sketch in his briefcase, she hurried to the chair, hoping the clothes would be decent. As she pulled the exquisite Chanel lace-over-silk cocktail dress from the tissue paper in the box, she sucked in her breath in appreciation, sorry she'd doubted him for a moment.

Like the other garments, the dress fit as if custom made. And although the strapless black left her shoulders bare, it would have been perfect for a night at the opera.

After she slipped the dress over her scandalous under garments, Craig picked up his coat and held out an arm to her. "That's how I want to think of you. Cool and discreet, a lady on the outside. And your insides are a bubbling cauldron with needs and fantasies only I can fulfill."

They walked through the lobby of the building, past the doorman, and no one suspected she was on fire for Craig's touch. Her jutting breasts, her stinging bottom, the tight panties wouldn't let her forget her newly awakened sensuality—not for one moment.

Craig opened the car door for her, and she gingerly settled into the seat. When he flipped the back of her skirt up, she gasped in surprise. The bare skin of her bottom rested on the cool leather, soothing her stinging flesh, yet another reminder of the evening ahead.

He drove to his apartment in silence, one hand on her knee, drawing indolent circles, a maddening hint of what might come next. He placed his hand on her waist as they walked the steps into his apartment building, and her blood simmered at the contact.

She couldn't wait to reach the privacy of his apartment and remove her clothes. With every step, her skirt swished against her bare bottom, her panties teased flesh aching for Craig's special brand of attention, and the tips of her breasts grew taut.

She had never been so aware of her body. She could think only of Craig, wanting him, needing him, hoping he would soon satisfy her need.

After a swift elevator ride to the penthouse, Craig unlocked the door and held it open wide. She grinned in delight at his new decor. Hundreds of bright neon helium balloons nestled against cantilevered ceilings. He'd strung a banner of glittering silver coins across the room. Gold kruggerands spelled the words, "Marry Me, Tracey."

Stained glass lamps emitted a soft glowing ambience, and the scent of jasmine wafted to her through the twelve-foot glass doors that framed the city's skyline and led to the balcony. Candles lit the hallway, and her gaze followed a path of rose petals to the bedroom.

He'd gone to so much trouble to make this night special and warm feelings of love made a lump rise in her throat. "Oh Craig, how romantic."

"There's a present for you on the sofa," he murmured huskily.

"But you've already given me the necklace and the bracelet."

"I intend to spoil you. Let me enjoy it."

She hurried into the living room, threading her way between the strings dangling from the balloons. Another jewelry box. She opened it, half expecting a pin or matching earrings to the exquisite pieces he'd already given her. But two delicate chains of diamonds were inside, each with a gold key, one set with rubies, the other emeralds.

Puzzled she turned to face him for an explanation. He'd strode across the thick carpet in silence and dropped to his knees at her feet. Taking the chain of diamonds, he snapped one onto each of her ankles. "These are the keys to my heart."

The collar around her neck, the bracelet on her wrist, and now the diamonds with the tiny dangling keys from her ankles marked her as his. She reveled in the special moment, knowing meeting him was the best thing that had ever happened to her.

If she lost him, it would be like losing a part of her soul. And as much as she wanted to make love with him, she feared she might disappoint him. Her stomach clenched. This time would be different. Craig would see to it. All she had to do was follow his directions and trust him.

Craig rose to his feet with the grace of a cat, and turned on his CD. Upbeat music flooded the room. "Would you like to dance?"

"Yes."

Craig grinned hot enough to ignite a brush fire. "You're overdressed."

She gave him a flirtatious wink and turned around so he could help with her zipper. His fingers grazed her neck, throwing a switch that jolted flutters of excitement through her. After the dress pooled around her feet, she began to step out of it.

"Don't move," he ordered.

She remained standing with her back to him, and he planted tiny kisses on her neck and shoulders. His fingers unfastened the leather bustier. Her breasts sprang free, aching and swollen for his touch. Craig's hands went to her hair, pulling out the pins holding her neat chignon in place.

"While we sit across the board room table, I imagine taking your hair down as you stand pliant and ready to do my bidding."

At his words, reminding her she'd agreed to obey his every wish, a shiver of fear made her quiver. As lock after lock fell against her shoulders, teasing the peaks of her breasts, her legs trembled.

"What is it you wish me to do?" she asked hesitantly.

"Answer me truthfully. Is your bottom still hot?"

"Warm." She suddenly recalled how he always collected on his debts, and she tensed her bare bottom that was conveniently turned toward him.

He pulled off her panties. "Not hot?"

"Warm," she repeated, refusing to let him intimidate her.

Craig patted her rear. "Bend over and pick up your clothes. Do it slowly."

The undercurrent of tension was strong enough to drown an Olympic swimmer. She stood in the middle of his living room for all intent and purposes naked, while he remained fully dressed. From his words, she expected his hand to strike her. As she bent over, she offered him a prime target. But she no longer required a slap to stimulate her arousal. Just the thought of what he might do combined with the memories of what he'd done and what he still might do to her brought waves of desire surging up from the deepest pool of her emotions.

She retrieved her clothes without Craig so much as touching her, and yet every yearning cell in her body acted as if it craved his touch. She wanted his hands caressing her breasts, her sensitive rear, assuaging the ache between her thighs. She longed to turn around and throw herself into his arms. Instead she placed her clothes on the back of the couch.

His hands spun her, and before she caught her breath, his lips claimed hers; at the same time he danced her around the room. As he hungrily kissed her, her head spun. She clung to him for support, closed her eyes, and floated on the savory sensations.

She tried to press her breasts to his chest, but he prevented this with an unyielding hand on her waist, allowing only their mouths to touch. He tasted of mint, and wine, and pure maleness. His steps became faster, bolder, and she opened her eyes to find herself dancing down the hallway of rose petals into his bedroom.

Soft indirect lighting cast his king-sized bed in shadows. Champagne rested in a silver ice bucket on the night table. Black silk sheets with matching pillows and an Italian lacquered headboard dominated the room.

"Take off your shoes," he instructed, and she gladly kicked off her high heels, leaving herself clad in the stockings with his jewelry around her throat, wrists, and ankles.

"Climb into bed," he invited.

She scrambled onto the cool, crisp sheets. Finally, he would stop teasing her and give her what she wanted. But then she turned around to find him at the foot of the bed staring at her, and she wasn't sure of anything.

She had to remind herself this was the same man who had strewn rose petals across the room. He seemed taller and sexier, more domineering, more sure of himself than she'd ever seen him before. When he didn't undress, a shiver of anticipation made her both eager and hesitant. She lowered her gaze in confusion. "What about you?"

"Lie back and bring your knees to your chest," he ordered.

She shimmied onto her back, and brought her knees to her chest, keenly aware of his scrutiny. Keeping her features deceptively composed, she glanced at his mocking smile and saw she hadn't fooled him for a moment. He was well aware of her unease but would accept nothing but her total obeyance.

"Now point your feet at the ceiling and support the backs of your calves with your hands."

"But—"

"Do it," he snapped. "Open your legs wider."

From between her parted legs, she watched him standing at the foot of her bed while she held herself open and ready for him. The position he demanded lifted her bottom off the sheets, exposed everything to his gaze, left her open, vulnerable, wanton.

He'd made her feel both decadent and like a lowly beggar. She was comfortable but miserable, alternately flushing hot with embarrassment and anger, then alternately eager for him to do something, anything to end this prolonged waiting. Within a few minutes she'd ceased thinking of anything except the burning ache between her thighs.

Craig removed his clothes slowly, walking around the room, yet always returning to stare at her. Each time he neared, she tensed. Finally the mattress at the foot of the bed sagged, and he kneeled between her widespread feet.

She'd never thought a man could look so beautiful. Craig's wide chest tapered to a rock-hard stomach. But his erection held her attention. He was large, thick, and more than ready. She wanted to touch him, to taste him, to urge him to take her.

He ignored her spread thighs and caressed her breasts. She groaned in disappointment. Damn him for never giving her what she wanted. He made her present herself to him then refused to take what she offered. His calculated teasing would soon drive her mad.

"Is there something you'd like?" he murmured, his tongue tracing a path between her breast and naval.

"Make love to me."

"You aren't ready yet."

"I am," she insisted, wiggling to brush against him.

"You're not even close. We're going to do this my way. You have no say when we begin. No say in what we do. No say in when we stop. You have to remember only one thing."

She could barely think, barely speak. "And what is that?"

"To remember the promise you made me."

His fingers parted the sensitive folds of skin between her thighs. If only he would ease the pressure building inside her. She gasped in disappointment when only cold air touched her there. "I didn't give you permission to torture me."

"Ah, but you did."

Craig sat back on his heels. "I'm going to hold you on the brink between pain and pleasure."

She shook her head, her hair twisting wildly on the pillow. "No."

"Yes. Now close your eyes."

The sheets rustled and the mattress sprang back then sagged once more under his weight. An ice cold droplet landed on her breast, and she jerked. He must have taken an ice cube from the bucket. As his warm tongue lapped away the cold, she sighed in pleasure and lost track of her thoughts.

Another drop fell on her bottom lip, and he sucked it away, ignoring her attempt to get him to kiss her mouth once more. The constant waiting and reminders they would do this his way or not at all strung her tight with tension. Cold drops fell on the inside of her thigh, and dripped toward her center, but he lapped them away without satisfying the aching need there.

He found her toes, her eyelids, her earlobe, and he spent several minutes on the hollow of her neck until she wanted to scream. Her breath came in shallow pants, and tiny animal whimpers came from the back of her throat.

"Craig, Please, I can't take any more."

"You don't have a choice. You are mine tonight to do with as I please."

An icy droplet trickled across her bottom, and his mouth teased and taunted, never landing where she wished. Her nipples hardened into points. Her blood hammered in her ears.

His fingers opened her wider, and he slipped a sliver of ice inside her. Despite her determination to obey his every command, her thighs attempted to squeeze closed, but his hands on her knees prevented her from squirming away. Then his breath found her, and his tongue stoked a heat hot enough to melt a polar icecap.

As he kept his promise, keeping her on the verge of pleasure, every muscle clenched, relentlessly building, hammering away at the last of her inhibitions. At any moment she would shatter. Every nerve ending would fire.

Her fingers dug into her thighs. Her skin prickled. She was about to explode.

But he pulled back. Damn him! How could he do this to her? She barely controlled a sob of frustration.

"Turn over."

She opened her eyes, thinking the world would spin as crazily as her thrumming thoughts. He'd piled the pillows high on the bed, one atop the other. "On your hands and knees, woman."

He guided her shaking limbs until she lay belly down over the mound of pillows, her bottom raised high. He didn't demand she close her eyes, but she still couldn't see him.

"Grab the posts of the head board and don't let go."

Raising her arms up, she clenched the cool, lacquered headboard, wondering if he intended to take her from behind. They'd never tried this position, and she wasn't sure she—

Whack. Smack. His hand struck her bottom several times in quick succession. The unexpectedness of his spanking after his tender teasing brought a violent clenching in her belly. Desire whirled over her like a tornado, the heat from his stinging slaps raising her temperature to a fever pitch.

She lost control of her thoughts—to a place of instinctive feeling. Her hips bucked, and he held the small of her back firm with his hand while his knees kept her thighs from clamping shut to try and ease her savage yearning.

His fingers slipped into the warm, wet, folds of her flesh and teased until only his firm hold on her prevented her from writhing onto the floor. Without warming, her body clutched tight, releasing the pent up tension in a magical flow of pleasure.

For a moment, she relaxed thinking she'd stolen the pleasure he'd denied her. But his fingers never stopped, and her muscles went taut again. The feeling was akin to climbing a mountain, and though she'd slipped back a pace or two, his fingers urged her relentlessly onward, barely giving her time to breathe.

A fine film of perspiration broke out on her flesh, and she tried to turn, grab him. She received a slap on her bottom, and he pressed her relentlessly back down onto the pillows.

"What are you doing?" she screamed. "I can't—"

"You can and you will."

Her hips moved up and down of their own accord. He knelt between her legs and rubbed his erection along her sensitive flesh. She screamed and bucked. A tiny orgasm gave her a momentary release. Not enough.

"Don't stop. More," she gasped.

"No more." He pulled away. "Are you thirsty? Would you like a drink?"

She barely heard his words through her dazed frenzy. He couldn't stop. Not now. Not when she needed him more than her next breath.

But he seemed immune to what he'd done to her. He helped her off the pillows and placed her on the edge of the mattress with her knees folded beneath her. Then he handed her a glass of champagne. Her eyes widened at the ring in the bottom of the glass. She plucked it out, and he placed it on her left hand, her only remaining limb that wasn't marked by a piece of jewelry.

"Your engagement ring."

She barely looked at the diamond. She wanted him badly enough to attempt raping him—not that he'd let her. He'd made it more than clear who was in charge. She would be the one submitting, and she didn't know whether or not she could take any more.

And yet Tracey had never felt so sensual in her life. His refusal to give her a choice had freed her from all responsibility for her actions. She could simply react, without guilt, without worry, without humiliation. How had he known she would respond so passionately? As she sipped the champagne, she trembled at the pent up sensations coursing through her.

She needed to walk, shake it off.

As if reading her mind, Craig smoothed the hair off her forehead, then cupped her chin, forcing her to look up at him. His dark eyes turned smokey. "Part your knees wide."

While she did what she asked, he made her look him straight in the eyes. Her stomach knotted. Her bottom burned. He had her sitting on his bed, her knees spread wide before him, dazed and longing for sexual release.

He took away her glass of champagne. "Place your hands on your thighs. Sit up straighter."

She'd never sat so straight in her life. As his hand wandered over her face, her shoulders, and breasts, every muscle tensed.

His handsome face broke into a pleased grin. "We need to talk about our marriage."

She groaned. "I can't think."

His hand dropped between her thighs, teased and tormented. She sucked in a breath, trying hard to remain still.

"Can you think now?"

His implication was clear. She would discuss whatever he wanted when he asked her to or he would make her suffer sweet torment until she did. She bit on her lower lip. "What is it... you wish to discuss?"

When she acquiesced to his demand, she thought he would remove his hand. He didn't. His fingers continued to dance inside her until she held back a scream.

"If you agree to marry me, I want you just as willing as you are right now—one day a week."

"Oh my, God!"

When she failed to get out another word in reply, his fingers worked harder. Her hips gyrated, seeking more.

He pulled his hand back, leaving her hanging. "One day a week," he demanded.

"Yes. Craig." She'd say anything. Do anything. If he would just end the unattainable pleasure-pain.

His palms touched her cheeks. "You understand what I'm saying?"

She nodded. One day of every week could be like these last few hours. He'd have her permission to do with her what he wished. An icy shiver slid down her spine. Giving him such control scared her and yet excited her to the very marrow of her bones.

Even now as she longed for him to give her release, in another way she wanted to prolong the exquisite pleasure of waiting. The fact that the choice was not hers lent an added degree of excitement.

And it hadn't escaped her befuddled brain that Craig hadn't yet allowed her to answer his marriage proposal. He'd merely set the terms. Only there was no merely about it. He wanted unquestionable submission—one day a week. Could she do that? Did she want that? She didn't know.

But she'd never felt such intense sexual longing in her life. And without even being satisfied fully, she knew she couldn't bear not to feel this way again. With her bottom stinging, with her sitting naked, her knees open and waiting for him to give her pleasure, she'd never felt so sexy in her life.

He scooped her into his arms and carried her into his glass and marble shower, setting her under a warm spray. The water cleared the fog from her mind, making the moment sharp and clear. He lathered his hands with a jasmine scented soap and then slowly washed her shoulders, breasts, and belly working his way down her front with the slippery soap before giving her back and bottom the same treatment.

When she didn't think she could stand his sensuous fondling for another second, he handed her the soap. Finally she got her chance to touch him. She caressed the muscles of his shoulders and his broad chest, and flat, tight stomach, barely teasing his jutting erection. Two could play this game.

She ran her hands down his thick thighs and hard calves, asking him to turn around. The feel of his warm flesh under her hands made her quiver with longing, and she washed his back and lean flanks quickly, her resolve to taunt him as he had done to her weakening. Her palms itched to caress the hard length of him until he lost control, threw her down and gave her what she wanted.

His mocking smile told her he knew what she'd tried to do. With just a small shake of his head, he turned away and she lost her chance.

Craig exited the shower first and wrapped a towel around his waist. He gestured for her to stand on the bath mat. Yesterday she would have cringed to stand naked before him under the bright lights. Today she wanted him to look at her. He took out a fluffy white towel, and she waited for him to wrap her in it. Instead, he insisted on drying her everywhere. Slowly.

As he patted the droplets from her flesh, the raging energies he'd created over the last several hours returned with hurricane force. Her knees threatened to buckle and sensing her weakness, Craig once again carried her across the room and settled her in bed.

He kissed her tenderly. She clutched him fiercely, pressing her breasts against his bare chest. While his tongue explored the recesses of her mouth, she clung to him, wriggling, trying to get him to fill the overpowering void inside her.

Once more he denied her. His lips traced a path over the hollow of her collar bone to the valley of her hips and lower until his mouth centered on her core.

Her fingers wound her way into his thick hair, and she arched up to him. Inside the tension that had strung her taut for hours was building, higher, harder, hotter. When he pulled away she screamed in frustration.

"I want . . . I must . . . Craig!"

Finally he thrust into her welcoming flesh, and she met him half way. Her burning bottom slammed against the mattress. Her fingers clawed at him. She couldn't draw in enough air. Her legs tightened around his waist.

He moved inside her fast, claiming what he wanted in a movement as old as time. She bucked wildly, and her desire peaked. Her entire body shuddered, spurted, climaxing in several electric jolts of passion.

She lost track of time. The pleasure went on and on and on. And when she could not stand one more second, his fingers slipped between the slick folds of sensitive flesh and sent her higher. The spasms wracked her again and again, acute, powerful, endlessly wondrous.

She screamed, and he swallowed it with a kiss. Hanging suspended between time and thought, she bucked her hips in wild abandon. Finally he pumped his seed into her, and she relished a tranquil moment in his arms. It took many minutes before her heart beat returned to normal, minutes before she regained her breath and her wits.

"I love you, Tracey."

"But would you have loved me if your experiment didn't work?"

"I knew it would work. I just wanted to prove that you could enjoy the physical side of love as much as I do."

Nestling against his chest, she snuggled closer. "I love you, too."

He smoothed the back of her head and drew her cheek against his shoulder. "Enough to marry me?"

"Yes." A tiny thrill shot through her. For the first time she looked forward to spending hour upon hour in his bed.

"And you agree to my conditions?"

"I have one of my own," she said lightly.

The muscles of his chest tensed. His eyes smoldered. "What?"

She tired to smother a chuckle and failed. "One day a week won't be enough. Let's make it two."

About the Author:

Ivy Landon is a pseudonym for a multi-published author who hopes her story will in turn shock you, and titillate you. Writing for **Secrets** was an opportunity to let her freedom of expression soar beyond all boundaries. She hopes you enjoy the reading as much as she enjoyed the writing. May all your dreams be spicy.

Secrets, Volume 2

Listen to what reviewers say:

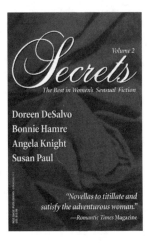

"*Secrets* offers four novellas of sensual delight; each beautifully written with intense feeling and dedication to character development. For those seeking stories with heightened intimacy, look no further."

—Kathee Card, *Romancing the Web*

"Such a welcome diversity in styles and genres. Rich characterization in sensual tales. An exciting read that's sure to titillate the senses."

—Cheryl Ann Porter

"*Secrets 2* left me breathless. Sensual satisfaction guaranteed…times four!"

—Virginia Henley, *New York Times* Best Selling Author

In *Secrets, Volume 2* you'll find:

Surrogate Lover by Doreen DeSalvo

Adrian Ross is a surrogate sex therapist who has all the answers and control. He thought he'd seen and done it all, but he'd never met Sarah.

Snowbound by Bonnie Hamre

A delicious, sensuous regency tale. The marriage-shy Earl of Howden is teased and tortured by his own desires and finds there is a woman who can equal his overpowering sensuality.

Roarke's Prisoner by Angela Knight

Elise, a starship captain, remembers the eager animal submission she'd known before at her captor's hands and refuses to become his toy again. However, she has no idea of the delights he's planned for her this time.

Savage Garden by Susan Paul

Raine's been captured by a mysterious and dangerous revolutionary leader in Mexico. At first her only concern is survival, but she quickly finds lush erotic nights in her captor's arms.

Winner of the Fallot Literary Award for Fiction!

Secrets, Volume 3

Listen to what reviewers say:

"*Secrets, Volume 3*, leaves the reader breathless. A delicious confection of sensuous treats awaits the reader on each turn of the page!"
— Kathee Card, *Romancing the Web*

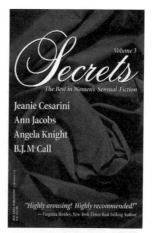

"From the FBI to Police Dectective to Vampires to a Medieval Warlord home from the Crusade—*Secrets 3* is simply the best!"
— Susan Paul, award winning author

"An unabashed celebration of sex. Highly arousing! Highly recommended!"
— Virginia Henley, *New York Times* Best Selling Author

In *Secrets, Volume 3* you'll find:

The Spy Who Loved Me by Jeanie Cesarini

Undercover FBI agent Paige Ellison's sexual appetites rise to new levels when she works with leading man Christopher Sharp, the cunning agent who uses all his training to capture her body and heart.

The Barbarian by Ann Jacobs

Lady Brianna vows not to surrender to the barbaric Giles, Earl of Harrow. He must use sexual arts learned in the infidels' harem to conquer his bride. A word of caution—this is not for the faint of heart.

Blood and Kisses by Angela Knight

A vampire assassin is after Beryl St. Cloud. Her only hope lies with Decker, another vampire and ex-mercenary. Broke, she offers herself as payment for his services. Will his seductive powers take her very soul?

Love Undercover by B.J. McCall

Amanda Forbes is the bait in a strip joint sting operation. While she performs, fellow detective "Cowboy" Cooper gets to watch. Though he excites her, she must fight the temptation to surrender to the passion.

Winner of the 1997 Under the Covers Readers Favorite Award

Secrets, Volume 4

Listen to what reviewers say:

"Provocative…seductive…a must read!"
—*Romantic Times* Magazine

"These are the kind of stories that romance readers that 'want a little more' have been looking for all their lives…."
—*Affaire de Coeur* Magazine

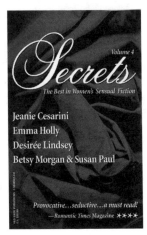

"*Secrets, Volume 4*, has something to satisfy every erotic fantasy… simply sexational!"
—Virginia Henley, *New York Times* Best Selling Author

In *Secrets, Volume 4* you'll find:

An Act of Love by Jeanie Cesarini
Shelby Moran's past left her terrified of sex. International film star Jason Gage must gently coach the young starlet in the ways of love. He wants more than an act—he wants Shelby to feel true passion in his arms.

Enslaved by Desirée Lindsey
Lord Nicholas Summer's air of danger, dark passions, and irresistible charm have brought Lady Crystal's long-hidden desires to the surface. Will he be able to give her the one thing she desires before it's too late?

The Bodyguard by Betsy Morgan and Susan Paul
Kaki York is a bodyguard, but watching the wild, erotic romps of her client's sexual conquests on the security cameras is getting to her—and her partner, the ruggedly handsome James Kulick. Can she resist his insistent desire to have her?

The Love Slave by Emma Holly
A woman's ultimate fantasy. For one year, Princess Lily will be attended to by three delicious men of her choice. While she delights in playing with the first two, it's the reluctant Grae, with his powerful chest, black eyes and hair, that stirs her desires.

Secrets, Volume 5

Listen to what reviewers say:

"Hot, hot, hot! Not for the faint-hearted!"
—*Romantic Times* Magazine

"As you make your way through the stories, you will find yourself becoming hotter and hotter. *Secrets* just keeps getting better and better."
—*Affaire de Coeur* Magazine

"*Secrets 5* is a collage of lucious sensuality. Any woman who reads *Secrets* is in for an awakening!"
—Virginia Henley, *New York Times* Best Selling Author

In *Secrets, Volume 5* you'll find:

Beneath Two Moons by Sandy Fraser
Ready for a very wild romp? Step into the future and find Conor, rough and masculine like frontiermen of old, on the prowl for a new conquest. In his sights, Dr. Eva Kelsey. She got away once before, but this time Conor makes sure she begs for more.

Insatiable by Chevon Gael
Marcus Remington photographs beautiful models for a living, but it's Ashlyn Fraser, a young corporate exec having some glamour shots done, who has stolen his heart. It's up to Marcus to help her discover her inner sexual self.

Strictly Business by Shannon Hollis
Elizabeth Forrester knows it's tough enough for a woman to make it to the top in the corporate world. Garrett Hill, the most beautiful man in Silicon Valley, has to come along to stir up her wildest fantasies. Dare she give in to both their desires?

Alias Smith and Jones by B.J. McCall
Meredith Collins finds herself stranded overnight at the airport. A handsome stranger by the name of Smith offers her sanctuaty for the evening and she finds those mesmerizing, green-flecked eyes hard to resist. Are they to be just two ships passing in the night?

Secrets, Volume 6

Listen to what reviewers say:

"Red Sage was the first and remains the leader of Women's Erotic Romance Fiction Collections!"

—*Romantic Times* Magazine

"*Secrets, Volume 6*, is the best of *Secrets* yet. …four of the most erotic stories in one volume than this reader has yet to see anywhere else. …These stories are full of erotica at its best and you'll definitely want to keep it handy for lots of re-reading!"

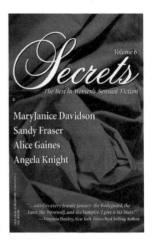

—*Affaire de Coeur* Magazine

"*Secrets 6* satisfies every female fantasy: the Bodyguard, the Tutor, the Werewolf, and the Vampire. I give it Six Stars!"

—Virginia Henley, *New York Times* Best Selling Author

In *Secrets, Volume 6* you'll find:

Flint's Fuse by Sandy Fraser

Dana Madison's father has her "kidnapped" for her own safety. Flint, the tall, dark and dangerous mercenary, is hired for the job. But just which one is the prisoner—Dana will try *anything* to get away.

Love's Prisoner by MaryJanice Davidson

Trapped in an elevator, Jeannie Lawrence experienced unwilling rapture at Michael Windham's hands. She never expected the devilishly handsome man to show back up in her life—or turn out to be a werewolf!

The Education of Miss Felicity Wells by Alice Gaines

Felicity Wells wants to be sure she'll satisfy her soon-to-be husband but she needs a teacher. Dr. Marcus Slade, an experienced lover, agrees to take her on as a student, but can he stop short of taking her completely?

A Candidate for the Kiss by Angela Knight

Working on a story, reporter Dana Ivory stumbles onto a more amazing one—a sexy, secret agent who happens to be a vampire.She wants her story but Gabriel Archer wants more from her than just sex and blood.

Secrets, Volume 7

Listen to what reviewers say:

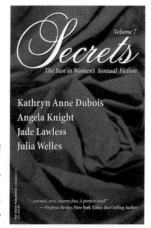

"Get out your asbestos gloves — *Secrets Volume 7* is…extremely hot, true erotic romance…passionate and titillating. There's nothing quite like baring your secrets!"

—*Romantic Times* Magazine

"…sensual, sexy, steamy fun. A perfect read!"

—Virginia Henley,
New York Times Best Selling Author

"Intensely provocative and disarmingly romantic, *Secrets*, *Volume 7*, is a romance reader's paradise that will take you beyond your wildest dreams!"

—Ballston Book House Review

In *Secrets, Volume 7* you'll find:

Amelia's Innocence by Julia Welles

Amelia didn't know her father bet her in a card game with Captain Quentin Hawke, so honor demands a compromise—three days of erotic foreplay, leaving her virginity and future intact.

The Woman of His Dreams by Jade Lawless

From the day artist Gray Avonaco moves in next door, Joanna Morgan is plagued by provocative dreams. But what she believes is unrequited lust, Gray sees as another chance to be with the woman he loves. He must persuade her that even death can't stop true love.

Surrender by Kathryn Anne Dubois

Free-spirited Lady Johanna wants no part of the binding strictures society imposes with her marriage to the powerful Duke. She doesn't know the dark Duke wants sensual adventure, and sexual satisfaction.

Kissing the Hunter by Angela Knight

Navy Seal Logan McLean hunts the vampires who murdered his wife. Virginia Hart is a sexy vampire searching for her lost soul-mate only to find him in a man determined to kill her. She must convince him all vampires aren't created equally.

**Winner of the Venus Book Club
Best Book of the Year**

Secrets, Volume 8

Listen to what reviewers say:

"*Secrets, Volume 8*, is an amazing compilation of sexy stories covering a wide range of subjects, all designed to titillate the senses. ...you'll find something for everybody in this latest version of *Secrets*."

—*Affaire de Coeur* Magazine

"*Secrets Volume 8*, is simply sensational!"

—Virginia Henley, *New York Times* Best Selling Author

"These delectable stories will have you turning the pages long into the night. Passionate, provocative and perfect for setting the mood...."

—*Escape to Romance* Reviews

In *Secrets, Volume 8* you'll find:

Taming Kate by Jeanie Cesarini

Kathryn Roman inherits a legal brothel. Little does this city girl know the town of Love, Nevada wants her to be their new madam so they've charged Trey Holliday, one very dominant cowboy, with taming her.

Jared's Wolf by MaryJanice Davidson

Jared Rocke will do anything to avenge his sister's death, but ends up attracted to Moira Wolfbauer, the she-wolf sworn to protect her pack. Joining forces to stop a killer, they learn love defies all boundaries.

My Champion, My Lover by Alice Gaines

Celeste Broder is a woman committed for having a sexy appetite. Mayor Robert Albright may be her champion—if she can convince him her freedom will mean a chance to indulge their appetites together.

Kiss or Kill by Liz Maverick

In this post-apocalyptic world, Camille Kazinsky's military career rides on her ability to make a choice—whether the robo called Meat should live or die. Meat's future depends on proving he's human enough to live, man enough...to makes her feel like a woman.

Winner of the Venus Book Club Best Book of the Year

Secrets, Volume 9

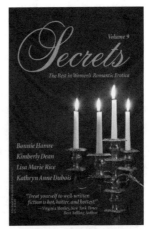

Listen to what reviewers say:

"Everyone should expect only the most erotic stories in a *Secrets* book. ...if you like your stories full of hot sexual scenes, then this is for you!"

—Donna Doyle Romance Reviews

"*SECRETS 9*...is sinfully delicious, highly arousing, and hotter than hot as the pages practically burn up as you turn them."

—Suzanne Coleburn, Reader To Reader Reviews/Belles & Beaux of Romance

"Treat yourself to well-written fictionthat's hot, hotter, and hottest!"

—Virginia Henley, *New York Times* Best Selling Author

In *Secrets, Volume 9* you'll find:

Wild For You by Kathryn Anne Dubois

When college intern, Georgie, gets captured by a Congo wildman, she discovers this specimen of male virility has never seen a woman. The research possibilities are endless!

Wanted by Kimberly Dean

FBI Special Agent Jeff Reno wants Danielle Carver. There's her body, brains—and that charge of treason on her head. Dani goes on the run, but the sexy Fed is hot on her trail.

Secluded by Lisa Marie Rice

Nicholas Lee's wealth and power came with a price—his enemies will kill anyone he loves. When Isabelle steals his heart, Nicholas secludes her in his palace for a lifetime of desire in only a few days.

Flights of Fantasy by Bonnie Hamre

Chloe taught others to see the realities of life but she's never shared the intimate world of her sensual yearnings. Given the chance, will she be woman enough to fulfill her most secret erotic fantasy?

Secrets, Volume 10

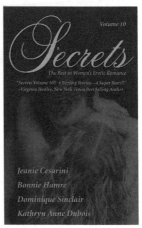

Listen to what reviewers say:

"*Secrets Volume 10*, an erotic dance through medieval castles, sultan's palaces, the English countryside and expensive hotel suites, explodes with passion-filled pages."

> —*Romantic Times BOOKclub*

"Having read the previous nine volumes, this one fulfills the expectations of what is expected in a *Secrets* book: romance and eroticism at its best!!"

> —*Fallen Angel Reviews*

"All are hot steamy romances so if you enjoy erotica romance, you are sure to enjoy *Secrets, Volume 10*. All this reviewer can say is WOW!!"

> —*The Best Reviews*

In *Secrets, Volume 10* you'll find:

Private Eyes by Dominique Sinclair

When a mystery man captivates P.I. Nicolla Black during a stakeout, she discovers her no-seduction rule bending under the pressure of long denied passion. She agrees to the seduction, but he demands her total surrender.

The Ruination of Lady Jane by Bonnie Hamre

To avoid her upcoming marriage, Lady Jane Ponsonby-Maitland flees into the arms of Havyn Attercliffe. She begs him to ruin her rather than turn her over to her odious fiancé.

Code Name: Kiss by Jeanie Cesarini

Agent Lily Justiss is on a mission to defend her country against terrorists that requires giving up her virginity as a sex slave. As her master takes her body, desire for her commanding officer Seth Blackthorn fuels her mind.

The Sacrifice by Kathryn Anne Dubois

Lady Anastasia Bedovier is days from taking her vows as a Nun. Before she denies her sensuality forever, she wants to experience pleasure. Count Maxwell is the perfect man to initiate her into erotic delight.

Secrets, Volume 11

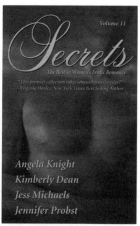

Listen to what reviewers say:

"*Secrets Volume 11* delivers once again with storylines that include erotic masquerades, ancient curses, modern-day betrayal and a prince charming looking for a kiss." **4 Stars**
—*Romantic Times BOOKclub*

"Indulge yourself with this erotic treat and join the thousands of readers who just can't get enough. Be forewarned that *Secrets 11* will whet your appetite for more, but will offer you the ultimate in pleasurable erotic literature."
—*Ballston Book House Review*

"*Secrets 11* quite honestly is my favorite anthology from Red Sage so far."
—*The Best Reviews*

In *Secrets, Volume 11* you'll find:

Masquerade by Jennifer Probst

Hailey Ashton is determined to free herself from her sexual restrictions. Four nights of erotic pleasures without revealing her identity. A chance to explore her secret desires without the fear of unmasking.

Ancient Pleasures by Jess Michaels

Isabella Winslow is obsessed with finding out what caused her late husband's death, but trapped in an Egyptian concubine's tomb with a sexy American raider, succumbing to the mummy's sensual curse takes over.

Manhunt by Kimberly Dean

Framed for murder, Michael Tucker takes Taryn Swanson hostage—the one woman who can clear him. Despite the evidence against him, the attraction between them is strong. Tucker resorts to unconventional, yet effective methods of persuasion to change the sexy ADA's mind.

Wake Me by Angela Knight

Chloe Hart received a sexy painting of a sleeping knight. Radolf of Varik has been trapped for centuries in the painting since, cursed by a witch. His only hope is to visit the dreams of women and make one of them fall in love with him so she can free him with a kiss.

Secrets, Volume 12

Listen to what reviewers say:

"*Secrets Volume 12*, turns on the heat with a seductive encounter inside a bookstore, a temple of naughty and sensual delight, a galactic inferno that thaws ice, and a lightening storm that lights up the English shoreline. Tales of looking for love in all the right places with a heat rating out the charts." **4½ Stars**

— *Romantic Times BOOKclub*

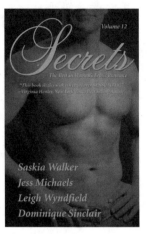

"I really liked these stories.You want great escapism? Read *Secrets, Volume 12.*"

— *Romance Reviews*

In *Secrets, Volume 12* you'll find:

Good Girl Gone Bad by Dominique Sinclair

Reagan's dreams are finally within reach. Setting out to do research for an article, nothing could have prepared her for Luke, or his offer to teach her everything she needs to know about sex. Licentious pleasures, forbidden desires… inspiring the best writing she's ever done.

Aphrodite's Passion by Jess Michaels

When Selena flees Victorian London before her evil stepchildren can institutionalize her for hysteria, Gavin is asked to bring her back home. But when he finds her living on the island of Cyprus, his need to have her begins to block out every other impulse.

White Heat by Leigh Wyndfield

Raine is hiding in an icehouse in the middle of nowhere from one of the scariest men in the universes. Walker escaped from a burning prison. Imagine their surprise when they find out they have the same man to blame for their miseries. Passion, revenge and love are in their future.

Summer Lightning by Saskia Walker

Sculptress Sally is enjoying an idyllic getaway on a secluded cove when she spots a gorgeous man walking naked on the beach. When Julian finds an attractive woman shacked up in his cove, he has to check her out. But what will he do when he finds she's secretly been using him as a model?

Secrets, Volume 13

Listen to what reviewers say:

"In *Secrets Volume 13*, the temperature gets turned up a few notches with a mistaken personal ad, shape-shifters destined to love, a hot Regency lord and his lady, as well as a bodyguard protecting his woman. Emotions and flames blaze high in Red Sage's latest foray into the sensual and delightful art of love." **4½ Stars**

—*Romantic Times BOOKclub*

"The sex is still so hot the pages nearly ignite! Read *Secrets, Volume 13*!"

—*Romance Reviews*

In *Secrets, Volume 13* you'll find:

Out of Control by Rachelle Chase

Astrid's world revolves around her business and she's hoping to pick up wealthy Erik Santos as a client. Only he's hoping to pick up something entirely different. Will she give in to the seductive pull of his proposition?

Hawkmoor by Amber Green

Shape-shifters answer to Darien as he acts in the name of the long-missing Lady Hawkmoor, their hereditary ruler. When she unexpectedly surfaces, Darien must deal with a scrappy individual whose wary eyes hold the other half of his soul, but who has the power to destroy his world.

Lessons in Pleasure by Charlotte Featherstone

A wicked bargain has Lily vowing never to yield to the demands of the rake she once loved and lost. Unfortunately, Damian, the Earl of St. Croix, or Saint as he is infamously known, will not take 'no' for an answer.

In the Heat of the Night by Calista Fox

Haunted by a century-old curse, Molina fears she won't live to see her thirtieth birthday. Nick, her former bodyguard, is hired back into service to protect her from the fatal accidents that plague her family. But *In the Heat of the Night*, will his passion and love for her be enough to convince Molina they have a future together?

Secrets, Volume 14

Listen to what reviewers say:

"*Secrets Volume 14* will excite readers with its diverse selection of delectable sexy tales ranging from a fourteenth century love story to a sci-fi rebel who falls for a irresistible research scientist to a trio of determined vampires who battle for the same woman to a virgin sacrifice who falls in love with a beast. A cornucopia of pure delight!" **4½ Stars**
—*Romantic Times BOOKclub*

"This book contains four erotic tales sure to keep readers up long into the night."

—*Romance Junkies*

In *Secrets, Volume 14* you'll find:

Soul Kisses by Angela Knight

Beth's been kidnapped by Joaquin Ramirez, a sadistic vampire. Handsome vampire cousins, Morgan and Garret Axton, come to her rescue. Can she find happiness with two vampires?

Temptation in Time by Alexa Aames

Ariana escaped the Middle Ages after stealing a kiss of magic from sexy sorcerer, Marcus de Grey. When he brings her back, they begin a battle of wills and a sexual odyssey that could spell disaster for them both.

Ailis and the Beast by Jennifer Barlowe

When Ailis agreed to be her village's sacrifice to the mysterious Beast she was prepared to sacrifice her virtue, and possibly her life. But some things aren't what they seem. Ailis and the Beast are about to discover the greatest sacrifice may be the human heart.

Night Heat by Leigh Wynfield

When Rip Bowhite leads a revolt on the prison planet, he ends up struggling to survive against monsters that rule the night. Jemma, the prison's Healer, won't allow herself to be distracted by the instant attraction she feels for Rip. As the stakes are raised and death draws near, love seems doomed in the heat of the night.

Secrets, Volume 15

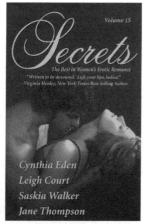

Listen to what reviewers say:

"*Secrets Volume 15* blends humor, tension and steamy romance in its newest collection that sizzles with passion between unlikely pairs—a male chauvinist columnist and a librarian turned erotica author; a handsome werewolf and his resisting mate; an unfulfilled woman and a sexy police officer and a Victorian wife who learns discipline can be fun. Readers will revel in this delicious assortment of thrilling tales." **4 Stars**
—*Romantic Times BOOKclub*

"This book contains four tales by some of today's hottest authors that will tease your senses and intrigue your mind."
—*Romance Junkies*

In *Secrets, Volume 15* you'll find:

Simon Says by Jane Thompson
Simon Campbell is a newspaper columnist who panders to male fantasies. Georgina Kennedy is a respectable librarian. On the surface, these two have nothing in common... but don't judge a book by its cover.

Bite of the Wolf by Cynthia Eden
Gareth Morlet, alpha werewolf, has finally found his mate. All he has to do is convince Trinity to join with him, to give in to the pleasure of a werewolf's mating, and then she will be his... forever.

Falling for Trouble by Saskia Walker
With 48 hours to clear her brother's name, Sonia Harmond finds help from irresistible bad boy, Oliver Eaglestone. When the erotic tension between them hits fever pitch, securing evidence to thwart an international arms dealer isn't the only danger they face.

The Disciplinarian by Leigh Court
Headstrong Clarissa Babcock is sent to the shadowy legend known as The Disciplinarian for instruction in proper wifely obedience. Jared Ashworth uses the tools of seduction to show her how to control a demanding husband, but her beauty, spirit, and uninhibited passion make Jared hunger to keep her—and their darkly erotic nights—all for himself!

Secrets, Volume 16

Listen to what reviewers say:

"Blackmail, games of chance, nude beaches and masquerades pave a path to heart-tugging emotions and fiery love scenes in Red Sage's latest collection." **4.5 Stars**

—Romantic Times BOOKclub

"Red Sage Publishing has brought to the readers an erotic profusion of highly skilled storytellers in their Secrets Vol. 16. ... This is the best Secrets novel to date and this reviewer's favorite."

—LoveRomances.com

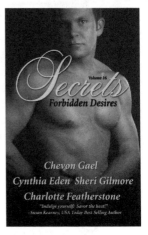

In *Secrets, Volume 16* you'll find:

Never Enough by Cynthia Eden

For the last three weeks, Abby McGill has been playing with fire. Bad-boy Jake has taught her the true meaning of desire, but she knows she has to end her relationship with him. But Jake isn't about to let the woman he wants walk away from him.

Bunko by Sheri Gilmoore

Tu Tran is forced to decide between Jack, a man, who promises to share every aspect of his life with her, or Dev, the man, who hides behind a mask and only offers night after night of erotic sex. Will she take the gamble of the dice and choose the man, who can see behind her own mask and expose her true desires?

Hide and Seek by Chevon Gael

Kyle DeLaurier ditches his trophy-fiance in favor of a tropical paradise full of tall, tanned, topless females. Private eye, Darcy McLeod, is on the trail of this runaway groom. Together they sizzle while playing Hide and Seek with their true identities.

Seduction of the Muse by Charlotte Featherstone

He's the Dark Lord, the mysterious author who pens the erotic tales of an innocent woman's seduction. She is his muse, the woman he watches from the dark shadows, the woman whose dreams he invades at night.

The Forever Kiss
by Angela Knight

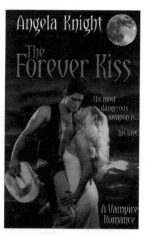

Listen to what reviewers say:

"*The Forever Kiss* flows well with good characters and an interesting plot. ... If you enjoy vampires and a lot of hot sex, you are sure to enjoy *The Forever Kiss*."

—The Best Reviews

"Battling vampires, a protective ghost and the ever present battle of good and evil keep excellent pace with the erotic delights in Angela Knight's *The Forever Kiss*—a book that absolutely bites with refreshing paranormal humor." **4½ Stars, Top Pick**

—Romantic Times BOOKclub

"I found *The Forever Kiss* to be an exceptionally written, refreshing book. ... I really enjoyed this book by Angela Knight. ... 5 angels!"

—Fallen Angel Reviews

"*The Forever Kiss* is the first single title released from Red Sage and if this is any indication of what we can expect, it won't be the last. ... The love scenes are hot enough to give a vampire a sunburn and the fight scenes will have you cheering for the good guys."

—Really Bad Barb Reviews

In *The Forever Kiss*:

For years, Valerie Chase has been haunted by dreams of a Texas Ranger she knows only as "Cowboy." As a child, he rescued her from the nightmare vampires who murdered her parents. As an adult, she still dreams of him—but now he's her seductive lover in nights of erotic pleasure.

Yet "Cowboy" is more than a dream—he's the real Cade McKinnon—and a vampire! For years, he's protected Valerie from Edward Ridgemont, the sadistic vampire who turned him. Now, Ridgmont wants Valerie for his own and Cade is the only one who can protect her.

When Val finds herself abducted by her handsome dream man, she's appalled to discover he's one of the vampires she fears. Now, caught in a web of fear and passion, she and Cade must learn to trust each other, even as an immortal monster stalks their every move.

Their only hope of survival is... *The Forever Kiss*.

Romantic Times Best Erotic Novel of the Year

Finally, the men you've been dreaming about!

Give the Gift of Spicy Romantic Fiction

Don't want to wait? You can place a retail price ($12.99)
order for any of the *Secrets* volumes from the following:

① **Waldenbooks and Borders Stores**

② **Amazon.com** or **BarnesandNoble.com**

③ **Book Clearinghouse (800-431-1579)**

④ **Romantic Times Magazine** Books by Mail (718-237-1097)

⑤ Special order at other bookstores.
Bookstores: Please contact Baker & Taylor Distributors, Ingram
Book Distributor, or Red Sage Publishing for bookstore sales.

Order by title or ISBN #:

Vol. 1: 0-9648942-0-3	**Vol. 7:** 0-9648942-7-0	**Vol. 13:** 0-9754516-3-4
ISBN #13 978-0-9648942-0-4	ISBN #13 978-0-9648942-7-3	ISBN #13 978-0-9754516-3-2
Vol. 2: 0-9648942-1-1	**Vol. 8:** 0-9648942-8-9	**Vol. 14:** 0-9754516-4-2
ISBN #13 978-0-9648942-1-1	ISBN #13 978-0-9648942-9-7	ISBN #13 978-0-9754516-4-9
Vol. 3: 0-9648942-2-X	**Vol. 9:** 0-9648942-9-7	**Vol. 15:** 0-9754516-5-0
ISBN #13 978-0-9648942-2-8	ISBN #13 978-0-9648942-9-7	ISBN #13 978-0-9754516-5-6
Vol. 4: 0-9648942-4-6	**Vol. 10:** 0-9754516-0-X	Vol. 16: 0-9754516-6-9
ISBN #13 978-0-9648942-4-2	ISBN #13 978-0-9754516-0-1	ISBN #13 978-0-9754516-6-3
Vol. 5: 0-9648942-5-4	**Vol. 11:** 0-9754516-1-8	
ISBN #13 978-0-9648942-5-9	ISBN #13 978-0-9754516-1-8	
Vol. 6: 0-9648942-6-2	**Vol. 12:** 0-9754516-2-6	
ISBN #13 978-0-9648942-6-6	ISBN #13 978-0-9754516-2-5	

The Forever Kiss: 0-9648942-3-8 • ISBN #13 978-0-9648942-3-5 ($14.00)